UNCLE ZEKE

Uncle Zeke

Ted Gary

Praus LLC
Portland, OR

This novel is a work of fiction. The characters, names, incidents, dialogue, and plot are the products of the author's imagination or are used fictitiously.
Any resemblance to actual persons or events is purely coincidental.

Cover design by Carol Gary

ISBN 978-0-9909021-0-2

Copyright © Ted Gary

All Rights Reserved

Printed in the United States of America

October, 2014

First Edition

Dedicated to my brother Walt
and to my longtime friend, Nick Pearce.

Acknowledgements

I would like to thank my wife, Carol, for her
loving encouragement and support, without
which *Uncle Zeke* would have remained a
rough idea rattling around in my head.

I would also like to thank Marya Curtis,
Corinne Pearce, Carol Pullin, and
Gail Shore for their valuable input.
The mistakes are all mine.

ONE

Within the span of forty-eight hours my carefully mapped life abruptly detoured from the interstate onto a bone rattling mish mash of back roads; rocks ricocheting in wheel wells like bullets, suspension parts slamming against the undercarriage, and tires skidding from side to side around each corner. I hate being out of control. …But I have gotten well ahead of myself.

As the CEO and sole employee of Klein InfoSec Associates, I had just spent a long and tiring week in California at Trilionne's headquarters, where I successfully – or so I thought – audited their information security procedures and controls. I had been counting on expanding my work at Trilionne in the future and also counting on them to provide a stellar reference to a prospective client I was courting. Instead, they cancelled my contract for next year, abruptly dumping me for a nationally known information security consulting firm. But of course, they still required me to submit my final report for this year's audit.

During the long flight from San Francisco to Boston, I consoled myself by looking forward to seeing Julie, my steady girlfriend for the past two and a half years. Prior to Julie, my longest serious relationship had lasted only eleven months before I cut it off. Julie is different – quite special. She is very attractive; some would say stunning. She has a girl-next-door look evocative of Sandra Bullock; dark brown hair she often wears in a ponytail; big, dark brown eyes glistening with vitality; and full lips that invite me to kiss her whenever appropriate and sometimes when not so appropriate. She is smart, too, earning her CPA and working her way onto the partner track at one of New England's most prestigious public accounting firms.

With all of that going for her, the thing I liked best was her feistiness. When we were first dating, I apparently had a habit of running fifteen or twenty minutes late for our dates. Unaware of my tardiness, I never thought twice about it. One time she set up a Sadie Hawkins date for her to treat me to dinner at the Back Bay Fish House. She asked me to meet her at the restaurant at seven o'clock. I arrived about seven fifteen and checked with the hostess, but Julie wasn't there. I waited five minutes and then started pacing back and forth with worry, an increasingly foreboding worry that surprised me with its intensity. Julie had never been late before, not even once, not even for five minutes. After ten more tense minutes of looking at my watch and then looking out the window, I pulled out my phone to text her. She arrived just as I hit send. I rushed over and hugged her and I said, "I was starting to worry about you. Maybe I had the time wrong. Were we supposed to meet here at seven, or was it seven thirty?"

Her brown eyes twinkled as she smirked and said, "I told you seven o'clock, but I didn't plan on arriving until seven thirty. You're always at least fifteen minutes late. From now on I don't plan on arriving until at least a half hour after the time we have agreed to meet. If one of us is going to be twiddling their thumbs waiting for the other, it's going to be you, not me."

I muttered, "Touché" before promising to be on time in the future. I admired her spunk.

As I took a sip of the drink the flight attendant had given me, I realized Julie must have gotten over "the marriage thing" because she hadn't mentioned it for almost three months. I am

8

not at all philosophically opposed to marriage, but I don't want to get tied down until at least my mid-thirties. By then, Julie and I would really know if our relationship was made to last, and we would be sure of our love for each other. Only then would it make sense to get engaged.

The flight attendant came back down the aisle and picked up our glasses in preparation for takeoff. She soon returned to the head of the aisle with the short seat belt flight attendants use to demonstrate how to fasten the buckle and then started in on the safety announcement that I nearly had memorized. The pilot announced we were number two for takeoff. He taxied the plane to the head of the runway, waited a few seconds, and then applied full power. As soon as we passed through ten thousand feet, I pulled out my iPad and Bose noise cancelling headphones.

I had until Wednesday morning to finish my network security report for Trilionne so I put off starting on it until the weekend. Instead of working during the flight, I was looking forward to a western movie marathon, having downloaded three classic Clint Eastwood films onto my iPad. Originally I planned to watch the movies during the evenings in my hotel room, but instead I spent those evenings searching for security vulnerabilities on Trilionne's network. As compensation for the extra hours I intended to reward myself on the long flight by watching *A Fistful of Dollars*, *For a Few Dollars More*, and then *The Good, the Bad, and the Ugly*, if there was time, and if I was still awake.

I watched the first two movies noticing how much younger Eastwood looked in the mid-60's compared to his recent grizzled appearance in *Gran Torino*. The seat belt sign came on, and the head flight attendant made the landing announcement in the middle of *The Good, the Bad, and the Ugly*. I repacked my carry-on items and waited to land and then head home with Julie.

I texted Julie, who I knew would be waiting in the cell-phone waiting lot, to let her know I would meet her outside baggage claim in ten or fifteen minutes. She was waiting for me as soon as I walked outside the automatic doors. She tooted the horn on her Camry to get my attention and popped the trunk open for my bags. I climbed into the passenger seat and leaned over for a long anticipated kiss. But this time kissing her was like kissing a Popsicle; cold and stiff with a hint of strawberry from her lip gloss. Something was bothering her, but pretending not to notice, I said, "Julie, I really missed you this week. It is great to be back home with you."

Julie nodded silently as she carefully pulled out into the flow of traffic and then said, "You're going to find some things a little different at home; actually, you're going to find everything a lot different. I've found a place living with an old friend from college and have moved all my things in with her. As much as I wanted you and me to work out, I am afraid this is the end of the line for us. I wish I knew a gentler way to break it to you, but I don't. You're just going to have to deal with the direct approach. Sorry."

I must have looked as clueless as a deer in the headlights and barely managed to say, "Whoa... Can we slow down for a second? When I left on Sunday afternoon we were fine; we were a happy couple. At least I thought we were. I come back five days later, and you announce you have moved out. What's the deal? Can we talk about this first? Is there someone else?"

Julie stared straight ahead and wiped a tear from her eye and stammered, "No. There's no one else. You just thought we were fine because you ignored me whenever I said I wanted to get married and have a family. You thought you could blow me off and I would forget about it. Well I didn't forget about it, and now I guess I am blowing you off. Life's too short for me to play your never-ending let's-wait-and-see games."

I put my hand gently on her knee and said, "You mean the world to me. I've obviously blown it. I had no idea settling down was so important to you. Let's step back and give ourselves a little time to work through this."

"David, I think a lot of you, too. I used to think we were the perfect couple with marriage in our future. But the truth is you and I each have completely different goals in life. It's clear to me that your consulting business is your number one priority. You travel all week meeting with clients and then spend half the weekend writing up reports. You say I am important, but if I am so important why do I only get whatever time is left over after your work? I don't think people are very important to you. If they are, it apparently has to be on your terms."

I replied, "Julie, let's not rush into breaking up. I can make some changes. Give me another chance. Please."

"David, I've given this a lot of thought. Three months to be exact, so I am not rushing into anything. It's too late for me to reconsider. I don't want our relationship to continue, to get married and have kids only because I forced your hand. The truth is if you wanted to settle down with me we'd already be engaged. It's too late. I can't continue to be with you because if I did, I'd always be wondering if you really loved me or if you were forced into something you didn't really want. Like I said, it's already too late."

Trying desperately once again to get her to give me another chance I said, "Sweetie, this is coming out of left field. I need some time to process it. I know I don't want us to end our relationship. Let's take the time..."

She interrupted, "David, you've stalled long enough. We're going to be at your place in just a second. I would really appreciate it if you'd just get out of the car, go inside, and not contact me. I didn't rush into this decision, and I don't need more time. I wish you and your business the very best."

I was shocked Julie wanted to breakup, but I was also totally perplexed by her complete unwillingness to discuss it. I liked feisty, but this wasn't feisty; it was off the chart unreasonableness. The storm within her must have been brewing for months, while I naively thought the status quo was as acceptable to her as it was to me. I had been relieved that she stopped discussing our relationship's next phase. How stupid.

Julie pulled over to the curb and popped the trunk from the inside. I stepped out of the car in a daze and stumbled around to the trunk to retrieve my bags. I closed the lid and wondered what had just happened. My head spun in bewilderment. What was going on? Julie's disappearing tail lights finally registered with me. She was really gone. I had never been dumped before; I had always been the dumper, not the dumped. Dumping was unpleasant. It always made me feel like a jerk, and I hated it. But, being dumped felt ten times worse. I felt like leftover food scraps that got chewed up in the garbage disposal and washed down the drain into the sewer.

I slowly trudged up the steps to the door of my brownstone and automatically reached into my pocket for the front door key. Where was it? I thought maybe I had tossed it into one of the many pockets of my soft-sided brief case. I knelt under the porch light in a daze looking into one pocket and then the next. I finally remembered I didn't take it with me because I had expected Julie to use her key to let us in. I was about to break out one of the window panes that bordered the door when I remembered the spare key in my wallet. I unlocked the door and stepped over the pile of mail the postman had shoved through the slot during my absence. My place had never felt this empty before. Julie was gone. Julie's things were gone, and the dust encircled spots where her purple Gardenias had been seemed to stare at me and say, "You jerk! You're going to have a lonely life. Maybe you should think about using some of your trust fund's millions to buy some friends."

I fell back into my leather recliner thinking, "I can handle this." Julie was probably just being emotional; maybe it was just that time of the month. I made a mental note to call her in the morning and try to talk some sense into her. Hopefully, she would realize how impetuous she was acting. I thought the best thing to do was to get some sleep and give her time to come around.

I meant to get out of the chair and go to bed, but instead I leaned back in the recliner trying to decide if I should attempt a last ditch effort to sweep Julie off of her feet or if I should play it cool and aloof. I spent the night oscillating between fitful sleep and bleary-eyed restlessness, and never did decide on a plan of action. Decisions about relationships are difficult. I never know for sure what the right answer is. Should I grovel, move on, or wait? How can a guy know?

TWO

By six o'clock the next morning I was too tired to be alert and too stiff to sit another minute in my recliner. I pushed myself out of the chair and dragged my butt into the kitchen where I made a pot of strong coffee. I drank two quick cups and headed for the shower where the blasting hot water both relaxed my stiff muscles and helped wake me up. After toweling off, I put on a pair of old jeans and a baggy burgundy sweatshirt. I looked out the window hoping Boston's typically dry July weather had somehow started to arrive. Instead, the dark, wet sky told me summer wouldn't be arriving anytime soon. I considered going for a run, but couldn't muster the motivation to go out in the warm, sticky rain. It was too early in the morning to call Julie. Instead I got started on the Trilionne report. I figured it would be best to give Julie a few more hours to stew about the mistake she was making.

Writing the Trilionne report started fast because I had already developed a template from similar reports for other clients. I only needed to tailor it to Trilionne's specific security strengths and weaknesses. Trilionne had fared quite well in the most recent audit, and it was evident Kyle Standall, their new Information Security Director, had implemented all of the security controls I had recommended last year, when I reported and demonstrated that many of their security controls were inadequate and not operating effectively. This year was different. My usual methods didn't let me penetrate very far into their network. Of course, given enough time I could have found more issues, but it would have taken more of an effort than most hackers would ever spend. I had made an effort to crack into the engineering server I accessed last year, but

Standall had put it behind its own firewall and apparently limited access to only a relatively few authorized people in their engineering department.

By one o'clock in the afternoon I completed the first draft and had given Julie plenty of time to reconsider her position. I texted her, "I miss you tons. Can we meet for coffee?" I would have bet she would reply within two minutes because she always kept her phone within reach. But I would have lost the bet. I would have bet double or nothing on the next two minutes, but I would have lost that bet, too. She was clearly ignoring me. How could she be so cold? There must be somebody else; maybe a partner in her accounting firm. I couldn't drive over to confront her because she hadn't told me the name of the friend she was staying with. I had seen her steeled determination before, but this was a hard-nosed bullheadedness I didn't know she possessed, a rigidity that troubled me deeply. It had to be caused by more than the marriage thing and all of the time I spent working. There must be someone else.

I continued to think about Julie and her stubbornness and eventually got around to thinking maybe this was all for the best. Maybe she was just now showing her true colors. It was probably a good thing she was showing how stubborn she really was, before we got married. Or worse yet, showed her true colors by two-timing me after we were married. Talk about dodging a bullet. It was much better for me to know now than later. Thank goodness she didn't know about the trust fund. She might have hidden her stubbornness and faithlessness until it was too late. In spite of this current episode, I wanted to give her one more chance, if she would take the initiative to reconcile and admit she acted rashly, but she needed to do it within a few days. If she came back, great. If not, I would just move on.

After a quick lunch, I edited the final copy of the Trilionne report. I originally thought the final report would only take about three hours to finish, but it took nearly five because I kept looking at my watch and wondering what Julie was doing. Next, in an effort to keep my mind off of Julie, I turned my attention to the pile of mail that had accumulated over the past five days. After tossing out the advertisements and other junk, a legal sized envelope caught my attention. The return address said it was from Pearce, Baker, and Boone, a law firm in Seattle, Washington. I opened the envelope and read the cover letter. It told me I was the sole heir to the estate of a Mr. Ezekiel Klein who had passed away four weeks earlier on June twelfth. I had never heard of Ezekiel Klein and wondered if he was possibly some long-lost, shirt-tail relative. However, that didn't seem possible because my parents told me I didn't have any paternal relatives. I was the last of our branch of the Klein clan; a fact Dad repeatedly mentioned in an attempt to nudge me into marriage and procreation. After thinking about it I concluded it had to be a mistake. After all, Klein is a fairly common name. The law firm must have been looking for a different David Klein, not me.

Just to be sure, I grabbed my cell phone and called the land line at my parents' house. When Dad answered, I started in with our usual banter, "Dad, this is David. How are you and Mom?"

"About the same as always. What's going on with you and Julie?"

Sidestepping his question, I said, "Hey. I just got a letter telling me I am the sole heir to the estate of some guy named

Ezekiel Klein. I assume it is some type of identity mix-up. You don't know any relatives by the name of Ezekiel Klein, do you?"

Dad took a deep breath and then held it for what must have been five seconds, but it seemed much longer. After the uncomfortable pause, during which I was concerned our phone connection might have been lost, he said almost to himself, "Yes, I do know, or did know, an Ezekiel Klein." He took another deep breath and continued with a shaky voice, "It is a long story, and I suppose you have a right to know the truth. It sounds like you're about to learn it anyway. I would prefer to talk to you about this in person. Can I take the train up to Boston tomorrow afternoon? You're at home aren't you?"

I felt my chest tighten as Dad refused to tell me what was going on. "Yes, I'm at home and I'm available tomorrow. But, I don't understand all of the mystery. What's this all about?"

"Like I said, I would prefer to talk to you about this in person. Let's meet for an early dinner and then we can talk about it. How about if I catch the three o'clock train and arrive in Boston around five twenty. Can you meet me at the station? And, can you come by yourself? It'll be better if Julie doesn't join us."

"Okay. I can come alone. I am sure Julie won't mind. See you at five twenty." Little did he know Julie wouldn't come with me, even if I begged.

I hung up, wondering what the mystery was and imagining a deep, dark family secret. My Dad normally was confident and controlled in every situation, but during our brief call he sounded completely shaken. But maybe I was blowing it out of proportion.

Dad and I maintained a distant but cordial relationship; a relationship I think is typical for most fathers and sons. We spoke by phone at least every few weeks, but never broached personal topics. Instead, we exchanged the usual pleasantries, and chatted about innocuous guy subjects like sports and the weather. Other than hints about getting married, Dad would never consider asking me about the details of my relationship with Julie, and if he did, I am sure I would find a way to avoid telling him what she meant to me, and I certainly wouldn't volunteer anything about the most recent episode.

When I was twelve or thirteen years old, Dad and I were driving back from the train after watching a Mets game. He seemed a little anxious, and when we were about one minute from home he asked me out of the blue, "David, do you know about the birds and the bees?"

Not wanting to admit my near total ignorance of the subject, I said, "Sure… I think so."

He breathed a deep sigh of relief and said, "Good." He pulled the car into the garage. We both went into the house and never spoke of sex again. I figured Mom had forced him into having "the talk" with me. I am sure he dutifully reported back to her that we had "the talk" and all was well.

Tomorrow evening couldn't come fast enough.

I leaned back in my recliner to carefully read the entire contents of the envelope. Ezekiel Klein's last address was in Packwood, Washington, wherever that was. Ezekiel had left instructions for the law firm of Pearce, Baker, and Boone to inform me I was the sole heir to his estate, which consisted

18

primarily of a house on eight acres in Packwood, a 2008 Toyota Tundra pickup truck, a little cash, and minor holdings in a few stocks. Thankfully, he didn't have any outstanding debts, but settling the estate sounded like more trouble than it was worth. The envelope included several legal affidavits I needed to complete and return. I set them aside until after meeting with Dad.

I went online to catch up on the latest information security articles, but my mind kept ping ponging between Julie and Ezekiel. How long would she ignore me? Who was this guy? Was she seeing someone else? What was the big secret? I read an entire article about the latest cross-site scripting vulnerabilities, but didn't retain any of it.

Rather than continuing to waste time reading, I turned my attention to Ezekiel. I entered his address into Google Maps and saw Packwood was a small town in the middle of nowhere, Washington. It was on Highway 12 about halfway between I-5 and Yakima – I had at least heard of Yakima. Packwood was ten miles south of Mount Rainier and nearly surrounded by the Gifford Pinchot National Forest. Talk about out in the boondocks. According to the aerial map, Ezekiel and a neighbor shared a T-shaped driveway connecting their properties to a road that led to Highway 12. Ezekiel's house was on the east end of the T, and about two tenths of a mile away, the neighbor's was on the west end.

The Zillow web site estimated his real estate to be worth $220,000. The 1,500 square foot house, with an unknown number of bedrooms and two bathrooms was on just over eight acres and backed up to the Gifford Pinchot National Forest. I entered Ezekiel's name and location into the PIPL web site and found out he had lived in Packwood for thirty years, didn't have a police record, and had a great credit rating. In ten minutes I had more information about Ezekiel, but nothing that really told me who he was.

I Googled "family tree" and Ancestry.com came up near the top of the list. I went to the site, paid their membership fee, and entered what little I knew about Ezekiel. Within a few minutes I discovered he was my Dad's older brother, an uncle of mine whom I didn't know existed. No wonder Dad wanted to talk about him in person. He had always claimed he was an only child. Dad had a lot to tell me; a lot of explaining to do.

THREE

Sunday afternoon, I took a cab to the Boston South train station and arrived fifteen minutes early. I could hardly wait to start unraveling the mystery of Ezekiel Klein, and maybe I was early because Julie made me see how rude it was to be late. Dad's train from New York was right on time, and he was among the first five people to reach the lobby. He wore a blue oxford shirt with a button-down collar underneath a maroon vee-neck sweater, khaki pants, and loafers, and he carried a small overnight bag. That was casual dress for Dad. I was surprised to see he might be spending the night.

People say I look just like my Dad, but I can't see a strong resemblance. Dad is five foot ten and weighs a pudgy 220 pounds. I am six one and weigh only 175; skin and bones by comparison. We both have brown eyes and wiry hair. However, mine is thick and brown, and his is thin and gray. I think people see the similarity in our noses, which doesn't speak well for either of us. Our noses are large enough to make it a challenge to look straight ahead in a strong cross wind. Of course they aren't really that big, but mine is big enough so I am more than a little bit self-conscious about it. If I thought Dad wouldn't be seriously offended, I would have had it fixed right after my twenty first birthday.

In spite of being well dressed, Dad looked like he hadn't slept since we talked on the phone the day before. His eyes were bloodshot, and his color was a shade paler than normal. I reached out to shake his hand, but he deked to the left and went around my outstretched hand to give me a hug. I couldn't remember the last time he hugged me. It was an awkward few seconds. Dad wasn't the touchy feely type, yet this hug seemed sincere.

As I stepped back to look at him, he said, "I booked a suite at the Copley Square Inn for the night. I thought we could go there and order room service so we can talk without interruption. I hope that'll be alright."

I generally avoided hotel food, but understanding he wanted complete privacy said, "Sure. That'll be fine. How was your trip up?"

He rubbed the back of his neck. "It was okay, but I was preoccupied thinking about how I would tell you about Zeke and worrying about how you would respond. Part of me has been afraid for a long time that this day would eventually come, and part of me has wanted it to come soon so I could get it over with; put it behind me. But let's leave it at that until we get to my room where we can talk in private."

We flagged a cab and rode in silence to the hotel. Dad checked in and received his cardkey for a room on the seventh floor. The awkward silence continued as we rode up the elevator and walked down the hall to room 723. It was a large one bedroom suite with a comfortable conversation nook containing two wingback chairs and a glass coffee table. I stepped over to the window which looked north towards the Back Bay, but the view I hoped to see of the water was obstructed by two tall brick buildings.

Dad dropped his overnight bag by the closet and made a bee line to the mini-bar where he pulled out three small bottles of scotch. Dad, usually a light drinker, looked like he expected this conversation to be very difficult. He unscrewed the caps, poured the contents of all three bottles into an empty glass, and before sitting down walked over to the window and closed the heavy drapes. He nodded towards the chairs, and we both sat down. I thought he was going to tell me about Ezekiel but instead he got up and walked over to the desk and picked up the room service menu. He looked at it for a minute and then brought it to me and said, "Order anything you'd like. It is on me."

I looked through the menu, which looked just like every other room service menu I had seen, and told him, "I'll have the club sandwich with fries and a Sam Adams." He called room service and ordered our dinners, adding an expensive bottle of merlot and a plate of cookies.

He walked back to his chair and sat across from me and took a long slow drink before starting to talk. "I don't know of an easy way to say this so I'll be direct. Ezekiel was my older brother. He is, or was, two years older than I. We were close, very close, best friends throughout our entire childhoods. Even as he entered his teen years and developed an interest in girls, we stayed the best of friends. When he got into high school, he made sure his friends tolerated me, and my friends thought it was cool that an older guy like Zeke would hang out with us younger middle school guys. When we were both in high school Dad, Zeke, and I had some of our best times together. We went to most of the Mets home games and afterward spent hours recalling the best plays. Zeke and I did so many things together I just assumed we would always be there for each other.

"As you may remember, your Grandfather was a strict, no-nonsense disciplinarian. He held himself to a high standard and expected Zeke and I would always do the same. We were both good kids, and I think we mostly measured up to Father's demanding and often unrealistic expectations. We never got into any serious trouble and always got excellent grades, especially Zeke. School was a cinch for him. I hardly ever saw him study, yet he was the valedictorian of his class. Father expected Zeke to go to one of the Ivy League schools, preferably Yale or Harvard. Either one would have given Father bragging rights down at the club. But when I was starting my junior year in high school, Zeke went off to college at Berkeley. He got a full scholarship based on merit because he was such a whiz. Of course tuition money wasn't an issue; Father could have paid the out-of-state tuition and never given it a second thought. However, Zeke was independent and wanted to make his own way in the world. Father was proud that Zeke earned the scholarship because it let him know Zeke wasn't just passing time waiting for his twenty-first birthday when he would come into his trust fund. Besides, he could brag about Zeke's full ride scholarship to his cronies down at the club. As long as I could remember, Father had told both Zeke and me we would become multi-millionaires on our twenty-first birthday. Zeke and I had talked about the cars we were going to buy. Zeke was going to get a Corvette, and I was leaning towards a Jaguar XKE. But I am getting off track."

A knock at the door interrupted Dad's monologue. He opened the door, and the waiter put the tray on the coffee table and opened the bottle of merlot. Dad signed the bill and as soon as the waiter left, he resumed, "When Zeke went to Berkeley it was during the Vietnam War. I think he wanted to do something radical, to be part of something that would change the status quo. He told me he had selected Berkeley because such cool things were happening in California. He wanted to protest the war, and he also mentioned something about California babes. We kept in touch with letters and

24

occasional phone calls. It wasn't like it is now when people call across the country every day without thinking much about it. Because we were Jewish he didn't come home on Christmas break. Instead, he made plans to come home in late March, at spring break. It was the longest we had ever been apart, and I could hardly wait to see him. I remember it clearly. He finished up his finals on a Thursday and he flew home on the following Friday.

"Spring had arrived early. The ornamental plum trees had already started to bud. Their blossoms were still weeks away, but the hope of springtime and the joyous expectation of seeing Zeke after so many months buoyed my spirits. Everything seemed so alive; the air, the garden, and most of all my heart.

"Mother, Father, and I were all so excited to see him that all three of us met him at the airport, and Father offered to take us all out to dinner at the club afterward. The Brighton Hollow Country Club was our family's place for birthdays, Mother and Father's anniversaries and any other special events. The club hosted a dance band on the first Saturday of every month, and Mother and Father planned their calendar to attend every one of the dances.

"During the drive to the club Zeke was conspicuously quiet and stared blankly out the side window. I asked him how he did in his classes, and he muttered, 'Okay. I am doing very well.' I wondered if something was bothering him, but I didn't give it much thought. Father drove us to the restaurant's entrance and let the valet park the car. We went into the dining room where Father had reserved his usual corner table. We idly chatted and then ordered our dinners. Right after the waiter brought our plates, Zeke dropped the bomb. I remember exactly what he said, just as if it happened yesterday. He announced, 'I need to tell you all about a big change in my life. I have accepted Jesus Christ as my savior; I have become a born again Christian.'"

Dad coughed, his voice trembled, and his eyes started to water. More scotch. I wondered if he was going to raid the minibar again.

He resumed his story, "Talk about doing something radical. Father turned beet red, and the veins on the sides of his neck bulged. I could see the throb of each heartbeat and was afraid he was going to have a heart attack. He took a drink of water to give himself a moment to regain his composure. Then he said to Zeke, 'If I heard you correctly I want to let you know in no uncertain terms I don't think your sense of humor is the least bit funny.'

"Zeke was clearly nervous but he looked Father directly in the eyes and said, 'I've become a Christian and I'm one hundred percent serious about it. I'm not trying to be funny.'

"Father took the white napkin off his lap, folded it and put it on the steak that he hadn't even tasted. He stood up and told Mother, Zeke and me to follow him because we were leaving. On the way out he told the maître d' an emergency had come up and we needed to leave. He told him to add twenty percent to the bill and put it on his tab. We all walked solemnly out to the entrance as if we were in a funeral procession. None of us looked the others in the eye during the wait for the valet to return with the car; we just stared at our feet. Father and Zeke stood ten or twelve feet apart. Mother stood between them shuffling her weight towards Father and then towards Zeke, her loyalty seemingly torn by indecision. Father didn't yell, but I had never seen him so tense. The valet brought the car around and we all climbed in. Father drove away from the club's entrance but pulled over at the edge of the parking lot. He turned around to face Zeke and said, 'We're Jewish. We're proud of our Jewish heritage. It is who we are. We are not, nor will we ever be Christians. Never! I am shocked you would even consider such a sacrilege. I am going to give you one chance and only one chance to recant your foolish decision. I want you to renounce this Christian nonsense right now and never ever mention it again. I hope I am being clear about this. I want to hear you renounce it right now!'

"Zeke knew Father could barely contain his outrage, but somehow he seemed at peace, and quietly said, 'I was afraid you'd react like this. I hoped you wouldn't; prayed you wouldn't, but I am not surprised. I thought you would be open to what I have become, who I now am. Clearly you aren't ready to do that. You need to understand I have made my decision. It is irrevocable. I haven't made it rashly, and I won't pretend otherwise just to keep you happy.'

"Mother didn't say a thing. She just tried to stifle her sobs. She gave Father a pleading look that said, 'Don't take this any farther.' But he was so pissed off I don't know if he could have backed off even if he wanted to. He ignored her pleading look and said, 'Ezekiel, I believe you when you said your decision is irrevocable. Now, you need to believe me when I tell you unless you recant this heresy right now, you're no longer my son. Your name will never again cross my lips. You will be dead to me! You will not receive a dime of your trust fund or of any inheritance!'

"I was torn in two by the father I respected and the brother I loved. I knew Father and Zeke had both dug into their positions. I knew they could both be stubborn asses. I wanted to say something to get one of them to back off, but I couldn't think of a thing. Even if I had thought of the right thing to say I don't know if I would have had the guts to say it. I was frozen by fear; fear of what this fracture could mean.

"Somehow both Father and Zeke sensed the discussion was over. We all sat quietly, fearfully. Father drove the car back to the airport where we had picked Zeke up less than two hours earlier, pulled over to the curb, and popped the trunk. Zeke hugged me, got out, opened Mother's door, kissed her, and closed the door. He grabbed his bag out of the trunk and walked off without bothering to close it. Father yelled at me to 'get out and close the damn trunk.' Zeke disappeared into the main terminal. I never saw him again. Never.

"We drove home in deathly silence, Dad parked the car in the garage, and we entered into the emptiness of the house. Father, Mother and I went into the parlor and sat down. I'll never forget how Mother cried. Her deepening sobs starting slowly like the faint sound of far off thunder, a deep rumble not heard as much as felt, the type of sound that spooks birds to flight, a thunder slowly but inexorably drawing nearer, increasing in volume and increasing in frequency until its power convulsed her body with tremors. Fists clenched. Her knuckles turned white. I'm sure her soft heart stiffened, as with rigor mortis.

"Father stared stoically straight ahead, afraid to make eye contact with his wife, who with each tremor was erecting an invisible barrier insulating herself from him, a barrier that grew higher and more impenetrable with each increasing sob. A barrier no amount of time would ever fully remove.

"I sat in dumbfounded silence unsure if I should silently slip away to my room or if I should somehow try to comfort my aching mother. I did neither, but sat in stiff silence, a silence during which I promised myself I would never again go to a Mets game with Father; a promise I kept. Mother's sobbing gradually slowed until she sat shivering as if she were cold. I didn't learn until this morning that she had comforted herself with an oath to continue her relationship with Zeke and to send him money; both without Father's knowledge and certainly without his consent.

"Our family died that night, not the individual members but the bond which had always been its strength, a bond which until that evening had promised a lifetime of togetherness filled with happy memories.

"After about five minutes of silence, Father announced he was retiring for the night. Mother got up and went into the bathroom and locked the door. I wanted to chase after Father and pummel his back with my fists until he came to his senses, but I was afraid of him and what he might do. Instead, I went up to my room and cried. I didn't sleep because I was hoping that I would hear Zeke return to the house. I hoped if he did return Father would take him back. We had been such a close family.

"Zeke never did come home again, and about seven the next morning I went down for breakfast. Father stopped reading the morning paper and walked over to me. After putting his hand on my shoulder he said, 'Zeke's gone. Dead! Don't ever try to contact him. It's best if you just let him go.'

"I was in a daze that first day after Father disowned Zeke. I didn't know it then, but I was in mourning. I went to my room and stayed there all day, not able to accept that Zeke might be gone for good. I got mad at Father, but didn't have the nerve to yell at him so I balled up my pillow to look like his head and pounding my fists into it until my arms were limp. The next day, I started to second guess myself and wondered what I could have done to prevent the blowup. Although I wasn't a party to the fight, I wished I could have done something that would have defused it.

"The next few days weren't much of an improvement. I tried to distract myself with reading or shooting baskets. But without warning a memory of Zeke would flash into my mind and I would be crying again. I felt like killing my Dad when I found out he had placed Zeke's obituary in the Jewish Post newspaper, requesting 'no condolences be sent'. But over time, my fits of crying gradually turned into incidences of occasional sadness. The days turned into weeks, and the weeks into months, and finally the months into years. And the pain lessened, but my guilt grew into an increasing hollowness I carry to this day.

"I never did forget Zeke, but neither did I try to contact him. I thought about it. In fact, I thought about it nearly every waking hour for months. But I didn't call him, nor did I write. Do you know why I didn't? It was because of the money. The damned money! I sold out Zeke for my trust fund. I was afraid if Father found out I had contacted Zeke he would disown me, too. I am totally ashamed. Now, it is too late."

Dad took another swallow and stared at the near empty glass he held in his lap. I had never seen him so distraught, so vulnerable. On one hand I wanted to say something to ease his pain, but on the other hand I was filled with questions that would only add to his sorrow. It seemed best to ask the questions because I was afraid we would never discuss Ezekiel again. I ventured, "Dad, I hope you don't mind too much if I want to understand more about what happened. You got your trust fund a long time ago, and Grandpa has been dead for more than ten years. Did you ever try to find Zeke? Did you ever try to reconnect with him?"

Dad swallowed a bite of his cold Rueben sandwich and said, "Not really. After my father died, I hired a private investigator to find out where Zeke lived and what he was doing. The PI discovered Zeke was living in a small lumber town in Washington and was an accounting manager at a saw mill. I had the PI fly out there and take some pictures. He sent me Zeke's address, his phone number, and a handful of photos. I looked at the pictures and knew right away he had found Zeke. The pictures were just an older version of the Zeke I remembered. He gave me a three page synopsis of Zeke's life; he had been briefly married, appeared to be active in a small church, and drove a pickup truck. Things like that."

I had to ask the obvious question, "Did you contact him?"

"I wanted to and even called him once, but then chickened out and hung up before he answered. I was afraid he wouldn't want to talk with me, or worse, he would tell me to go to hell. The truth is I was afraid he might want to meet with me and tell me what he thought of my betrayal. I was afraid I wouldn't be able to look him in the eye. He had to know that I sold him out for my birthright. He had every right to hate me."

"Oh, Dad. Do you really think he would have slammed the door in your face if you reached out to him? I really doubt it. Of course he could, but how could have that have been worse than this?"

Dad slowly replied, "I know. I know. You're right. But it's obviously too late now. I put money ahead of Zeke. I should have told Father to keep his damned money. I should have told him Zeke was more important to me than a fat trust fund. Should of, could of…, but I didn't. The money was bitter sweet. Whenever I spent any of it on something for myself I couldn't help but ask myself if whatever I was buying was more important to me than Zeke, and it never was; never. That's why I gave much of it away."

"Does Mom know about Zeke?

"I told her last night. She couldn't believe it. She was shocked, but she told me we all make mistakes. I don't deserve her. She's much too good for me. She listened to my story, my terrible story, and when I was finished she came over to the couch and sat next to me. She hugged me, and we cried together. I don't deserve her.

"This morning, I called my mother to tell her about Zeke's passing. She had already been notified. In fact, she had flown out to his memorial service. She had always stayed in touch with him – mostly through mail. Shortly after Father disowned Zeke, Mother rented a post office box and used it to secretly correspond with him. They stayed in contact throughout the years. Her annual trips to Mexico with her lady friends were really trips to secretly meet with Zeke. He was diagnosed with stage three prostate cancer about a year ago, and she saw him one last time about three weeks before he died."

"If Grandma kept in touch with him, why didn't she let you know?"

"I asked her that very thing. She said it was because she thought I had disowned Zeke just as Father had. She thought I didn't want to know anything about him. She told me how much I meant to Zeke, and how much he wanted to reconcile.

But he thought I never wanted to see him again. I was such a fool."

As I stood up and walked over behind his chair I made a mental note to call Grandma sometime soon. I put my hands on his shoulders and said, "Dad, I'd like to think that if I was in your shoes I'd have done things differently, but I am not at all sure I would have. I am afraid I would've done exactly what you did. I hope not, but who knows?"

He reached his hands up to mine and said, "Well there you have it. The skeleton is out of the closet. I'm not sure why Zeke wanted to make sure you learned about him, but it is clear that he wanted to expose our ugly secret."

"I wonder why he left everything to me. Grandma must have told him I don't need any of it. He could have given it to a charity or to friends. I'm going to do everything I can to understand why he left it to me."

"You may never know."

"True, but I am certainly going to try and found out."

I looked at my watch, and saw it was after eight. We hadn't even finished our dinners. I walked around in front of Dad and said, "It is getting late. I should be going. Are you going to be alright?"

He smiled and said, "Yes. I'll be okay. It means a lot to me that you and your mother understand. That you don't despise me."

"Dad, I could never hate you, you know that don't you? I am going to call Zeke's lawyers tomorrow and then figure out what the next steps are. I'll keep you in the loop unless you don't want me to."

"Yes, please do."

Dad stood up and we hugged again. We walked over to the door, and I left with my mind full of questions about Zeke; questions I was going to try to answer.

FOUR

My next on-site client meeting, at Braxter Enterprises, was scheduled to begin three days later, in Vancouver, Washington. Three weeks earlier, Theron Chandler, Braxter's Chief Security Officer, had sent me an email requesting a proposal for me to audit their InfoSec program using the International Standards Organization 27001 security framework. His email explained they wanted me to perform the audit because I had a top-secret security clearance and because I was also a certified forensics examiner. I didn't understand why they would need someone with top-secret clearance or a forensics examiner, but I was glad they did because it gave me justification to charge my highest hourly rate.

I responded with a detailed proposal one week later, and as soon as he received it, he called me to tell me in detail what he wasn't willing to write in an email that could be forwarded, or worse, intercepted by an electronic eavesdropper. After I picked up the phone, and we exchanged a few pleasantries, Theron jumped right into his explanation, "Braxter is an electronics company that, according to our website, manufactures Radio Frequency Identification technology."

To let him know I was somewhat familiar with the technology I interjected, "RFID chips, right?"

Without acknowledging my interruption he continued, "The chips are like little radios that get programmed with identification information, and then they can be scanned by a handheld device that reads the information. We sell tons of those chips but they're low priced commodities, and we don't make much profit on them. As our website explains, we are a leading supplier of active RFID chips. These little guys can broadcast their data up to a range of about one hundred yards. Big box retailers program them with data like part numbers, quantities, manufacturing dates, etc. and then attach the chips to pallets of merchandise in their warehouses. The chips tell the inventory tracking systems exactly how much of each item they have in their warehouse, and it even lets them know what inventory is the oldest and should be sold first – all without someone needing to walk through the warehouse to perform a manual inventory count."

I interrupted again, "I read Braxter's website and have a basic understanding of RFID technology. I'm more than happy to help you with your information security, but I don't understand why you need a consultant with a top-secret security clearance or a forensics examiner."

"That is the interesting part; we need you to work with one of Braxter's lines of business not mentioned on our website. We have an unpublicized division which does all of its business with the Army, Navy, Marines and the intelligence agencies. We developed special microchips and highly efficient antenna systems allowing tactical command centers to track the movement of nearly every asset they have on the ground. That includes everything from people to rocket launchers to tanks; they use it in virtually anything that has a value over $2,000. One of the unique features of our technology is that in low-power mode it transmits data only every ten minutes to conserve battery power. But it also listens for a signal telling it to go on high alert. When the devices are on high alert they can be reconfigured on-the-fly to transmit their information up to 1,000 yards at three times per second and to give the command center real-time location data.

I raced to scribble notes as fast as I could while Theron continued. "As you can imagine, a range of 1,000 yards is not enough for many tactical situations. The Department of Defense and the spook agencies build our military line of devices into their assets, and our devices send each asset's exact position to a relay that extends the transmission range as far as needed. They usually send the signals up to the GPS satellite network where the asset's globally unique ID and its location are then sent back to the tactical command and control center. It tells the commanders exactly where everyone and everything of value is positioned. This information serves multiple purposes. It lets commanders redirect assets to areas of greatest need, and it helps prevent troops being killed by friendly-fire. It even helped the Army recover a munitions shipment that was stolen and on its way to the Afghanistan black market."

I didn't know what to say other than, "That sounds extremely valuable."

Theron went on to say, "Braxter calls the technology Kilroy in honor of the World War II 'Kilroy was Here' graffiti. The military considers Kilroy to be a top-secret strategic system and is rightfully concerned that foreign nations are currently trying to hack into Braxter's network and steal the design specifications so they can clone the system."

I interjected, "I've heard some news stories a few months back about the Chinese using advanced persistent threat exploits to hack into companies like Intel, Google, and Dow Chemical to steal their intellectual property and manufacture knockoffs without spending the time or money to design the products from scratch."

Theron explained, "We do want to hire you to perform the ISO audit I mentioned in my email, but we are really looking for a much more thorough audit than normal. We need you to go over our security controls with a fine toothed comb. I suspect we'll also need you to forensically examine some of our computers for evidence of espionage. Your original proposal was only for four weeks. I estimate the project we have in mind may take up to four months. I need you to revise your proposal, but don't go into detail about what you will be doing because I don't want to leave a paper trail for anyone with curious eyes. You only need to change the four weeks into four months and change the resulting prices. We are willing to pay your $325/hour rate, plus normal travel expenses for you to commute from Boston each week for the duration of the project."

I told him I would send my revised proposal by FedEx the next day.

Theron accepted the revised proposal and within two days returned a signed Statement of Work along with the PO number I would need for billing purposes. We had scheduled the Braxter engagement to start the week following the Trilionne project, and I was excited to get started with it and to put the Trilionne fiasco behind me. Wednesday's meeting would be a kick-off with Theron and Braxter's primary security stakeholders; people from information security, physical security, IT, and even software development engineers. I would start interviewing them immediately after the meeting to get a complete understanding of their security program. Theron had promised to schedule a series of one-on-one interviews for Wednesday afternoon, Thursday, and Friday morning.

To prepare for the meetings, I spent the first part of Monday morning developing an introductory presentation for me to explain to the Braxter staff what the audit would entail and what information I would need from each person. I also spent about an hour refining the questionnaires I would use with their IT and engineering people to gain an understanding of their software development process and information security program.

I wrapped up the Braxter preparation by eleven thirty and had about thirty minutes to kill because I didn't want to call Ezekiel's lawyers until nine in the morning, Pacific Time, which was three hours behind Boston time. I couldn't help thinking about Julie. I still hadn't heard from her, and I missed her a lot more than I expected to. I wondered if she was having second thoughts; no I hoped she was having second thoughts. Listening to my Dad's regrets the night before had made me much more circumspect about the value of relationships. I had second thoughts about walking away from Julie merely because I *thought* she was being stubborn or disloyal. I planned to wait for her outside her office at five thirty that evening, which was the time she normally left work, to see if I could convince her to come back or, failing that, at least to talk with me.

At noon, I called Pearce, Baker, and Boone and told the receptionist I was calling in response to a letter I had received from one of their attorneys, a Ms. Carolyn Anderson. The receptionist put my call right through. I introduced myself to Ms. Anderson and told her I was calling in regards to Ezekiel Klein's last will and testament. She told me she couldn't divulge the full estate details until she verified my identity. However, she was willing to tell me Ezekiel had named David

Klein as the sole heir, and he didn't appear to have any outstanding debts, but she would leave that for the probate to confirm. She also told me she was in custody of a sealed letter for me from Ezekiel and she could only release it to me in person or if I sent a notarized affidavit proving I was David Aaron Klein who resided at the address to which the letter I had received was mailed.

I wanted to meet with Anderson face-to-face in case she had known Ezekiel personally and could tell me about him. As long as Julie was playing hard to get I didn't have any reason to return to Boston for the weekend. After some quick figuring, I realized if I left Braxter by noon on Friday, I could drive from Vancouver, Washington to Portland and then catch a commuter flight from Portland International to SeaTac or to King County Airport and could be in downtown Seattle by three thirty, or shortly after. I asked Ms. Anderson if she could be available at four in the afternoon on Friday to meet with me. She agreed, and I gave her my cell phone number and asked her to contact me if anything came up. If Julie came to her senses before Friday I could always change my plans and return to Boston instead of going to Seattle.

I also planned to rent a car at the airport in Seattle and drive it to Packwood after the meeting with Anderson so I could spend the weekend digging into Ezekiel. According to Google Maps it would only take two and a half hours to drive from Seattle to Packwood, depending on traffic, which I assumed would be heavy on a Friday evening.

I called the airlines and cancelled my Friday afternoon return flight from Portland to Boston and booked a one thirty flight from Portland to King County Airport, just south of downtown Seattle, and I also booked a rental car for pick up at the airport. I was all set for the next chapter in the mystery of Ezekiel Klein.

I had several hours free before trying to intercept Julie at five thirty so I went for a three mile run and then got back to the security reading that I hadn't been able to focus on the prior Saturday. At four forty five, I took a cab to Julie's office building and arrived twenty-five minutes later. I wanted to be ready just in case she left work a few minutes earlier than normal. I stood off to the side in the lobby where I could observe the bank of elevators which went up to the fifteenth floor where she worked. At five thirty five she exited from the middle elevator, tied her hair back in a ponytail, and started walking through the crowded lobby to exit at the main doors. I was relieved to see she was alone because I didn't want to create a scene in front of her co-workers. I quickly caught up and got in step with her, on her right side. She didn't notice me until we reached the main doors. When she finally realized I was walking beside her, she was taken aback and brusquely said, "David, what are you doing here? I asked you to leave me alone. You do remember that don't you? I hope you aren't going to force me to get a restraining order."

"Yes. I remember you asking me to leave you alone, but I just had to try talking with you one more time. If you won't talk with me, then I won't keep bugging you. I promise. You won't need a restraining order, but I really would like you to give me a chance for us to talk. Just a few minutes, please?"

She slowed down and said, "I guess I owe you that. Let's go to the Starbucks up the street and we can talk for a few minutes there. Only ten minutes. Fifteen tops."

"Thank you," I murmured.

We walked in silence to the coffee shop, which was surprisingly busy for an early evening. Julie asked for a Grande decaf, but I bought each of us Ventis because they take longer to drink. We took the only available table, a two-top in the dimly lit corner. I lowered my voice to ensure the other coffee drinkers couldn't hear my creaking voice and said, "Julie, I've been thinking a lot about last Friday. I've gone from being shocked, to resentful, to rueful. You were right about me not seriously considering marriage. I did blow it off and honestly, I thought you would just wait for me to take the next step, if and when I was ready. That was wrong of me, and I am sorry. I should've taken you seriously. Please accept my apology."

She raised one eyebrow and warily said, "Apology accepted, but don't think it changes anything."

I continued as Julie ran her finger in circles around the rim of her coffee cup, "I don't know what is next for us; I don't know if anything is next for us. I can't honestly say I'm ready for marriage, and I think we would both agree it wouldn't be a good idea to move towards marriage unless I'm positive... unless both of us are positive marriage is what we want. We would both need to be sure I'm ready for it, and we both know I'm not, at least not yet. I understand you aren't willing to continue our relationship unless it is headed for something permanent. I get that. I really do. But it doesn't mean I like it. Anyway, I'm not here to try and convince you that you should move back in. I am here to apologize, which I have already done. And I'm here to ask you if we can still be friends while I try to figure out if I'm ready to get married. I know it might be awkward, but it would make me feel much better if we could talk every once in a while. What do you say?"

Julie's eyes started to moisten, but she kept her composure and said, "I am willing to try being just friends; it would have to be strictly platonic, but I am willing to try it; at least in a little while. I think we should give ourselves a couple of weeks before we talk again. I want us to be able to step back from us being a couple. That way we can see if being only friends will work."

I told her giving ourselves a couple of weeks made sense, but I didn't like it one bit. I thanked her for meeting with me; we hugged platonically and went our separate ways. As I walked away, I thought about how relieved I was that at least she agreed to talk again in a few weeks. I realized it wasn't only because I wanted to see her again, which I did; but because it meant I hadn't hurt her so badly she never wanted to talk with me. That would have been unbearable.

I took a cab back to a deli which was only a block from my condo and bought a takeout tuna sandwich and salad for dinner. I then walked home where I ate in silence. After dinner, I searched LinkedIn for potential clients in Portland, Seattle, and anywhere in between. I found a couple of prospective companies in both Portland and Seattle where I had second-level connections I could ask for introductions to get my foot in the door. I was thinking I might want to spend some extra time in the Northwest to find out more about uncle Ezekiel. He had certainly piqued my curiosity.

After dinner, I watched the last half of *The Good, the Bad, and the Ugly* and then packed for the trip to Vancouver. It was going to be a ten day jaunt, and I needed to take business casual clothes for the Braxter meetings, and I wanted to take casual clothes for the side trip to Packwood. I packed four dress shirts, two pairs of slacks, underwear, socks, my dress shoes, and my running gear. I could send laundry out at the hotel which allowed me to travel light enough to avoid checking baggage. I didn't need to pack my toiletries because I always kept a full set in my suitcase. I planned to wear jeans, a sweater, and Nikes for the flight. They would do double duty while I was in Packwood investigating uncle Ezekiel.

FIVE

Tuesday morning I arrived at Logan an hour early for my nine o'clock flight through Chicago to Portland. First class had checked in full so I couldn't upgrade to first class. But, I took advantage of priority boarding to beat the crowd. I shuffled down the narrow aisle, hefted my roller bag into the overhead bin, and squeezed into my aisle seat, with my knees crammed against the back of the seat in front of me. As long as I was charging Braxter an extra $50/hour for my top-secret clearance rate, I would personally pay the difference between coach and first class for the future flights between Boston and Portland. Braxter had made it clear in their purchase order that they would only reimburse me for economy air fare, but I could easily afford to pay the extra money for first class and besides, I would write it off as a business expense.

A young man about nineteen or twenty years old sat in the middle seat next to me. He wore faded blue jeans with a hole in the right knee, an untucked wrinkled tee shirt, and a pair of sandals. He reminded me of how I liked to dress when I was his age. He said "Hi. I'm Ben." I introduced myself and noticed he was holding a microeconomics textbook. I took a chance and begrudgingly violated my personal rule that forbade me from engaging fellow passengers in idle conversation; a rule I enacted after being bored nearly to death by nervous fliers who tried to take their minds off of the flight by babbling nonstop. I pointed at the book and made the brilliant observation, "It looks like you are studying economics."

He said, "Yes, business administration. I am getting my MBA at Northwestern, and have one more chapter to read for a test tomorrow." Then he asked me, "What do you do?"

I replied, "I run a small information security consulting company."

He turned toward me, as much as his narrow seat allowed, and asked, "I've heard the term 'information security' mentioned here and there, but I don't really know what it means. One of the guys I live with is studying engineering and has mentioned 'InfoSec' a few times. He told me it means information security, but I don't have the slightest clue what he was talking about. Would you mind giving me the Reader's Digest overview?"

I knew it was a going to be a long flight and it wouldn't hurt to be sociable for a few minutes. I started in with an abridged version of my standard explanation that I hoped wouldn't be too technical. "Information security is concerned with preserving the confidentiality, availability, and integrity of information. It nearly always applies to electronic information, but can also apply to paper records. Confidentiality, integrity, and availability are called the CIA triad of InfoSec. Confidentiality means only authorized people should be able to access the information. Hackers and other bad actors make all of this difficult because they try to steal credit card information, proprietary intellectual property, and other information; any of which compromises confidentiality. Integrity means the information can be trusted to be correct. Bad guys hack into systems and modify data, like bank balances or student transcripts, which compromises information integrity. Availability means pretty much what you would probably guess; making sure information is there when people need it.

Hackers can launch what are called denial of service attacks against websites by sending such a large number of web page requests all at once that the website gets completely overloaded. As a result the web pages don't get sent to valid users. This kills availability. Some hackers threaten to launch denial of service attacks against corporate websites, like on-line banking sites, unless the corporation which owns the website pays a protection fee to keep the hackers from attacking. Does any of this make sense?"

Ben nodded and replied, "Yeah, it does, but is it really that big of a deal? How many hackers are there, and realistically, what are the chances they'll attack a single company?"

Ben, like most of the population, didn't have a clue about the scale of cyber-attacks. I asked him, "If you connected a new web server to the internet and didn't protect it by putting it behind a firewall and configuring it securely how long do you think it would take before someone tried to hack into it?"

Ben shrugged and then replied, "I don't know. I would think most never get attacked. Based on that, the average must be at least a month before it gets hit? Am I close?"

"I'm afraid not. According to the Internet Storm Center, a group which monitors intrusion attempts, it would almost certainly be attacked in less than ten minutes. Pretty scary, huh?" Ben just sat there so I tossed out another question, "How many times do you think the US nuclear defenses are attacked each day?"

"Well since I was way off last time, I am going to guess about once per hour. That works out to about twenty-five times each day. Am I closer this time?"

"Not so much. They get attacked on average ten million times per day which works out to be about more than one-hundred times each second. Of course the nuclear infrastructure is highly protected, causing most and hopefully all of the attacks to fail. The good news for people like me who are in the InfoSec business is the bad guys, with their automated tools, make sure we have plenty of demand for our services."

Ben laughed and said, "Maybe I should ditch business school and study information security."

I grinned and said, "I wouldn't do anything rash."

I thought I might have overloaded Ben with my sobering facts; I didn't think he knew whether to believe me or not, but he asked, "How tough is it to protect computers from the hackers?"

I continued my monologue, "It was a lot easier before everything was connected to the internet, but now the internet paves a four lane electronic freeway from anyone who has a computer right up to the front door of corporations. Nearly all corporate computers are connected to the internet, and that connection opens all of those computers up to the risk of cyber-attacks. Of course, corporations use firewalls to protect their corporate networks from the bad stuff on the internet, but even the best firewalls can't be one-hundred percent effective."

"What does a firewall do?"

"Firewalls are called firewalls because they're like those heavy, metal doors that keep fire from spreading from one part of a building to another, but in this case they keep bad actors from getting from the internet into the corporate network. I tend to think of them as being like security guards who only let authorized people into a building, only in this case they, theoretically at least, allow only authorized internet traffic. InfoSec would be easy if corporate networks didn't need to connect to the internet. The problem is employees who work for the corporations need to use the internet for research, customer interactions and the like. This means firewalls can't block all internet traffic because if they did the employees couldn't do their jobs. The idea is for firewalls to selectively block network traffic and allow only valid traffic."

Poor Ben. By the time I had finished my Reader's Digest overview, it had turned into an overly detailed explanation, and we had reached our cruising altitude and were well on our way to Chicago. Ben was glassy eyed and mumbled something about needing to study for his midterm. I'll bet he was wishing he had developed his own personal rule forbidding conversations with fellow travelers. He thanked me for the explanation and politely plugged his ear buds into his ears and started reading. I didn't have room to pull my laptop out; instead I grabbed my iPad and started reading *The Hunt for Red October*, an old Tom Clancy novel I had downloaded several weeks before.

We arrived in Chicago on time, and I had thirty minutes to eat before boarding my flight to Portland. I scarfed down a dry sandwich in the terminal's food court and hurried to my gate. After boarding, I took my window seat on the right side of the plane and resumed reading my Clancy novel. The book was entertaining, and the time quickly passed. Shortly before we started our descent, I noticed the Pacific Northwest was covered with a low, gloomy cloud layer extending as far as I could see to the north and to the west. The clouds must have been no higher than seven or eight-thousand feet high because several snowcapped mountain peaks poked their heads through as if they were reaching for the sunlight that can be rare in the Northwest, even in summer. The pilot came on the intercom and pointed out Mount Adams, St. Helens, the one without its top, and Rainier, the one farthest to the north.

We started our descent into a cottony cloud bank, and I waited for our wheels to touch the tarmac. The pilots must have been still thinking about mountains, or napping, or else playing games on their cell phones because the landing slammed us down into our seats, causing a few passengers to curse under their breath. After the plane taxied off of the active runway, the pilot came on the intercom and said, "Ladies and gentlemen, we have attacked the city, and the city has surrendered! Seriously, I want to apologize for such a terrible landing. I've been flying these big birds for more than twenty years, and that is the worst landing I've ever made. I don't have any excuses, but again, I apologize. I hope the rest of the day is smoother than our landing. I'll be standing outside the cockpit while you deplane in case anyone wants a personal apology."

At least he had both a sense of humor and the common sense to admit the landing was terrible. After getting off of the plane, I walked to the Hertz Gold Club reader board that was only about a hundred yards east of the main terminal. My Nissan Altima was ready and waiting. I set my bags in the back seat and headed two miles east to the I-205 Bridge that would take me north over the Columbia River into Washington. Braxter's headquarters were on the east side of Vancouver so I arrived in twenty minutes.

Because of the time change, it was still early afternoon in Vancouver. After driving by Braxter to be sure I could find it in the morning, I drove to my hotel in downtown Vancouver hoping they would let me check in a few minutes early. Fortunately, my room was available and it even had a nice view of the Columbia River.

I spent the rest of the afternoon reading up on the advanced persistent threats the Chinese had allegedly used against Intel and the other high tech companies. My reading confirmed what I already suspected; the hackers had probably searched the internet to find some valid employees' email addresses. They then sent infected emails to the employees. When an employee opened the email, the infected email would silently install malicious code on the employee's computer. This is often how hackers establish a foothold behind the attacked company's firewall. It is analogous to a criminal being able to sneak by the security guard to gain access to the inner parts of the building. Only in this case, it was a software program that gained access to the corporate network.

The malware, once running behind the firewall, could use the internet to reach back out to the hacker's command and control software and receive instructions about what it should do next. The command and control software could tell it to do any sort of nefarious deed such as cloning itself on other computers or searching hard drives for documents containing phrases such as "company proprietary". The command and control software could then tell the malware to send the documents to the hacker. These types of attacks are called advanced persistent threats because they are clearly sophisticated in nature and because they can often operate for months, or longer, without detection.

After I finished my reading, I thought back over the shocking number of U.S. companies that were attacked by the Chinese and wondered why the good old United States of America hadn't made a self-righteous, internationally visible protest with the Chinese government. The attacks were clearly illegal, and it would have made sense for the feds to impose trade tariffs, sanctions, or other penalties. Then it dawned on me; the feds had likely been caught with their own cyber hands in the Chinese's cookie jar. They couldn't very well raise hell because they were guilty of the same thing. Of course, I was merely speculating, but my explanation was plausible enough to satisfy me. I think Tom Clancy would have liked it, too.

Although it was only five-thirty in the evening local time, it felt much later to me. I wanted to stay up until at least ten Pacific time; otherwise I would wake up too early the next morning. I called the front desk to get a suggestion for a running route near the hotel. The desk clerk told me there weren't any good places nearby and suggested I use a treadmill in their fitness center. Treadmills aren't my first choice, but I used one anyway in hopes of increasing my energy level before going out for dinner.

I changed into my running gear, grabbed my iPod, and walked down to the gym. It was a typical cramped hotel gym with two exercise bikes, three treadmills, an exercise mat, and a few dumbbells. After selecting a playlist of blues songs, I warmed up for five minutes at a jogging pace and then kicked the pace up to eight and a half miles per hour. I ran at this speed for five miles and felt pretty good. Then I began to cool down at a gradually decreasing pace. After ten minutes of cool down, I toweled off and walked back to my room to shower.

I dressed, grabbed my iPad, and walked to the Altima to look for a decent place to eat. After wandering around for ten minutes I spotted an Applebee's and pulled in. I always feel self-conscious eating by myself and sometimes wonder if other people in the restaurant think I am a social pariah because I don't have any friends to go out to eat with me. I asked the hostess for a booth in the back corner and sat facing the back so I could avoid making eye contact with anyone who might have thought I was a social misfit. I ordered a Cobb salad and returned to *The Hunt for Red October.* After paying my tab and driving back to the hotel, I went to my room, stripped to my underwear and crawled in bed to read for a few more hours.

Travel appeals most to those who do it the least. Mention traveling to a white-collar migrant who travels each week to reap his fees, and he will probably envision endless airport security scans, crawling boarding lines, cramped airplane seats, salty restaurant food, and carbon copy hotel rooms that all are ironically compensated for by earning points in loyalty programs promising more security scans, boarding line, airline seats, restaurant food, and hotel rooms. I try to ignore the loneliness; using social media updates, texts and phone calls in a vain attempt to maintain relationships, relationships that can only be successfully built with understanding smiles and compassionate nods and tender touches. Not being able to even talk with Julie made me feel sad and empty. I fell asleep thinking about both Julie and the project I would start working on the next day, but mostly about Julie.

Six

My meeting with Theron Channel was scheduled for eight thirty so I left the hotel at ten after eight to give myself plenty of time for the ten minute drive and for checking in at the visitors' entrance. Braxter Enterprises was located in a non-descript, sprawling one story building set back about one hundred yards from the main road. Like many of the IBM facilities I have visited, the entrance was tastefully landscaped with large concrete planters that served a dual purpose of being attractive while blocking a terrorist or disgruntled employee from driving a bomb-laden vehicle within thirty feet of the front door. Braxter wasn't taking any chances in terms of letting anyone drive into their lobby. The exterior walls were about fifty percent brick and fifty percent heavily tinted glass to let in natural light while preventing prying eyes from seeing inside.

I walked through the front doors and immediately confronted a uniformed, but unarmed, security guard manning a gated entrance. I signed in at the guard station, and the guard called Theron to come down to authorize my entrance and escort me inside the building. The physical security was pretty standard, but I had expected better, given Braxter's top-secret projects. Theron walked out through the gate, we shook hands like old buddies. He informed the guard I would be working with Braxter for the next four months. The guard carefully checked my driver's license and compared my face to the picture. After satisfying himself that I was indeed David Klein, he issued me a temporary contractor's badge and motioned me through the gate.

I followed Theron down a busy hall, walking quickly to keep up with his frenetic pace. He looked to be about 5' 7" tall – a little shorter than I had remembered. I estimated his weight to be about 250 pounds, which made him more than just a little pudgy. He was one of those pregnant looking guys who carried his extra weight almost entirely in his sagging stomach; his butt and legs were slender. How he kept his pants from falling down as he power walked was an unsolved mystery to me. His dress shirt was untucked, but part of the shirttail was stuck in his waistband, revealing the tag on the back of his Levis. It advertised a twenty-nine inch inseam and a forty-six inch waist. I then glimpsed part of a suspender clip attached to his waistband near the tag; suspenders worn under his dress shirt. Mystery solved.

He turned right, and I followed him down an empty corridor. Theron slowed for me to catch up and commented, "This part of Braxter houses our commercial operations, and the security here isn't nearly as tight as it is in the part of the building which houses our government/military operations."

We took another right turn and came to a second guard station. This one was manned with two extremely serious looking armed guards. Theron told them who I was, and they pulled out a copy of my top-secret clearance papers the Defense Intelligence Agency had apparently sent to them. One of the guards carefully compared my physical characteristics to my description and photo. Next, he asked me to place both hands, palm-down, on the glass surface of a machine resembling a small photocopier, and the machine scanned my hands much like a photocopier would. The guard explained I would need to wait a couple of minutes for my fingerprints to be sent back to Washington DC and be digitally compared to the set of prints on file there.

While we waited he had me step over to a photo machine that looked just like the photo machines I had seen at the Massachusetts Department of Motor Vehicles. He took my picture and the machine laminated it onto a new contractor's badge that clearly displayed my name and picture. In a few minutes the machine that had scanned my palms beeped and then flashed a green light. The guard explained that a digital representation of my right thumb print was being programmed into the fingerprint scanning door-lock. Every time I needed to enter the restricted area I would be required to use two-factor authentication; the first step was to swipe my contractor badge on the door scanner. The second step was to put my right thumb on the scanner for two seconds. I asked, "Why does it need two seconds to scan my print? That seems slower than other scanners I have seen."

The guard smiled and replied, "It isn't just checking your fingerprint. It also confirms that your thumb has a pulse. That way if someone steals your badge and cuts off your thumb they won't be able to enter the restricted area because your severed thumb won't have a pulse."

As I gulped, I am sure my pulse quickened while I managed to say, "Uh huh. Makes sense."

I thought I was all set to enter the secure work area, but the guard pointed to my bag and said, "You can't take anything inside that can store data. That means no smart phones, no laptops, no tablets, no USB drives, and no cameras."

I responded, "I have one of each in my bag."

He pointed to my right and said, "You can put them in one of those lockers against the wall. Here's a key to locker six. You can retrieve your stuff on your way out." I removed the contraband devices from my bag and locked them up. The guard motioned for me to hand my bag to him, and he inspected its every pocket. I could tell these guys took physical security seriously, and I could only assume they were serious about information security as well.

The security guard's last step was to run a metal detecting security wand up and down each of my arms and legs and then up and down my torso. I was clean, and he finally cleared me to move forward. Only then were Theron and I allowed to proceed down the hall. On the way I said, "The fingerprint scanner and the photo machines look pretty new. How long has that security checkpoint been in operation?"

Theron replied, "They were both installed about a month ago. We realized we needed to take our security to the next level."

We continued down the hall until we came to a cafeteria. It was larger than other corporate cafeterias I had endured, and Theron explained that Braxter subsidized the cafeteria to encourage people to eat on the premises instead of taking the extra time to eat at one of the nearby restaurants. Theron bought a couple of cinnamon bagels with cream cheese, and we left the cafeteria and quickly reached the conference room where our first meeting was scheduled. The conference room table was similar to the utilitarian Formica topped tables I had seen at other Department of Defense suppliers. I suspected that when DoD personnel came on-site Braxter didn't want to appear like they were frittering money away on non-essentials like comfortable or stylish furniture. Eight metal chairs surrounded the table and matched its bland décor. Theron and I sat down across from each other, and I immediately noticed how tightly his shirt was stretched across his protruding stomach. Two of the buttons were holding on for dear life. I was afraid one would pop off, shoot across the table and put one of my eyes out. Of course, I kept these thoughts to myself.

I turned my attention back to Theron and heard him say, "The rest of the team won't be joining us for about twenty minutes. I thought I could spend a few minutes bringing you up to speed. I gave you some background when we spoke on the phone, but now that you're here I can give you more details. You will remember we provide Kilroy to the military. The Department of State has included it on the US Munitions List so Kilroy is required to comply with ITAR."

I interrupted, "I am not familiar with ITAR. What is it?"

"It stands for International Traffic in Arms Regulations. In a nutshell it means we can't provide Kilroy or any information about it to any foreign entities. If we do, Braxter is subject to heavy fines and our executives could face jail time. That's a serious concern, but not as serious as the concern about unfriendlies getting their hands on the technology. As you likely know, the U.S. spook agencies monitor a significant percentage of the internet traffic. They continually search for intelligence information going across the wire. Apparently, they happened across a communication referring to Kilroy by name, and it gave a partially accurate description of Kilroy's capabilities. The DoD notified us saying we have a leak inside the Kilroy division. They're putting the screws to us to not only increase our security, but to use all possible means to determine if any unauthorized information has been leaked. That is where you come in."

"How many people work in the Kilroy division, and how's it organized?"

He chomped a bagel bite. "It is a fairly small group. We have two hardware engineers and two firmware engineers. Together they develop the device hardware and software. Two additional software engineers develop the command and control software. The quality assurance team has two people, and we have one technical writer who develops the user manual and the various service manuals. We have one person in sales, but he's stationed in Virginia. Besides that we have a couple of accountants, two IT people, one security person besides me, and the division VP, Joan French. I can't believe any of these people would be stealing Kilroy information, but then again who in the CIA would've suspected Aldrich Ames of spying for the Ruskies? Anyway, you need to audit our security with a fine-toothed comb. You'll report your findings directly to me and to French, but only to the two of us. Any questions before the rest of the team arrives?"

Theron took another chomp, and I nodded. "Yeah. I had planned to give the team a presentation about the ISO 27001 security principles and my audit procedures, but the PowerPoint presentation is on my computer, and it's locked in the locker. Any chance I can get it?"

"Don't worry about giving a formal presentation. Just give them a verbal overview. After the meeting, I'll take you to your cubical. It has a computer you can use. Is there anything else on your computer you need?"

I shrugged my shoulders. "I guess not, but I am not a hundred percent sure."

Theron wiped his mouth with the back of his hand and mentioned, "By the way, you won't be able to get out to the internet from any computers in the Kilroy division. It's an inconvenience. Actually, it is more than an inconvenience. It is a pain in the butt, but we're pretty locked down. We can't afford to lose our defense business. It only accounts for ten percent of Braxter's revenue, but makes up more than 30 percent of our profits. No need to tell that to the DoD though."

At nine thirty, the Kilroy technical team began arriving in the conference room. By nine thirty five, five people had joined us; four men and one woman, and Theron started the meeting by asking me to introduce myself to the team. I kept my introduction brief and superficial because I didn't want anyone to think they might be under suspicion of espionage. I explained I had been retained to perform a standard ISO 27001 security audit.

After I wrapped up my introduction, Theron asked everyone to go around the table and introduce themselves. He nodded to the woman who was sitting almost directly across from me. The dark circles under her eyes and her worried expression had caught my attention earlier, as she walked in. She appeared to be in her early forties and wore her blonde hair in a ponytail, a dark blue jacket over a white blouse, and a dark blue skirt that matched the jacket. She smiled pleasantly at me and then introduced herself, instructing me to call her Joan. As I had surmised, she was Joan French, the VP heading up the Kilroy Division. She instructed her team to cooperate with me in every way and asked me to let her know if I was getting anything less than full cooperation. I always appreciated it when an executive sets a strong tone-at-the-top for cooperation because it always makes my job a whole lot easier.

The man to Joan's right introduced himself with a terse, "Harold Barry, firmware lead. I also manage the hardware guys." He fit my stereotype of a nerd engineer. His brown hair was a day or two past needing to be washed and a month or two past needing to be cut, and his shirt looked like it had never seen the hot side of an iron. His button down collar wasn't buttoned, and its pocket contained two pens and a mechanical pencil.

Next was an Indian who sat to my immediate left. He looked to be in his early thirties and was dressed neatly in business casual attire; a maroon long sleeved shirt and tan Dockers. He was absolutely verbose compared to Harold and said, "I am Shankar and I manage the software engineering team that develops Kilroy's command and control software. Let me know how I can help you."

The person on my right was a balding man about fifty-five years old. He looked me directly in the eye and said, "I am Ronald, the QA lead. My team does our best to make sure the stuff these guys develop works like it is supposed to." He grinned and continued, "Sometimes it's quite a challenge. By the way you can call me either Ron or Ronald. I answer to either one. Just don't confuse me with The Ron." I must have looked confused because he nodded towards Theron and said, "He's 'The Ron' Get it? Theron." Everyone groaned. Ron was the joker on the team. It seems like every team has at least one.

The last person introduced himself, "I am Mike one of the two IT guys. I can help you sort out our network and servers. Just let me know if you have any questions." Mike was dressed casually in a University of Oregon Ducks tee shirt and blue jeans.

Theron explained that Karl Matson, the other security person, was out because his wife had just gone into labor with their first child. He told me to catch up with him when he returned to work in a few days. He then reminded everyone that he had scheduled one-on-one times for me to meet with each of them separately to interview them about their security procedures and policies. He told them that, although I was a contractor, I had been fully vetted and had a top-secret clearance. They could and should share any information with me. On that note he adjourned the meeting and offered to show me to my cubicle, which was right next to his.

My cube wasn't as Spartan as I thought it would be. It was well lit, and the ell-shaped work surface provided plenty of room for me to spread out. One of the cubicle's side walls held two short book shelves and a locking cubby-hole storage area. Theron instructed me about the 'clean desk' policy, "Don't leave any papers on your desk when you are away from it. If you need to go to the restroom, lock your papers up first. We actually prefer you work paperlessly and keep all of your notes on the computer. That way you can't accidentally leave papers lying around.

"Your computer is a laptop, but it's never to leave the building. You can take it with you to conference rooms for meetings but don't try to leave with it. All of the data on the hard disk is encrypted with 1024-bit encryption. If you leave it idle for more than two minutes the screen saver will come on, and you'll need to log back in when you return to it. Mike from IT should be here in a couple of minutes. He'll give you your login credentials and your initial password, which you will need to change right away. He'll also ask you to scan one of your fingers on the laptop's built-in scanner. When you log in you'll need to use your password and scan your fingerprint." He grinned and continued, "Your laptop's fingerprint scanner isn't very sophisticated. It won't check for a pulse so don't let anyone cut your finger off."

In terms of information security Braxter was miles ahead of Trilionne, and Theron Channel was light years ahead of Davis Chandler, Trilionne's Chief Information Security Officer. I knew I was going to enjoy my assignment at Braxter even though I wasn't sure if I would find the suspected leak, or not.

Theron told me he had sent an email to my work account to inform me of my schedule for interviewing the other personnel, and I looked forward to diving in.

SEVEN

My first meeting was with Joan French, whose office was only about thirty feet straight down the hall from my cube. Her door was ajar, and when I knocked, she stood up from her large oak desk and motioned me to come in. As far as executive offices go, hers was unremarkable. I wondered if the masculine desk was Braxter's standard issue executive desk or if it was a power statement on Joan's part. Two guest chairs faced her desk; I assumed so she could hold small meetings without needing to move to the round table and four chairs situated in the corner. Photos of what I guessed were her sons hung on one of the walls. Both boys were in their late teens; probably high school graduation pictures. They certainly looked like brothers, but I didn't see a strong resemblance with Joan. She walked over to the table carrying her coffee cup, and we both sat down.

Joan pulled at the skin at the base of her throat and said, "Theron speaks highly of you and says you're recognized as an expert by information security industry leaders. I hope you can ferret out any irregularities here. As Theron has undoubtedly told you, it looks like we might have a leak, and if we do the consequences will be severe. Worst case we could lose our government contract and face a huge fine. My career here would be over."

I could feel the pressure building. "I hope you realize it'll be nearly impossible for me to prove you don't have a leak. Just because it can't be found doesn't prove it isn't there. Do you have any reason to suspect anyone on the team?"

Joan had crossed her legs under the table, and I could see her left foot in my peripheral vision shaking like a fall leaf in a wind storm. Her high heel shoe looked like it could fly into orbit any second. She replied, "No. I'd be shocked if anyone on the team was stealing from us. Besides, everyone on Kilroy has undergone an extensive background check, and everyone has a secret security clearance; Theron's is top-secret."

"They all have recent credit checks?" Joan looked puzzled so I added, "That could show if anyone's in a financial bind and needs some extra money?"

Joan took a couple of quick breaths. "I don't know. Our standard hiring practice is for every candidate to authorize us to perform periodic background checks. I'll make sure we've checked everyone's in the past ninety days."

I lowered the volume of my voice and spoke a little slower in hopes she would relax a little. "That's a good place to start. My first step will be to make forensic copies of everyone's hard disk. Then I'll search each disk for anything suspicious. I'd like to make the copies after hours to avoid tipping anyone off that we're looking for malfeasance. I'll need the admin passwords for everyone's computers. Can you get those for me? I'd rather not ask Mike because, if he is the perpetrator, I don't want to tip him off."

"Sure. Corporate IT has a copy of our admin passwords. I can get them without alerting Mike."

"I'm going to need five one-terabyte external hard drives. I'll use the external drives to store the copy of each person's hard disk. I could buy my own drives but security won't let me bring them on site."

"I'll have them for you within two days. What else?

Joan appeared to relax somewhat; at least her foot slowed its up and down motion. I added, "I have my own software to analyze the hard disk copies. Is there any way for me to bring my laptop on premise?"

"Send me an email describing it, including its serial number. I will forward it to the security guards, and they'll let you bring it in."

"By the way, is it common for you to authorize people to bring in their own devices?"

"It was until about four or five weeks ago when we tightened our security up."

That's not what I wanted to hear. "It sounds like it would have been pretty easy for someone to copy the specs onto a portable USB drive or even to their own laptop until recently. Is that correct?"

She bit her lower lip and said, "I am afraid so."

"Okay. You need to understand it isn't very likely I'll be able to find out who copied the files. I'll try, but you can't expect miracles."

"I get it, but I need you to do everything you can. If we have a leak and don't stop it, heads will to roll, and mine will roll farthest."

"I'll do everything I can. There is something else I need. Soft copies of all of your security documentation, including documentation about how HR performs background checks on new hires, physical and environmental security, access control policies, security incident management procedures, business continuity management plans, and anything else you have. Can you get those to me by tomorrow?"

"My admin, Greg, will email them to you within the hour. I know exactly where they are because I reviewed some of them myself just last week."

"Great. That means I can start reading them right after lunch. One more thing; how would you like me to keep you updated on my progress?"

"Email me at the end of each week. Summarize what you accomplished and tell me your objectives for the next week."

Sensing the meeting was over, I stood up and told Joan, "You'll have my status report every Friday. But if you ever have questions please get ahold of me right away."

She nodded and I walked out of her office and back to Theron's cube so he could take me to my appointment with Harold, the nerdy lead firmware engineer. Theron said, "I thought I would let you do the toughest interview next."

I walked into the windowless conference room which Theron had reserved for my interview with Harold, who was already there waiting for me with his back towards the open door. He was reading a glossy paper that looked like it was a datasheet describing some type of hardware component, but I didn't know for sure because I couldn't read more than the headline. Harold barely glanced up as I circled around the table to sit across from him. I recalled Harold's job was to write the firmware enabling the Kilroy hardware to send its location signals to the command and control center. I almost chuckled aloud at the aptness of Harold being a firmware engineer because firmware is a type of software that doesn't interact with humans. It controls hardware or mechanical devices, such as anti-lock braking systems or engine controllers. The firmware Harold wrote didn't interact with people, and apparently he didn't either.

If I am honest with myself, which I occasionally try to be, I must admit I take some form of twisted pleasure when I meet people I consider to be true, card carrying techno-nerds. Maybe it's because people sometimes think I am a nerd, a label I would like to avoid because of the social awkwardness connotation. I believe I have reasonable social skills, and I prefer to think of myself as being 'technical'. The fact that I know people who are much higher on the 'Steve Urkle' nerd scale than I am serves as proof I am not really a bona fide nerd. As I said, I'm technical, and that is a good thing because it implies I can tackle challenging problems, in my case challenging information security problems.

I smiled at the top of Harold's head and said, "As you know, I'm here to perform an audit of Braxter's information security and need to ask everyone some background questions. First, what is your overall assessment of Braxter's security; what are the strong points and what areas do you think could be improved?"

Harold continued to look down at the datasheet but replied, "I'm not stupid. You're here to find the person who's stealing information. That's right isn't it?"

I was momentarily taken aback by his blunt question and wondered why stealing was the foremost subject on his mind. Was he guilty? He continued to stare at the paper sitting on the table between us. His ongoing lack of eye contact increased my suspicion. I didn't know if he was feeling guilty, or if he was merely nervous about answering my questions, or if he was just uncomfortable talking at all. His reason didn't matter. I couldn't let the truth about why I was there tip off the entire

Kilroy team, and I needed to get the conversation on track. I calmly replied, "As I said in our meeting, I'm here to perform an ISO 27001 information security audit. Why would you think I'm looking for someone who is stealing information?"

He finally looked up at me and gave me an incredulous stare. "There's been lots of talk about security lately, and in the past five or six weeks security has gotten a lot tighter. Any idiot would notice it. I can't even bring my droid phone into our work area anymore."

"So, security has gotten tighter. Do you see areas that aren't as tight as they should be?"

"No. Everything is already plenty tight."

Talking with him was like cross-examining a hostile witness. "You also mentioned you think I'm looking for someone who's been stealing information. Would it be possible to do that… to steal information?"

"Maybe not now. Before, it would have been simple. Anyone could have done it."

"How's that?"

"All of our product specifications were stored on a file server that anyone on Kilroy could access. Anyone could copy them. I know because I used to read the specs myself during my breaks and during lunch. Nobody told me I couldn't, and I wanted to know how all of Kilroy's systems interact. Some people might think it's a waste of time, but I am technical and like to understand the details. Of course, now I can only read the specs which directly pertain to my work. What's wrong with letting people see the bigger picture?"

"Did you make any copies of the specifications?"

"Didn't need to."

"Why's that?"

"I have a photographic memory and pretty much remember everything I read. I don't need to make any copies. It is all stored up here," he said while tapping the side of his head. "Why? Do you think I stole secrets?"

"No," I lied. Harold's defensive attitude put him on my list of suspects, but I certainly didn't have enough information to accuse him or even mention my suspicions to anyone.

He looked right at me with his dark brown eyes and said, "Good, because I didn't."

"Can you tell me about the security controls that are in place to protect the firmware you write?"

He furrowed his brow and said, "Sure. We recently implemented a software control system that locks down all of the code I write. My code is in a special file repository that holds all of the source code for the entire Kilroy project. It is like a computer vault that holds the company jewels. Whenever I need to make a change to my firmware code, I am forced to check it out from the software control system, and each check-out action gets recorded in the system's audit logs. Every time I check any software out and make changes, it is all recorded, and I am required to document why I checked it out and what changes I made. I even have to get approval from management. Talk about big brother watching over my every move. People from Quality Assurance and from Security review each change to make sure I haven't introduced any defects or security vulnerabilities. Our software development process is top notch. It has to be. If my code has defects, people die."

"Do you have documentation describing Braxter's software coding standards?"

"Of course."

"Would you email a copy of it to me?" I wanted to see if the document he would send would be exactly the same as the document Joan promised to have her admin, Greg, send to me. Part of my audit was to determine if everyone was using the latest version of the standards.

Harold appeared to relax a bit and replied, "Sure, I'll do it as soon as I return to my cube. Is there anything else, because I have lots of work to do? My next firmware release is scheduled for next Monday, and I still have one module to completely rewrite."

I lied once again, "No. You have been quite helpful. Thanks for your time."

As I was standing up to leave, Harold asked, "You know why you're here, don't you?"

"As I told you, I'm here to perform a security audit."

He sneered, "That's what they want you to think. You're really here to be their scapegoat. If the DoD can prove that someone has stolen specifications from us and you don't catch them, you're going to take the blame, not Joan and not Braxter. I hope they are paying you a lot because you're going to be toast."

I walked back to my cubical thinking about what Harold told me and worried that he might be right. Klein InfoSec Associates, the consulting business I had poured years of my sweat into, would go down the toilet if a story got out that I was incompetent. I put the thought out of my mind and checked my email. Joan's admin, Greg, had sent me all of the security documents Joan had promised. I put off reading them until after lunch. I walked down to the cafeteria to get some food I could bring back to my desk, where I expected to spend the rest of the afternoon reading the documents.

In spite of its small size, the cafeteria offered a couple of hot entrées and had a deli station where the cooks could make a variety of customized sandwiches. I ordered a tuna on whole wheat, and loaded up my tray with a green salad and a giant cookie I shouldn't have taken, but I rarely resist the aroma of fresh, soft chocolate chip cookies. I added a large glass of water and took it all up to the cashier. The total was $4.85. I love subsidized cafeterias. What a deal.

I went back to my desk and started reading the physical and environmental security document. It was thorough and well written, and it was as boring as watching paint dry. By page twenty I was thinking I should have gotten a caffeinated soft drink instead of water. It would be totally embarrassing to fall asleep at my desk on my first day. I willed myself to read the rest of the document and made a few notes to remind myself that the policies and procedures described in the document reflected best practices.

Next, I plowed through two documents describing access control policies and human resource background checks. I discovered Braxter had only been performing in-depth background checks for Kilroy team members for the last two years, and employees who were on the payroll prior to that time weren't required to authorize Braxter to perform a detailed background check. I made a note to find out which existing employees, if any, refused to authorize the detailed check. Anyone who refused would warrant a little extra scrutiny. I wondered if Harold refused.

I had enough time to at least start reading the business continuity plan. It was a three-hundred page tome that documented all of the data backup procedures, plus procedures to get the entire Kilroy production line and IT systems back in working order in the event of a natural disaster or even a man-made disaster, such as a bomb. Reading it raised my boredom to a new level. Restoring IT systems after a disaster, even a simulated one, is tremendously complicated and rarely goes according to plan. The next disaster recovery test for the IT systems was scheduled for early September, and I made an entry on my calendar to be on hand to see if they could get all of their systems back on line according to plan.

I managed to stay reasonably alert until five thirty, when I finally finished the business continuity plan. Like the documents I read earlier it was complete and clear. I called it a day and headed back to my hotel. Usually when I am on an on-site assignment I spend an hour or two each evening reading documents I didn't have time to read during the day. Not with Braxter because they wouldn't allow me to take anything out of the building. I looked forward to having a free evening.

Several hours of daylight remained by the time I returned to my hotel so I quickly changed into my running gear and drove to a high school I had seen while driving back from Braxter. It had a nice track where I ran wind sprints to increase my cardio capacity. I alternated between sprinting at about ninety-five percent of my maximum effort for half a lap and then jogging the next half a lap to recover. I repeated this routine for sixteen laps then slowly jogged a couple of laps to cool down.

I picked up a small meat lover's pizza on the way back to my hotel room and ate it while the pizza was still hot, before showering. After I showered, I pulled out my iPad to read my Clancy novel and fell asleep around ten thirty.

*****

I awoke at five thirty in the morning because my internal clock was still on east coast time. After a quick shower I got dressed and headed to Braxter, stopping at a coffee shop for a large coffee and a yogurt and fruit parfait because the Braxter cafeteria wouldn't be open until seven thirty.

I planned to spend most of the day interviewing the remaining Kilroy team members. Ron, the software quality assurance team manager explained that in addition to evaluating the software for functional defects, his team also scrutinized all of the software for security vulnerabilities. He told me everyone on his team had been trained on secure software development practices and secure software evaluation practices. He was clearly proud of his team. Ron also told me all of the QA team members had consented to in-depth background checks.

Next, I interviewed Shankar, but didn't learn anything new. Shankar substantiated everything Ron told me, which was a positive; I would have been concerned if he hadn't. Last for the day, I interviewed Mike, one of the IT guys. Mike was assigned solely to support the Kilroy project, although his manager Susan Dickenson, had broader responsibilities. As I listened to Mike talk, it became clear that he took his work seriously. By the end of the day I had interviewed all of the key people except for Karl, whose wife had just delivered a healthy baby boy. I planned to catch up with him the following week, after he returned to work.

After I left work I followed what was starting to become a routine. I returned to my hotel, changed into my running gear and went for another run at the high school. On the way back to my hotel, I stopped at a deli and picked up a roast beef on whole wheat sandwich to eat in my room. The deli sold fresh smelling cookies, but I didn't want to start piling on extra pounds. After scarfing my sandwich, I drove into Portland and explored the Pioneer Square area. I arrived downtown in twenty minutes, parked my car in a public garage, walked down to the Willamette River, and came to a wide walkway bordering the west side of the river. I walked downstream along the river and then crossed over on the Steel Bridge's pedestrian ramp to the Eastbank Esplanade. Runners, bikers and skaters sped by, several times so close I was almost hit. In spite of the eclectic traffic I decided that unless I planned to run wind sprints at the track I would drive into Portland to run along the river and then grab dinner because running along the scenic river was much more inviting than running on a boring track. I made a mental note to Google running routes near downtown Portland and see what else might be available.

I walked south towards the Hawthorne Bridge where I crossed back to the west side of the river. A couple holding hands and making eyes at each other strolled towards me. The woman's brunette hair reminded me of Julie, and I was immediately hit with a melancholy mood. I could almost smell the perfume Julie wore on our first date. Sometimes my emotions are like the wind; unseen and as a rule unnoticed, but at times very powerful, so powerful they can overshadow my rational thoughts. Being reminded of Julie was a blast of wind making me feel terribly alone.

I knew honoring Julie's request not to contact her for two weeks was going to be nearly impossible. According to my count, I had to wait another eleven days, eleven days that would seem like eleven weeks, weeks that would drag on at a glacial pace. If I kept missing her, maybe I was ready for marriage and ready for a job that didn't require such constant travel. I wondered if Julie was thinking of me. But mostly I was afraid she was seeing someone else.

I walked deep in thought back to where I had parked my car and got on I-5 to drive back to Vancouver. I reached my room at eight thirty and went online to order a dozen red roses to be delivered to Julie's work the next day. I requested the florist include a plain card saying, "Thinking of you, David." And I was – thinking of her, wishing we were back together.

Next I emailed Pat Hoard, a private investigator I had used two years before on a consulting gig in Boston. His diligent surveillance gave me the evidence I needed to prove one of my client's Chief Information Security Officers had a serious gambling problem that drove him to sell intellectual property to the competition. I gave Pat what little information I had to help him track Julie; her last address, which was mine, description of her Camry, names of her family members, and her employer's address. It wasn't much to go on, but Pat knew how to connect the dots, and I authorized him to spend up to 120 hours to find her current address and to take pictures of everyone she was spending time with. Pat would probably assign the surveillance to several off duty Boston cops so they could watch her 24/7 for a few days. It was going to cost me more than ten-thousand dollars, but it was well worth it for me to know if she had dumped me for someone else.

Afterwards to distract myself, I searched online for more information about Packwood. It really was located in the middle of nowhere. I remembered the town was nearly surrounded by the Gifford Pinchot National Forest so I went to the GPNF web site to get more information. I had no idea that both Washington and Oregon contained multiple, adjoining national forests. The Gifford Pinchot forest all by itself was huge; nearly 1.4 million acres. But it connected with other national forests that connected with yet other national forests. Assuming trails were in place, it looked like someone could hike from the border between California and Oregon all the way to Canada without leaving national forest property. I wondered what the Gifford Pinchot forest was like. I assumed it had lots of trees, but I had no idea whether they were hardwoods like in New England, pine, fir, or something altogether different. After about forty-five minutes of digging around, I turned my laptop off and took *The Hunt for Red October* to bed and read until I fell asleep.

Normally, I sleep like a rock and then wake up without recalling even a hint of a dream. That night was different. A particularly vivid dream woke me from a deep sleep and then puzzled me for more than an hour. I dreamt I was a detective trying to solve the crime in the murder-mystery game of Clue. All of the characters in my dream were people from the Kilroy project. They were all gathered together in an old, three story Victorian mansion. Professor Plum was a brilliant recluse, whose shifty brown eyes darted around the room from one object to another, always avoiding direct eye contact with the others. He wore a purple, velvet smoking jacket with leather patches on the elbow. His bushy eyebrows peeked over his thick black rimmed glasses while he smoked his Sherlock Holmes pipe. Although in costume, I could easily tell he was

Harold because he answered my questions with curt denials and indignantly proclaimed his innocence. He claimed he and Colonel Mustard were in the library arguing about the symbolism in Kafka's *The Metamorphosis* at the time the murder apparently occurred.

Theron, a paunchy version of Colonel Mustard, corroborated Professor Plum's alibi. The Colonel wore a pith helmet and a yellow field jacket stretched tautly across his sagging belly. Three war medals hung proudly on his right breast. He answered my questions with military precision, but didn't provide any useful insights as to who might have committed the murder. After questioning the Colonel, I knew the process of elimination was getting me closer to identifying where the murder had occurred, the murder weapon, and the actual murderer. I checked both Professor Plum and Colonel Mustard off of my list of suspects.

Mrs. Peacock was next in line. She styled her hair in a French braid and wore a low cut blue dress that revealed two inches of ample cleavage, a sultry version of Joan French. I peppered her with questions about the murder, but she too, convinced me of her innocence. That narrowed things down to the last character in my dream, Reverend Green.

Shankar was Reverend Green. He wore an olive green robe over a white clerical collar. The process of elimination told me I had my man. Consequently, I confidently began my interrogation. However, the Reverend had a bullet proof alibi. He wasn't even in the house when the murder was committed. Instead, he was working late at the church. He told me the church custodian could corroborate his story if I wanted to double check his alibi.

According to the Clue rules, the game winner – hopefully me – would need to identify the character who had perpetuated the murder, ascertain the murder weapon, and determine the room where the crime occurred. As I exhausted the suspects, my initial optimism evaporated. I quickly became stressed out, frantic actually, as I tried to solve the mystery. I ran from the ballroom to the library then on to the study and fired additional questions at each of the characters. I desperately revisited every possibility of character, murder weapon, and room. It was clear a murder had been committed, and it was equally clear none of the characters had done the deed. I double checked all of my conclusions just to be sure I hadn't overlooked a thing, but still it was obvious neither Professor Plum, Colonel Mustard, Mrs. Peacock, nor Reverend Green had committed the crime.

Lying in my bed at three fifteen in the morning, I felt like a complete failure. I didn't and still don't believe dreams tell the future. However, I couldn't help wondering if there wasn't some meaning to mine. Was I unable to identify the murder because it was one of the team members not in the dream, or did I fail because the murderer wasn't part of the team at all? I wasn't able to come to a conclusion, but neither was I able to go back to sleep. After an hour of tossing and turning, I turned on the light and returned to Tom Clancy.

Eight

The next morning I successfully navigated my way through Braxter's security checkpoints and arrived at my stark cubical at seven forty five, just after the fecal matter hit the fan. As I was unlocking my desk, I received a text message from Joan saying, "my office ASAP." I quickly walked to her office and knocked on the partially open door. She was on the phone but waved me in and pointed to one of the two chairs across from her desk. I quietly sat down and listened to her side of what was a very one-sided conversation, a conversation where she was grimacing while nodding her head and listening. Joan was conservatively dressed in a white blouse worn under a gray blazer. Her blonde hair was parted in the middle and hung down to her shoulders. She rubbed her eyebrows with her free hand and her face held a tight stare. As I watched her listen to the caller, I couldn't help but picture her being dressed up as Mrs. Peacock, but I didn't think the real Joan would flash cleavage, at least not at work. She was too businesslike.

In between long periods when I could hear her caller ranting but couldn't make out his words, I heard her say, "No, Sir. ... Yes, General. ... No, of course not... Yes, this is my only priority... I didn't think we needed to hire a big security firm... He is reportedly the best money can buy ... I will get back to you just as soon as I know something... Yes, by five o'clock your time... Certainly." I heard the other party slam the phone down before Joan had a chance to say goodbye. She gently hung up the phone and immediately started filling me in.

She wiped her ashen cheeks. "That was Brigadier General Matthews. He's the pompous ass who oversees the Kilroy program for the Army. As I am sure you surmised, he's extremely upset at me and at Braxter. He threatened to cancel our contract and take legal action to transfer all of our Kilroy intellectual property to Calkins, our number one competitor. I don't know if he has legal authority to do it, but it doesn't really matter because either way he wants to make my life a living hell. I hate working with newly minted generals who can't resist throwing their weight around. Matthews and I have worked together for more than seven years, and he was actually human when he was a lowly Colonel."

I asked, "What's got him so worked up?"

"Last night the Defense Information Systems Agency intercepted a Kilroy specification as it was being sent through a circuitous internet route to the People's Republic of China. The people at DISA don't know who sent it but are assuming it originated at Braxter. Of course, the Army has their own copies of all of the Kilroy documents, but it would never occur to Matthews that they could be the source of the leak. Thankfully, the specification was a high level design document describing Kilroy's overall operation, and it didn't divulge any details about how it actually works. The Chinese will know our forces have Kilroy, but Matthews doesn't think they have enough information to compromise it or reverse engineer it. Unfortunately for us, he is probably right about Braxter being the source of the leak. We're guilty until proven innocent. I told him we had hired a top notch consultant to help us find the leak. He thinks I should have hired a large firm with a national reputation. He told me you'd better find the leak or you won't ever find a DoD contractor who will use your services in the future. He isn't making idle threats, and I am sorry you got pulled into this mess."

There goes Klein InfoSec Associates. Right down the toilet. "Did you give him my name?"

Joan leaned back in her chair, her legs crossed and her top foot madly waving up and down. "Yes, I'm afraid so, and I think he wrote it down and plans to have one of his people check you out. I'm afraid if you don't find the leak he really will blacklist you."

This isn't how I envisioned my Braxter engagement; I didn't sign up for this. "I told you not to expect miracles."

"You... we had better not fail."

I folded my arms across my chest and said, "Joan, if you're having second thoughts about me and want to switch to a nationally known firm, go ahead. I'll only bill you for the contracted minimum of two weeks. You need to have complete confidence in whoever you use. If you stick with me, I'll expect your full support."

Joan shook her head in denial and said, "I hired you. I trust you. And, I don't want Matthews to push me around. Screw him. I'm going to stick with you unless they force me not to."

I was relieved that Joan was supporting me, but I wondered if she had the juice to stand up to Matthews if he insisted I be replaced. Only time would tell. I said, "By the way, I had an idea that might help... if we get lucky. Have you considered planting an Easter egg in the specifications so you can track where they came from?"

"I am not sure what you are talking about. What's an Easter egg?"

"It can be several things. I am thinking of hidden text buried in each document that will tell us where each specific copy originated. Information like the date it was last modified and the address of the server where it was stored. We would embed different Easter eggs in the copies we send to the Army. Then if a stolen document is intercepted the Easter egg would tell us if it came from Braxter or from the Army. "

Joan leaned forward. "How would we hide the message?"

"The specs are written using Microsoft Word and then stored in both their original Word format and also in Adobe's Portable Document Format. The method I have in mind is pretty simple, but sometimes simple solutions are the best. Let's say we wanted to bury a message that says, 'April 3, 2014 – Braxter Document Server'. I would enter the text into the specification's footer area at the bottom of each page. I would then shrink the message to a one point font size and change its color from black to white. It would be invisible when viewed on a computer screen or when printed on white paper. If someone were to print it out on colored paper the font size would be too small for the message to look like anything other than a faint white line across the bottom of the page. The only way someone would be able to read it is if they enlarged an electronic version at least six hundred percent, and that is pretty unlikely."

Joan smiled and said, "Aren't you a devious one. I like it."

"Harold told me new firmware is scheduled to release in a few days. Can we use the new release as an excuse to update and reissue all of the specifications? That would give us the opportunity we need."

She let out one huge breath, and color started returning to her cheeks. "I don't see why not."

"I see one potential problem. Who is going to bury the Easter eggs in the documents? It has to be someone with access to the final versions and someone you totally trust."

"How 'bout Ron? As the QA lead, he verifies and validates each of the final documents. Plus, I totally trust him. I've worked with him for more than ten years. He's never given me any reason to doubt his integrity."

"Okay. Ron it is." I hoped Joan knew her people as well as she thought she did.

I thought for a moment and then continued, "You know we could already be too late. This could be like locking the barn doors after the horses have escaped. Any document already in the wild won't have an Easter egg. We can't help that, but we can tell everyone the new release contains new, state-of-the-art capabilities which obsolete the prior version. Because hardly anyone knows the Kilroy big picture, people shouldn't be suspicious if they don't know specifics about the new capabilities. If anyone at Braxter or even the Army is stealing documents they'll want to get the latest versions, and if DISA or the National Security Agency intercepts the specifications being sent to the Chinese we'll know where they originated and will be able to narrow our search."

Joan thought for a moment and said, "The Easter egg idea is good, but it isn't going to be enough. We need to get more aggressive in looking for a mole here at Braxter. If we lose another document General Matthews will yank our contract. What else can we do?"

"What is the status of the external hard drives I asked for?

"You should have them by the end of the day."

"Okay. I will start making copies of the key peoples' hard disks this weekend. I was planning to analyze five drives at a time and then analyze five more. If you want us to move fast, I will need another three drives. That will let me copy data from all of hard drives and analyze them later. How soon can you get the additional ones?"

"I'll expedite them and you'll have them by Monday afternoon. And I'll make sure the security guards let you bring things in and take them out without being inspected. They won't like it, but too bad. I'm the boss. What else?"

"I need the names of all the Kilroy people who refused to authorize the detailed background investigations. Also, I think you should hire a private investigator to look into everyone's financial status. It would be good to know if anyone has an unusual amount of debt or if anyone has recently had a significant increase in assets – an expensive car or a vacation home. As you might imagine, high debt can motivate people to look for alternate income sources, and sudden asset increases can signal someone is receiving payoffs. Although I doubt anyone at Braxter would be stupid enough to deposit illicit funds in their bank account or brokerage account, we still need to check it out."

"Is there anything else?"

"Two things. First, I need Theron to show me how your security information and event management software is configured."

"Can you dumb it down a little for me so I'll know what you are talking about?"

"Sorry. You may not know it but everyone's computer and every server on the network can be configured to send a record of all user activity to centralized security information event management software, where it can be analyzed. For example, it can record each time you log in to or out of your computer, and it can record when and where you save a file. If you save it to an external USB memory device that action can be recorded. Saving files to USB memory devices is against policy because it is theoretically possible to smuggle a memory device out of the building, but that doesn't mean it isn't happening. We can configure the SIEM software to record all events of interest, and we can configure it to automatically look for anomalous activity and alert us if it sees any. Theron can fill me in on how the system is configured, and we can reconfigure it, if needed, to capture all of the events that could help us. It is like the ultimate 'big brother' software. It collects evidence we can hopefully use to detect and prosecute any unauthorized behavior."

"David, you have carte blanche to do whatever you think is required. If we have a leak, we've got to stop it and stop it quickly."

"Second, I need a place to work that is more private than my cubicle. If people see a stack of hard drives on my desk they aren't going to believe I am merely performing an ISO security audit. We can't tip anyone off."

Joan thought for a second and then said, "Let me speak with the building supervisor. There are a couple of unoccupied offices in the Kilroy area. We set them aside for visits from the army brass, but I know I can get one allocated to you."

"One more thing, I need 24/7 building access. I will need to do some of my digging after hours to avoid raising undue suspicion among the staff."

"Consider it done."

"Joan, I don't know if Theron told you this or not, but starting next week, my contract calls for me to work four ten-hour days. We set it up this way so I can commute back and forth from Boston. I will start by early afternoon on Mondays and leave by noon on Fridays. Today I need to leave at noon even though I'm not returning to Boston. I've got a meeting late this afternoon in Seattle to deal with the estate of an uncle who recently passed away. If you can authorize the 24/7 access right away I will try to return Sunday afternoon, if not Saturday night, to begin copying everyone's hard drives."

"You'll have it before you leave today. Oh, one more thing… Unless and until you are told otherwise you report directly to me. I'll inform Theron later today. And here's my business card with my cell phone number, in case you need to reach me after hours."

I left Joan's office and returned to my cube by way of the cafeteria. I bought a large cup of coffee and a bagel with lox and cream cheese. Walking back to my desk I realized I needed to reprioritize my work. Finding the leak, if it existed, was clearly priority number one. I moved the security audit to priority two and for the time being would only work on it if I had slack time. I checked the instant messaging system to see if Theron was available because I needed to discuss the security information event monitoring system with him right away. His status showed "available" so I sent him a message asking him to meet me in the conference room ASAP.

Theron and I arrived at the conference room at the same time. I motioned for him to enter ahead of me and closed the door behind us. We sat facing each other on opposite sides of the table, and I was relieved that the shirt Theron was wearing wasn't too tight for him and that I didn't need safety glasses to protect my eyes from speeding buttons. Theron looked a little irked that I had pulled him away from whatever he was working on and said, "Tell me, what lit your hair on fire first thing this Friday morning?"

"I just met with Joan, and the Army reamed her out because they intercepted a Kilroy specification on its way to China. She wants my full attention focused on finding the leak, assuming the document was sent by someone at Braxter. She told me to do whatever it takes to track it down."

Theron interrupted me and with an irritated tone said, "Hold on. Why did Joan assign this to you and not to me?"

Joan had put me in a tough situation by cutting Theron out of the loop and not telling him I would be reporting directly to her and not to him. I rationalized it would be easier to play dumb than to tell him I wouldn't be reporting to him any longer and said, "I think Joan grabbed me because you weren't in the office yet, but you should ask her yourself. I am just guessing."

Theron settled back in his chair and said, "Okay. What do we need to do?"

"I told Joan we needed to make sure the security information and event management software is configured to monitor as much activity as possible and to analyze the activity to identify anything suspicious. I assumed you have SIEM software. Please tell me you do."

"Of course! It's a top of the line system from JCNSoft. We just upgraded to the newest version. It really rocks."

"That's a relief. How do you use it?"

Theron smiled like a grandmother being asked to describe her newest granddaughter. "You may know JCNSoft thinks an awful lot of their software. The Kilroy project couldn't justify purchasing it for ourselves. So we joined forces with Braxter's corporate security group and split the cost between us. That made sense because Kilroy was already using the corporate Security Operations Center. The SOC is manned 24/7 with analysts who monitor all of our security systems. Kilroy generates lots of cash for Braxter, but not enough for us to afford staffing our own SOC 24/7. It may not be ideal, but sharing the SOC makes sense because it lets us afford better systems and around-the-clock staffing."

Theron was so proud of the Security Operations Center that I didn't have the heart to tell him I was concerned that sharing the SOC might not be worth the risk of giving all the people in corporate security visibility of Kilroy's security systems. I asked him again, "How is the SIEM being used?"

"We've enabled second-level logging on all of Kilroy's PCs, servers, and firewalls. Whenever any of those devices do anything of interest, a log event is sent over the network to the SIEM. The SEIM's rules tell it what to watch for, and when it sees something of interest, it notifies whoever is on call in the SOC for them to investigate. We configured the rules to look for the normal things such as multiple failed login attempts which can indicate someone is trying to crack into one of the systems. Of course, the firewall logs much more information, especially if someone outside of Kilroy attempts to access one of the Kilroy systems, which should be impossible."

"It looks like you have set it up fairly well. However, I want to take it to the next level. First, let's enable third-level logging to record every time anyone accesses a file. I know the logging overhead will slow the systems down some, but if anyone notices, we'll tell them nothing has changed. We definitely don't want to raise suspicions. Can you change the logging level without letting anyone know?"

Theron wrinkled his nose and said, "Is that level of logging really necessary? It sounds a little paranoid to me."

I smiled and said, "Yeah. It is a bit over the top, but the stakes are too high not to do it."

Theron nodded and said, "I guess you're right. If someone really is stealing Kilroy specs they're pretty sophisticated because our security is top notch."

"You're right on both counts. I have just gotten started with the security audit, but haven't seen anything to make me concerned."

"Okay. I have administrator rights to all of the systems and can make the changes remotely. Nobody will suspect a thing."

I continued, "Second, in addition to sending the logs to the SEIM, I want them sent to a backup system logger. That way we can periodically compare the data in the main SEIM to the backup data. If anyone tampers with the corporate SEIM data we will know it. Oh, I don't want corporate security to know anything about the backup system. How long before the backup system will be operational?"

Theron replied, "That is going to take a couple of days. Let's say Wednesday of next week."

"Not soon enough. We need it by end-of-day Monday. When you reconfigure the systems for third-level logging you should also set them up to send their log events to both the primary SEIM and to the backup."

I pushed back from the table to indicate the meeting was over and reminded Theron I'd be leaving early for the weekend. I spent the rest of the morning trying to come up with other things I could do to catch the thief. Nothing immediately came to mind, but I knew I needed to keep working on it. I felt like I was playing a game of chess against a grand master. I hoped I was up to the challenge.

NINE

I left Braxter right at noon and drove to the airport and returned my rental car. My flight to Seattle to meet with Carolyn Anderson at Pearce, Baker, and Boone was on-time and uneventful. I sat in a window seat on the right side of the plane, and the clear skies let me see the snow splotched Cascade mountain range stretching out alongside our route. The forested foothills south of Mount Rainier surrounded the area where I thought Packwood must have been located, and I looked forward to visiting it that evening.

The mid-sized rental car, another Altima, was ready and waiting for me, and its GPS even directed me to the correct building without any wrong turns down Seattle's one way streets. I parked in the building's underground parking facility and took the elevator up to the 33rd floor. I arrived fifteen minutes early, but the receptionist buzzed Anderson without making me wait.

A tall, blond, attractive woman entered the reception area and called for David Klein. I walked over, shook her hand, and introduced myself. She asked me to call her Carolyn, and I asked her to call me David. She was younger than I expected; late twenties or early thirties I guessed; probably only a few years out of law school. Her tailored pant suit fit her slender body perfectly. I couldn't help stealing a quick glance at her left hand to see if she was wearing a wedding band, and she wasn't. I surmised from her last name and Nordic looks she was some flavor of Scandinavian.

Carolyn turned and started walking down the hall she had entered from. "Let's go to my office." Her office was one of the farthest from the reception area. Its small size and lack of windows let me know she was near the bottom of the firm's pecking order. As I sat down in the chair across from her desk, I inquired, "I'm curious. Why would my uncle choose a big Seattle law firm to handle such a moderate estate? Estate law is pretty common; there must be dozens of less expensive firms he could have used between here and Packwood."

A faraway look briefly dimmed Carolyn's eyes as she said, "Zeke and my father were best friends. My family is from Packwood. While I was growing up, Zeke was like an uncle to me; in fact I called him uncle EZ. It's ironic that I knew him as an uncle, but he wasn't, and you never met him but he was actually your uncle."

"Yeah, it is. It sounds like you've known him for years. I didn't even know he existed until I got your letter."

Her dazzling blue eyes started to tear up. "Zeke always looked out for everyone. He wanted to help my career by sending a little business to Pearce, Baker, and Boone. Right after he was diagnosed, he had me draft his will. It was a thoughtful gesture. I tried to talk him out of it because we do corporate law and civil litigation, not estate law, but he was adamant. My boss teased me about it, but told me I could do it since Zeke was a family friend. I spent several nights and weekends reviewing my old estate law text books. Honestly, I hadn't thought about estates and probate since taking the bar exam."

She took a folder off of her desk and said, "Before discussing the contents of Zeke's will, I need to see photo ID matching the address we sent the letter to. It is really just a formality because you look a lot like Zeke, and he kept a picture of you from your MIT graduation on his mantle."

93

I wondered how he got my picture as I pulled out my wallet and showed her my Massachusetts driver's license. She quickly glanced at my photo and was completely satisfied I was truly Zeke's nephew. She pulled the papers out of the folder and said, "As mentioned in the letter I sent to you, you're the sole heir to Zeke's estate. But just to set the record straight, Zeke gave many of his things away to the church and to friends between the time he was diagnosed and the time he passed.

"EZ was a very generous man who didn't have much use for material possessions. Things just weren't important to him. He never locked the front door of his house, and he always left the keys in his truck's ignition. After he died, I knew I needed to lock up his house to prevent anyone from pilfering any of his things. My folks and I turned his place nearly upside down looking for his house keys, but we never did find them. I had the locks rekeyed. Here are the new keys along with a couple of others I found in the house." She paused before saying, "I am getting off track. I mentioned he gave many things away in case you notice some things are missing; tools, a few of his clothes, some of his furnishings."

"When we spoke on the phone, you mentioned a sealed letter…"

"Yes, I have it right here. You can take it. But before you go, I have several papers you need to sign." She slid three papers and a pen across the desk towards me. I scanned each paper and after signing each one, slid them back to her.

I hoped to prolong our conversation to learn more about Ezekiel and said, "Carolyn, my uncle is a complete mystery to me. I want to learn more about him; to understand the type of person he was. In fact, I am going to spend at least part the weekend in Packwood looking through his things to get a sense of what he was like. I'd also like to talk with some of the people who knew him well. Do you think your Dad would have some time to meet with me?"

Without hesitation, she answered, "I'm sure he would. I'll call him in just a few minutes and let him know you might be stopping by. When you turn off the highway to get to Uncle EZ's you'll head south on a gravel road for about 300 yards. The road will stop at a large turnaround. Then you can go either to the right or to the left. If you head right, you'll come to Mom and Dad's. If you go left you'll come to EZ's." She pulled a piece of paper from a yellow legal pad and wrote down a phone number and sketched the layout of her parent's place relative to Zeke's. "Here's their phone number, and their names are Carl and Angie."

"Did his friends call him EZ?"

"Many of us did. It fit him well and seemed natural. That or Zeke. No one called him Ezekiel."

"By the way, I am working on a consulting assignment in Vancouver and may drive up to Packwood on several more weekends. If you are ever in Packwood on a weekend I'd appreciate it if you would show me around."

Carolyn laughed and said, "Nobody needs to be shown around Packwood. You can walk through the entire town in less than fifteen minutes. You'll have the whole town memorized after your first hour there."

I could feel my face reddening and said, "I guess I'm used to larger places." I stood up to leave but then remembered the papers. "Would it be possible for you to make copies of these papers before I go?"

"Sure. Wait here and I'll be back in just a minute."

While Carolyn was making copies, I looked around her office. It was devoid of personal affects except for her University of Washington law school diploma dated two years earlier.

She handed the copies to me and said, "I don't know why I didn't mention it earlier, but Sunday is Mom's birthday. I'm leaving for Packwood tonight. If you would like to meet for coffee tomorrow at ten I can tell you a few things about EZ. Afterwards, I can introduce you to Mom and Dad."

"That's very generous of you. Where should we meet?" I grinned and said, "I gather from what you said Packwood doesn't have more than a few coffee shops."

"It has exactly one. It's the Mountain Coffee Company. If you can't find it, ask anyone."

"Great. I'll see you tomorrow at ten."

Carolyn and I walked back to the reception area. She shook my hand and said, "Tomorrow at ten."

Ezekiel, Zeke, and now EZ. He sounded friendlier and more laid back with each new moniker. I had already wanted to learn about Ezekiel, but now I wanted to learn about Zeke and EZ even more. I became even more curious to understand what made him tick.

It was four thirty by the time I got to my car, and I thought I might be able to beat the rush hour traffic by leaving immediately for Packwood. But after thirty minutes of driving, I had only gone ten or twelve miles. My rumbling stomach reminded me I had skipped lunch so I wanted to find a place to eat and read Zeke's letter. Hopefully, the traffic would thin out while I ate so I could make better time to Packwood.

I found a decent looking restaurant in Federal Way and took a booth in the back where I would hopefully be undisturbed. After ordering a Cobb salad and diet cola, I broke the seal on my envelope and began reading Zeke's typewritten letter.

Dear David,

I can imagine you were surprised, or perhaps upset, to learn your father had a brother. Many times I have wanted to contact you. However, I believed that if your father had wanted you to know about me he would have told you; so, I kept my silence in deference for his apparent wishes.

You are probably wondering why I was not part of the Klein family. I went to college at Berkeley and filled my weekends with the usual foolish indulgences; smoking dope, getting drunk and spending nights with women I didn't care about, women whose names I couldn't even remember the next morning. After a few months of exercising my freedom I felt completely empty and life seemed futile. However, I started paying attention to my roommate who was a Christian. To make a long story short, he and his friends had a peace and love I had never seen before, a love I didn't have and couldn't summon. It drew me to them like a stray cat to a warm lap. At first I didn't want anything to do with Jesus because, as Jews, we were taught He was just a man and after He died, His disciples absconded with His body and then claimed he was resurrected. Over the course of three or four skeptical and searching months I gradually came to believe the Bible's account of Jesus. I made a deliberate decision and surrendered to Him by asking Him to be my Lord and Savior.

I knew I needed to tell your grandparents about my decision and wanted to do it in person. I had hoped Mom and Dad would be open minded enough to accept my newfound faith. However, my hopes were fruitless. Dad felt like I had disowned and disrespected our Jewish heritage. He responded in kind and disowned me. I didn't expect him to have such a strong, visceral response, but I knew it was a possibility. If I had known he would disown me, I still would have become a Christian, and I still would have told him. But I must admit the lingering pain of estrangement from the family never completely left me. It would go into remission for a time, sometimes months, but then I would see two young boys having a good time with their father, and my happy childhood memories would overtake me.

Although I dearly missed my family, I believe losing my trust fund was actually a huge blessing. Through the loss of my trust fund God showed me I needed to lose my old, selfish life so I could find new life; abundant life, a life of adventure and transformation that comes from learning to hear and obey the voice of Jesus. The trust fund and all the things it could buy, things that could never satisfy me, might well have distracted me, if not blinded me, from seeing the true light of life.

Although Dad and I never spoke again, Mom and I kept in touch, surreptitiously like a spy and his handler. She visited me once or twice a year and filled me in on the family. You are the apple of her eye, and she never tired of telling me how wonderful you are. Her visits kept my family connection alive, and rekindled my desire to reunite, especially with your father. However, fear of more rejection sapped my courage.

At times I resolved to contact your Dad and you. Mom told me when you were going to graduate from MIT. I bought a plane ticket and planned to crash the graduation ceremony. I attended the commencement, took a picture with a telephoto lens of you receiving your diploma, and then lost the courage to contact you and your parents. To this day I don't know if I made the right decision; probably not — fear rarely motivates noble actions.

You are also probably wondering why I included you in my will. Although I was briefly married I never had children of my own, and I strongly desired to have a connection with the next Klein generation. You are the closest I can come to that. I hope you will have a family and there will be a memory of me for at least another generation or possibly two.

David, I don't have any idea what you think about spiritual things. If you are like most, you are wrapped up in day-to-day living and don't give them much thought. You can correctly surmise I would like you to come to know Jesus, the Messiah. If you would like to know more about what it means to be a Christian I encourage you to start reading the Bible I left for you in my house. Start reading in the book of Matthew. It is the first book of the New Testament, which is kind of like the sequel to the Torah for Jews. I encourage you to also attend an Alpha Course – several are available in Boston. It is a no-pressure introduction to Christianity where you can freely express your questions and your doubts, and hear what others believe. If you are interested in it you can find all the information you need about it online. But it is your decision, and I don't want to put pressure on you.

I believe the best gifts are those that are freely given, without any strings attached. The things I have bequeathed to you are yours to do with whatever you desire. You can sell them, keep them, rent them out, or do whatever you would like. You are not under any obligation to me.

One more thing, would you please tell your Dad I deeply regret our estrangement and I don't hold him at all responsible. If he feels at all responsible for it, please tell him I forgive him, and ask him to forgive me.

Your long lost uncle,

Zeke Klein

P.S. I left some pictures for you at the house.

Zeke's letter left me dumbfounded. How could people let religion divide a father from his son and an older brother from his younger brother? Although I grew up Jewish, my religion was more of an ethnic thing than a faith thing. I heard the stories about Moses and the Red Sea and Daniel in the lion's den. They were fine stories, but they were only stories; like Santa and the Easter Bunny probably are to Christians. I certainly didn't understand why anyone would divide a family over folklore.

I paid my bill and resumed the drive to Packwood. The traffic had cleared somewhat, but time no longer mattered because I was lost in my thoughts. The more I thought about the whole Zeke situation the more I felt like something had been stolen from me; an opportunity that could have been wonderful, very wonderful, like a family reunion where everyone is laughing and smiling. I never got to see my Dad enjoy time with his only brother. I never got to play ball with my uncle. Instead we were pieces of families who thought their fractured lives were normal – all in the name of religion.

It was nine thirty by the time I reached Packwood, and the sun had just set behind the mountains. Except for Duffy's Grill, which had a few cars parked out front, the whole town appeared to have closed up for the night. I pulled into the Gifford Pinchot Motel and got a room for two nights. I read for an hour and then went to bed.

TEN

I awoke at five forty, much too early for a Saturday, and lay in bed thinking about Julie; wondering if we would ever get back together. I was adrift without someone special to go home to, someone who would miss me when I was away, someone I could make smile, the kind of smile that says, "I am happy just to be here with you." Part of me wanted to call her and tell her I couldn't bear to be apart from her, that I wanted to get on the next plane for Boston and spend the rest of my life with her. But I was afraid that I wasn't really ready for a marriage commitment, and I was afraid she wouldn't answer my call or worse yet, she would answer and then tell me she had moved on to someone else. Maybe it would be easier to let her go, to forget about wooing her back, to look for someone else, someone special I could make a fresh start with. I decided the best option was to continue with the silent separation and give my emotions time to settle, and give Pat time to find out if Julie was seeing someone else.

I tried to go back to sleep, but after all of the time wondering about Julie, I was wide awake. It was too early to get breakfast so I put on my running shorts and shoes to go for a run to see Packwood in the breaking morning light. The Gifford Pinchot Motel where I was staying was on Highway 12, at the east end of town, so I headed west. The sun hadn't yet fully risen over the Cascade Mountains behind me, and a thin layer of low, misty fog had settled close to the ground, giving the valley floor a surrealistic almost eerie feel. I saw the silhouettes of countless evergreen trees standing above the still fog like sentries guarding the small town.

101

I ran past a gas station, a combination liquor store and tobacco shop, a few other small shops, Taylor's Food Mart, Duffy's Grill, a vacant lot, a burger joint that advertised breakfast and another motel; all within the first three blocks. I looked up and down each of the cross streets as I ran past them, but didn't see any other businesses, except for a small beauty salon located in the owner's home. Highway 12 was obviously Packwood's main street. In the fourth block I passed a secondhand store, two vacant buildings which were once restaurants, a community library, a small auto repair shop that looked like a throwback to Mayberry, and a defunct grade school, half of which had been converted into the county sheriff's substation and the other half into a local museum that I suspected recalled an earlier time of more prosperous days. That was it. My legs hadn't even fully loosened up and I had seen nearly everything Packwood had to offer. Carolyn was right when she told me nobody needs to be shown around Packwood.

I continued running west on Highway 12's wide shoulder and enjoyed the silence offered by the total lack of traffic. My run promised to be quiet and peaceful, an opportunity to think more about my dysfunctional family and what I might want for a family of my own. When visiting new places, I always found running to be a great way to explore the unfamiliar surroundings and to contemplate. Compared to driving I moved slowly enough to get a good feel for the area and had brain cycles left over to mull over a variety of problems and opportunities. The sky continued to grow lighter, and the surrounding mountains were no longer only dark silhouettes. Their lush evergreen trees stood in tight formation, elbow to elbow, and completely hid the forest's floor.

I was unexpectedly shaken from my peaceful musing by a sudden cacophony of snapping branches. The ruckus came from within the fog-blanketed woods less than twenty yards to the right of me, to the north of the highway. I turned in time to see a huge deer, his head and huge antlers rising above the fog, coming right at me. The big buck was more the size of a horse than the size of Bambi. I stopped, unsure if I should run, yell, or fall down and play dead. Gigantor, the buck on steroids, stopped about 15 feet from me and glared. He had lifted his head so high his antlers lay across his broad back. Snot dangled from his flaring nostrils like dirty icicles from a leaky gutter. He pounded the road with his right front hoof as if to say, "One wrong move and I'll grind you into the pavement." I slowly backed away from him, careful not to look directly at him or make any moves he might interpret as aggressiveness. Thankfully no cars were coming because I didn't even consider checking for traffic before backing onto the highway. I had just crossed the center line when his harem of oversized deer scampered up behind him. I heard more noises behind me, turned and saw five or six deer on the south side of the highway crossing the road to the north. Pandemonium reigned. Some of them started one way and then abruptly reversed direction, their hooves skidding on the hard pavement. I was surrounded by a terrifying herd of schizophrenic deer that was guarded by an alpha male.

Gigantor apparently realized I wasn't a threat to him or to his women and seemed to relax knowing his harem was out of danger. He lowered his head, strutted across the highway to the south side while his ladies fell in line behind him. I was too scared to be envious. Their noise diminished quickly as they disappeared into the fog enshrouded forest, but I could still smell their unpleasant, strong musky odor. It stunk like wet diapers that had been ignored for a week of stifling hot summer days. Then it occurred to me that I just might have wet myself. I looked down at my crotch which was thankfully dry.

Still shaken, I opted to cut my run short and turned around to head back toward town. From then on I paid closer attention to the woods shouldering the road. I didn't want any more surprises. What if I had encountered a grizzly bear instead of deer? It occurred to me I hadn't seen the Mountain Coffee Company, where I was to meet Carolyn so I made sure to look more carefully down each of the side streets. I found it nestled behind three cedar trees on a side street. A lone car parked in front of it. I made a mental note of its location so I could easily find it later. I was almost back to the motel when I saw Mount Rainier towering above the ground fog, between two of the lesser mountains. The rising sun reflected off of Rainier's majestic, snow covered mass. I stopped to capture the stunning scene with my iPhone's camera and promised myself a visit to Mount Rainier National Park where I would get a much closer view. I walked the rest of the way back to my room to give myself a chance to cool down before showering.

I put on a blue oxford shirt, jeans and Nikes and then walked down to a burger place called Duffy's Grill because I hadn't seen any other places in town that advertised breakfast. I arrived just as it opened at seven and was the first customer. I sat at a booth which looked out at the highway and opened up the menu. I hoped they hadn't invented some type of breakfast-burger akin to a breakfast-burrito and was relieved to learn they served a full menu of normal breakfast items from opening until eleven, when they started serving lunch. I ordered the logger's breakfast just to see how the locals dined.

Wow! The waitress served my order on an oversized plate that was the same size as the serving plate my mother would use to serve a full turkey at Thanksgiving. My dainty repast contained enough calories to keep a small village nourished for a week; three eggs, two bacon slices, four sausage links, a slab of ham, two pancakes, hash browns, and a biscuit. I envisioned my arteries clogging with cholesterol and grease. The breakfast should have been served with a coupon for a reduced price on bypass surgery. It tasted great but I was afraid to eat even half of it.

I walked back to my motel and realized I still had plenty of time to check out Ezekiel's place before my coffee date with Carolyn. I put his keys into my pocket, grabbed the printout I had made from Google Maps, and drove up the highway looking for the turnoff to Wilson Lane. I rose above the fog as I gained elevation, and the sky brightened noticeably. I found a dirt road where I expected to and drove to the tee intersection where I turned left. There wasn't a mailbox or any other indication of what might be at the end of the drive, but I tried it and drove slowly because of the many potholes; some threatened to high center my rental car and leave me stranded and at the mercy of marauding deer. My car crept into a dark tunnel of encroaching Douglas fir trees and western red cedars that seemingly held their many arms out far above the driveway.

After about a hundred yards, I emerged into a better lit clearing and stopped the car to look around for someone who might be able to tell me if this was Ezekiel's place. I saw an older Toyota Tundra pickup parked in the left bay of a triple-wide carport. The center bay was empty except for a large wheelbarrow, and the right bay was mostly filled with rows of neatly stacked firewood. A row of tall doors spanned the middle carport's back wall. I guessed some sort of storage area was behind the doors.

Zeke's two story house, at least I assumed it was his, stood on the left side of the clearing about fifty feet from the carport. I say a clearing, but it wasn't bare dirt or even lawn, but a treeless patch of ground splotched in countless clumps of salal with their shiny, prickly leaves. Oregon grape and ferns competed with the salal for the muted light passing through the tree canopy. If this was Zeke's place then yard work wasn't high on his priority list. The entire landscaping was completely natural except for the clearing where the trees had been removed, and a few rotting stumps remained to tell the truth. According to a bumper sticker I had read while walking through Portland, "Stumps don't lie."

The house looked almost as natural as the encompassing forest. Clear stained cedar siding gave it a woodsy look, a wraparound porch girdling the house's front and two sides created a comfortable, homey ambiance, and two weather-worn wooden chairs nestled against a small hot tub that invited cozy conversation, conversation with Ezekiel I would never have.

I walked quietly up to the front door while listening closely for any signs of life. Closed drapes prevented me from looking through the main windows. I knocked several times while peeking through the door's glass porthole, but didn't see or hear anyone moving inside. Next, I tried one of the keys Carolyn gave me. The first one slid easily into the lock, unlocking the door and confirming this was Ezekiel's place. I peered inside, but couldn't see beyond five or six feet down the dark entry way. I hollered, "Hello," and hearing nothing took two steps inside. The combination of the tall trees blocking out the direct sunlight and the closed curtains made the interior dark. I walked forward slowly groping my way along the wall for a light switch which I finally found and turned on the hall light.

I found myself standing in the living room, a room reminding me of a small hunting lodge. Three stuffed deer heads hung on the far wall staring blankly at me with glassy eyes. Two of them were relatively small non-threatening deer trophies mounted on either side of the head of Gigantor's huge twin, the deer that threatened me during my morning run. The evil twin had his mouth open wide as if yelling, "Ezekiel might have been able to kill me, but my brother is going to get you!" I was glad Uncle Ezekiel had killed the stinking bastard. No wonder his brother threatened me earlier; unbeknownst to me our families may have been feuding for years. A black bearskin rug was splayed across the hardwood floor on the far end of the room, a man's room with no signs of a woman's touch anywhere.

The living room and halls were spotless. No dust rested on the window sills or tables. Vacuum cleaner tracks were visible in the hallway carpet, and each of his three house plants thrived. I wondered if Carolyn's mother had cleaned the place in anticipation of my arrival.

An austere kitchen was to the right of the living room. It, too, was spotless. A microwave oven took up about a quarter of the counter space, leaving little room for preparing meals. I wondered if Zeke cooked and ate the animals he killed. The kitchen opened into an atrium-like, family room two stories tall. The room was naturally lit with floor-to-ceiling windows, but surrounded by the woods, only muted light entered the room. Two brown leather recliners and side table faced a cozy wood stove. His answering machine's red light was blinking and the LED display showed he had seven messages; probably all from telemarketers informing him he could get a reduced interest rate on his mortgage or computer techs informing him that his computer was unprotected. A reading lamp, Zeke's well-worn Bible and a thick photo album sat on the side table. I pictured Zeke reading his Bible while staying warm by the fire, but wondered why two chairs and not just one.

I sat in one of the recliners and picked up the photo album to nose around in Ezekiel's world. Page after page showed him enjoying times with different friends; camping, picnicking, hiking, eating, hunting, cutting firewood, and more eating. Ezekiel didn't lack friends. A manila envelope was inserted into the album between the last page and inside back cover, and I peeked to see what secrets it might hold. It contained five 8x10 photographs of a much younger Ezekiel on his wedding day. Two photos were of him and his wife, two were of the wedding party, and one was a shot of the extended families. The only person I recognized beside Ezekiel in the family photo was my grandmother. I wondered how she was able to sneak out to attend his wedding. A legal sized envelope was stuck inside the manila envelope, and I wouldn't have noticed it if it hadn't prevented me from sliding the photos back inside. It contained a faded newspaper article dated June 24, 1978 about a drunk driver whose pickup truck crossed over the center line in front of a couple on their honeymoon. The bride, Ellen Klein, died on the scene, and the groom, Ezekiel Klein escaped with only abrasions and a broken leg. Poor Ezekiel; family seemed to have brought him nothing except loneliness and heartache.

I slowly stood up, returned the photo album to its place on the side table and looked up to the second floor, where I saw a railed walkway and what looked like three bedroom doors. I backtracked towards the front door to reach the stairway, and as I ascended the stairs, a display of framed photographs caught my eye. Three were scenic pictures of mountains, lakes and animals. Four others were of people I didn't recognize. At the top of the stairs I was stopped dead in my tracks by the photograph of my parents and me in my senior year of high school that Grandma had insisted we have taken for her. Grandma must have had a copy made for Ezekiel.

The first bedroom looked like a guest room because it was devoid of personal affects and had no clothes in the closet. Ezekiel must have used the second bedroom as a den or office. It had a large desk against the wall where the bed normally would have been. A closed laptop sat in the middle of the desk, and a printer was off to the side. A large gun safe stood in the corner. Curious, I pulled the key ring out and on my third try found the match to the lock. The safe had three drawers and spaces to hold six rifles, but the rifle spaces were taken by two powerful looking bows and a quiver of razor-sharp hunting arrows. The first drawer held a pistol wrapped in a soft cloth, which I removed to get a better look at the gun. It was an unloaded 45 caliber Springfield Armory semi-automatic. Additionally, two loaded ammo clips and a holster sat next to the pistol's original packaging. My first thought was to take it with me on my next run, but I put it back in the drawer because I didn't know the first thing about shooting. The next two drawers were loaded with more ammo, cleaning supplies, hunting knives, and other hunting paraphernalia, such as elk calls and deer scent.

I opened the walk-in closet door and discovered what looked like a miniature combination of Cabela's and REI stores. A row of camo clothing, two backpacks, trekking poles, a small tent, two sleeping bags, snow shoes, three pairs of skis, ski poles, boots, crampons, an ice axe, rope, and much more were are neatly packed onto the closet's shelves. Uncle Ezekiel must have been one of REI's best customers. What was I going to do with all of this stuff?

The third bedroom was larger than the other two. I could tell it had been Ezekiel's because clothes were in the closet and in the oak chest of drawers. I checked out the sizes, and he and I were the same size, even our feet were the same size, but I didn't need, or want, any of his clothes. I felt like an intruder as I snooped through his things. At the same time, I wondered what I was going to do with all of his things and when I was going to have time to do it. I wondered if I could hire someone to clean and sell everything. As I pondered my options, the alarm clock on Ezekiel's nightstand reminded me it was time to head back to town for coffee with Carolyn.

Eleven

I arrived a few minutes early, and the Mountain Coffee Company was noticeably busier than it was when I had run by it earlier. Three people stood in line ahead of me waiting to get their morning caffeine hits. The aroma of fresh, rich coffee and the voices of friends chatting filled the small shop. Carolyn hadn't yet arrived, so instead of getting in the line to order my drink, I sat down at an open table to wait for her.

A slender man sipped his coffee at the next table. Gray hair hung from underneath his Stihl cap. He wore a long sleeved camo tee shirt with frayed cuffs and faded jeans; workmen's jeans; the type with a double layer of denim on the knees. Once-bright orange suspenders with "Stihl" written lengthwise down each strap held his pants up. Being a city boy from Boston, I wasn't sure what to make of his ensemble. The suspenders and cap matched in their exaltation of Stihl, whatever Stihl was, but the camo shirt conflicted with the bright orange. Was he trying to be invisible or not? Just as I was trying to solve the puzzle, he leaned towards me, stuck out a strong hand and said, "Hi. I'm Burt. How are you on this fine summer morning?"

Not accustomed to such outgoing strangers, I returned his smile and shook his hand. "I'm doing okay. My name is David. Glad to meet you. How are you?"

"Fine, just fine. Everyday above ground is a good one."

Burt looked up when a man who was about the same age as he walked into the coffee shop and raising his voice to be heard over the other voices Burt hollered, "Coffee's paid for." The man, who was dressed in jeans, a red tee shirt, and a Coors cap waited in line to get his already purchased coffee and then walked over to join Burt at his table. As he sat down, Burt said, "Herb, this is David. David, Herb."

We shook hands, and Herb asked, "David, you new to Packwood?" I notice Herb's puzzled expression as he looked at my button-down oxford shirt.

I shook my head. "Just visiting. Actually I am here to tend to my late uncle's estate."

"Zeke Klein?"

I cocked my head to one side and raised my eyebrows. "How'd you guess?"

"It's a small town. We all know everyone and everyone else's business; at least we try to. I heard Zeke left his place to some relative from the east coast."

"That's me."

"Sorry about his passing."

"Thanks."

"We both worked at the lumber mill. ...For more than twenty years. So we knew each other pretty well. He was a bean counter, and I was a sawyer. We didn't see eye to eye on many things, him and me."

"Is that so?" I said hoping Herb would continue.

Burt and Herb gave each other a knowing glance. Herb's eyes narrowed and his fists tightened as he said, "Zeke was a strange one. Seeing as how you are dressed like you're from the city and sound like you're from the east, you would probably call most of us red necks, and I suppose we are. We mostly drive pickups, like our Buds – sometimes a little too much, cuss a bit, and spend our free time hunting and fishing. Zeke was only kind of a redneck, more like a pink neck. Didn't really fit with the rest of us. He drove a pickup and liked to hunt and fish, but I never saw him have more than one beer, and he never swore, at least not that I personally heard. He was one of those born again Christians, the kind that somehow always has a smile pasted on his face. It couldn't have been real; had to be some sort of act. You know how Christians are – always thinking they're better than everyone else."

Burt leaned toward Herb, put a calming hand on his forearm, and asked me, "You one? A born again Christian?"

"Not me," I replied.

"Thank God," Burt whispered to himself as he leaned back in his chair.

Herb continued as if Burt hadn't interrupted him, "I ran into him at the store one Saturday morning, after I had gotten well lubricated the night before. My head felt like a bass drum in a marching band, I must've reeked of beer and looked like a hobo, but he stopped to chat with me, him wearing his big, phony smile. I know he thought he was better than me so I asked him, 'You think you're better than me just because you don't get drunk, don't you?' He continued to smile and answered, 'No, Herb, I don't. But, I do think I am better *off* than you because I don't get drunk.' He thought I didn't see through him, but I did."

Burt put his hand back on Herb's arm and added, "He was the best hunter in the valley and could sneak up on any animal in the woods. Expert bow hunters are like ghosts. When he wasn't huntin' or fishin' he spent a lot of time at his church.

Maybe I should say it the other way; when he wasn't at church he spent time huntin' or fishin' – never missed his church."

I looked out the window and saw Carolyn walking up to the front door. My escape had arrived. "Nice talking with you. The person I'm meeting just arrived," I said as I rose up to leave.

I met Carolyn right as she walked in the door and said, "Good morning. What can I get for you?" She was wearing a blue jean jacket over a red plaid cotton shirt, snug blue jeans, and a black baseball cap. I could see her blonde ponytail cascading like a waterfall through the half-moon opening above the adjustment strap on the back of her cap. Every guy in the place took a second look. I immediately felt over dressed and made a mental note to downgrade my wardrobe the next time I met Carolyn in Packwood, if there was a next time.

"A large coffee would be perfect. …With a little cream."

Before I could order, Burt waved her over to their table where unfortunately there was room for us to join them. I hoped she wouldn't sit down, but the three of them were apparently well acquainted. I ordered our coffees, added a little cream to Carolyn's, and took them over to the table. Carolyn started to introduce us, but Burt said, "We've already had the pleasure."

I couldn't resist and said, "Herb was just telling me about how Zeke thought he was better than everyone else."

Carolyn took a slow sip of her coffee, turned to glare at Herb, and then began her scathing cross examination. "Herb, who was it who bailed you out after your DUI so you didn't lose your job?"

Herb slouched back in his chair. "Zeke."

114

A bulging vein ran from Carolyn's hairline down the middle of her forehead reminding me of Angelina Jolie when she smiled, but Carolyn wasn't smiling. She pressed on, "Who gave you half of his elk during the strike in '98?"

"Zeke."

"Who was it who loaned you his chain saw after yours broke down so you could cut your firewood for the winter?"

Herb squirmed in his chair. "Zeke…"

"Zeke, Zeke, Zeke. Maybe you think Zeke thought he was better than everyone else because he treated you so much better than you ever treated him. By the way, did you ever pay him back the $500 bail money?"

Herb mumbled, "Not that I remember."

"As the attorney for his estate, let me notify you of your obligation to pay it to David Klein," she said pointing to me. "When are you going to pay it back?"

"I'll get back to you on that. I think it's time for me to be going," Herb said, and wet his lips.

Burt stood up and mumbled, "Me, too."

Carolyn watched them go, took a deep breath and said, "David, I am sorry you had to hear Herb's ranting about Zeke. I didn't mean to go off, but I guess I am pretty defensive when it comes to EZ."

"I wouldn't have missed it for the world."

"Some men are so insecure. When they see a real man like Zeke, they can't help but try to cut him down to their size."

Carolyn took another sip and leaned back in her chair, "What can I tell you about uncle EZ?"

"Did he ever mention his family?"

"Only once. When I was eleven or twelve years old my grandparents had just spent two weeks visiting us. After they left, I asked EZ why his parents never visited him. As he thought about how to answer his face lost its glow, as if he had stepped out of the sunlight and into a deep shadow. He said 'sometimes people have big disagreements and don't want to see each other anymore.' I asked him if he missed his Mom and Dad, and he said he thought about them nearly every day. I felt bad about making him sad and never asked about his family again. I think he could tell I felt bad because he reached his hand out and put it on mine and told me his Mom came to visit him whenever she could."

"Did he ever mention his brother, my Dad?"

"No, but I knew he had a brother because I had heard quite a bit about you."

"So he didn't explain what happened with his family?"

"No, and it was none of my business."

"He explained it to me in the sealed letter you gave me. As you might surmise with a last name of Klein, our family is Jewish. The short version is that Zeke went away to college at Berkeley and became a Christian. He came home and told my grandparents about his conversion, and my grandfather disowned him. They never spoke again, and Zeke and my Dad never spoke again either. It's a mess. Apparently, Zeke walked out on a trust fund worth several million dollars. I don't pretend to understand his Christianity, but it must have meant a lot to him."

"Hmm. I didn't know about the trust fund, but about five years ago, I overheard EZ and my Dad talking. EZ said something about the Klein *geld fluch*. Afterwards, I asked Dad what they were talking about, and he played dumb and said it was nothing. I could tell he was fibbing so I Googled it to find out what *geld fluch* meant. It's German for 'money curse', the Klein money curse." I certainly didn't see why Zeke would consider money to be a curse. I was rather fond of it.

"Money curse? What's the curse all about?"

"I have no idea."

Carolyn glanced at her watch and said, "I should be getting back soon. Why don't you follow me up to the house, and I'll introduce you to Mom and Dad? I know they're looking forward to finally meeting you."

"Sounds good."

We walked to our respective cars. Hers was an old full-sized 4-wheel drive Ford pickup with a gun rack hanging just in front of the rear window. Rusty scratches in the once white paint and numerous minor dents screamed that the truck was not a typical soccer Mom's SUV. It was not the ride I expected a young, urban attorney to drive; male or female. I would have liked to have seen her wrestle it through the tight turns of the Pearce, Baker, and Boone parking garage. I got in my Altima and followed her up to her parents' place.

During the short drive, I caught myself wondering if Carolyn and I might have a romantic future together, but I immediately realized I was getting way ahead of myself. Even though her carefully cultivated, yet casual, beauty snared my imagination, and even though I admired her forthright manner with Burt and Herb, and as much as I was plotting how to see her again, I wasn't ready to write off Julie in exchange for a possible romance with Carolyn. Instead I hoped Carolyn and I would become merely good friends, but in my case it was incongruous to use the phrase *merely good friends* because I had no one I could honestly count as a good friend so there was nothing *mere* about the possibility.

TWELVE

Carolyn and I both drove our vehicles into the Anderson's driveway. Carolyn parked her pickup next to the detached garage that housed a three year old BWM 328i with its hood open and its front wheels elevated by ramps. I parked behind the pickup and walked up to Carolyn who waited for me. She nodded towards the BMW and whispered, "Dad's retired and has too much time on his hands. He's always checking the oil and the belts and hoses for me. I have it serviced regularly, but he worries it will break down and leave me stranded on some desolate back road."

We walked around to the front of the Beemer, and Carolyn said, "Dad, this is David, uncle EZ's nephew. David, this is my Dad, Carl." Mr. Anderson wiped his hands off on a rag and we shook hands. He was six feet tall and because I didn't see any extra pounds I guessed he weighed about 185. His short hair was a mixture of mostly blonde with gray around his temples. Carl smiled and said, "Carolyn, why don't you go inside and introduce David to your mother. I'll join you in a couple of minutes and then we can chat. By the way, everything looks good under the hood. It shouldn't give you any trouble."

Carolyn and I walked toward the house, a simple two story wood structure about the same size as Zeke's, but it was stained a barn red with forest green trim. The front door opened as we approached, and Carolyn's mother came out smiling. She looked more like Carolyn's older sister than her mother; the family resemblance left no doubt they were closely related. Mrs. Anderson hugged me like I was her long lost son. "You must be David. We've been looking forward to meeting you ever since Carolyn told us you were coming to Packwood. Zeke was like family to us. Please come in." Carolyn said, "David, this is my mother, Angie. Let's all go in and sit down." We went into the homey living room furnished with a dark leather couch, a couple of recliners, and a mission style oak rocking chair with seat and back cushions that were upholstered in well-worn burgundy colored leather. A lamp and a short stack of books sat on an oak end table beside the rocker. Like Zeke's place a wood stove stood along an outside wall. A large bookcase stuffed with books stood at the opposite wall. I sat at one end of the couch, and Carolyn sat on the other. Mrs. Anderson settled in one of the recliners and started working on a half complete knitting project.

We looked at each other for a minute before Mrs. Anderson broke the uneasy silence, "Carolyn tells me you live in Massachusetts. Did you come all the way out here just to see Zeke's place?" I explained I was in Vancouver on business and expected to be in Washington for several months, and I wanted to learn as much as I could about Zeke. She nodded in understanding, but didn't volunteer anything about him. The silence started to settle back in, but Mr. Anderson walked into the room before it became awkward. He sat in the rocker and said, "David, I hear you want to learn something about Zeke. That correct?"

"Yes, sir."

"Carl will do just fine."

"Okay. Carl, I didn't even know I had an uncle until after he died. My family disowned him so he's a complete mystery to me, a mystery begging to be explored. Carolyn said he was like family to you so I am hoping you will be kind enough to indulge my curiosity."

120

"Zeke, he was one of a kind, but it is difficult to describe him because he was a complex person; complex, but in a straightforward and simple way. That sounds so stupid that I can't believe I said it. I don't know what your religious persuasion is, but the best way I can describe Zeke is to say he was the most genuine disciple of Christ I've ever known. There are a lot of tarnished Christians in this world; I count myself one of them, but Zeke, he was the real thing."

Mrs. Anderson interjected, "I first met Zeke at the mill. He was the head accountant, and I was the accounts payable bookkeeper. Carl and I had only been married a couple of years, but it wasn't working out. I knew Carl had a temper before I married him, but like a lot of foolish young women, I thought I could change him. I tried, but it just made him mad. One time I came into the office with a black eye that makeup couldn't quite hide. Zeke noticed it, and asked me what happened. I lied and told him I had run into the medicine cabinet door. He let it drop, but I was pretty sure he hadn't bought my lame story."

Carl, took over the monologue, "I felt terrible about hitting Angie and was ashamed to face her, so after work I went to the Blue Ox to have a few beers. I was on my third or fourth one when Zeke sat down on the stool beside me. He said, 'Carl, I saw Angie's black eye, and she told me she ran into the medicine cabinet door. It must have been quite a door because it nailed her pretty good.' I thought Zeke was going to light into me for hitting a woman. But he didn't; instead he said, 'Carl, sometimes we do things we hate ourselves for. Then we do them again and again, hating ourselves a little bit more each time. We promise ourselves we'll try harder next time, but in spite of our trying we mess up again. Sometimes we need to ask for help. If you want help, I know someone who will help you. But, Carl, don't ever hit her again because if you do, I will beat the living snot out of you.' With that he stood up and walked out leaving me not sure what to think."

I was surprised at Carl and Angie's openness with me, a near stranger. If I was in their place I wouldn't be sharing my screw-ups with anyone. However, I was glad to be learning more about Zeke.

Angie picked up the narrative as if she and Carl had told this story several times before. "I considered leaving Carl, but I really didn't have anywhere to go. I was too ashamed to go back to my parents. Besides, I kept telling myself Carl didn't mean to hurt me and I just needed to be more careful not to make him mad. Things got better for a couple of months, but then Carl had a real bad day at work, and I burned the fried chicken for dinner. He didn't hit me, but he did push me. I tripped and hit the back of my head on the corner of our coffee table. Carl immediately felt horrible and took me to the emergency room where it took nine stitches to sew me up. The next day at work, Zeke asked me what happened. I told him I tripped and fell, which was almost true."

Carl said, "After work I stopped by my regular watering hole, the Blue Ox, for couple of beers. I had more than a couple and then Zeke, he walked in. He asked me what happened to Angie, and I told him it wasn't any of his business. He asked me again, a little louder this time, and I stumbled off of my stool and took a swing at him. He sidestepped, and I missed. I swung again, and he stuck out his foot and tripped me. I fell flat on my face but popped back up madder than a hornet. I took another swing; he sidestepped it again and then smashed the heel of his hand into my nose, flattening it against my cheek. My face was so bloody that I couldn't see well enough to hit him back, which was a good thing because I would have likely missed and taken another blow to the face for my trouble. Zeke quietly walked out of the bar. The owner gave me a towel and I stumbled out to my truck and drove myself to the emergency room where the same doctor who sewed Angie up set my nose. He mentioned that our family was particularly accident prone and we needed to be more careful."

I couldn't help interrupting, "Let me get this straight. The most genuine disciple of Christ you had ever seen intentionally broke your face. Your ideas of the perfect Christian and mine aren't even in the same zip code. Being Jewish, I admit I don't know much about Christianity, but I'm sure I heard Christians are supposed to love their enemies, turn the other cheek, and not return evil for evil; not do things like break people's noses."

Carl chuckled and then replied, "Back then I would have agreed with you one hundred percent. I thought Zeke was a phony. But since then I have learned God seems to care more about the overall condition of our heart than the few times we might screw up. Zeke, he screwed up. I admit that. But now I see the bigger picture. Because you're Jewish I assume you are familiar with King David and how he committed adultery and then committed murder in an attempt to cover it up?"

"Yeah. I vaguely remember the story."

"The Bible said this when the prophet Samuel was looking for the person God wanted to be the next king of Israel, 'the Lord does not see as a man sees; for man looks at the outward appearance, but the Lord looks at the heart.' God was referring to David's heart. There must have been something about

David's heart that caused God to want to select him as the next king, yet I believe God knew David was going to mess up big time. God surely knows each person is nothing if not a bundle of contradictions."

I nodded, because I knew I was a bundle of contradictions, but I wasn't sure if God knew or cared.

Carl continued his explanation, "Being Jewish, you probably aren't too familiar with the New Testament, but in the book of Acts, God has this to say about David, 'He's a man whose heart beats to my heart, a man who will do what I tell him.' The bottom line is David screwed up big time, but God, He knew David loved Him and really wanted to please Him. I came to learn that, although Zeke screwed up sometimes, he really and truly loved God. I'll bet when Zeke entered the pearly gates he heard God say, 'He's a man whose heart beats to my heart, a man who did what I told him.'"

Angie picked up the baton and continued, "Carl came home and told me what had happened. He was still steaming, and I was afraid he was going to get his gun and go after Zeke. About the time I got him calmed down there was a knock at the door. I opened it, and Zeke stepped inside. Before Carl could do anything, Zeke walked over to him and said, 'Carl, I am so sorry. I judged you for mistreating Angie and then did exactly the same thing myself. I call myself a Christian, but I am such a hypocrite. I need to ask you to forgive me.'"

Carl said, "I told Zeke to get his phony ass off of my property and to never come back. He walked to the door, but before leaving he turned and said, "I don't blame you for hating me. I deserve it, but I do want you to know I am very sorry." He pulled an envelope out of his jacket pocket and

124

while laying it on the floor said, 'I hope this is enough to cover your medical bill. If not, let me know and I will pay it.'"

Angie sniffled and said, "After he left I opened the envelope thinking it might contain a hundred dollars or so. Back in those days trips to the emergency room weren't nearly as expensive as I hear they are now. Our bill was $180 and they were going to let us pay it on time, over six months. I opened the envelope and found ten crisp one hundred dollar bills. I don't see how Zeke would have had so much cash on hand. He must have borrowed it from the mill's safe and then replaced it before anyone noticed it was missing. I told Carl we couldn't accept so much money and to my surprise he agreed. He asked me to give $820 of it back to Zeke. He took a twenty out of his wallet and added it to eight of the bills and put it back into the envelope.

"The next day at work I ran into Zeke in the hall. He was so ashamed of himself he wouldn't look me in the eye. I told him he gave us too much money and our bill was only $180. I handed the envelope back to him, but he wouldn't take it. He said, 'Tell Carl the rest is for the pain I caused him. I'm just glad he hasn't pressed charges for assault.' He turned, walked into his office, and closed the door. I'd never seen Zeke be so despondent. I put the money in my purse and tried to concentrate on accounts payable.

"That evening Carl asked me if I gave the envelope back to Zeke. I told him how bad Zeke felt and how I tried, but Zeke wouldn't take it back."

Carl nodded toward Angie and took over, "Part of me was happy to have the extra money, but part of me was a little puzzled. Why would he give us so much extra? He must have been truly sorry about hitting me. Anyway, I figured it would be a lot easier to ignore the pain in my nose if I had a new hunting rifle to keep my mind occupied. I'd been looking at a new Winchester 270 and scope, but didn't have the money. It cost just over $700, but even with Angie and me both working I didn't have the extra money. To make a long story short, I bought the Winchester and tried to put Zeke out of my mind.

"Angie and I were getting along fine, but then she messed up the check book and our rent check bounced. The landlord reamed me out and threatened to evict us. It was a Friday. I know because I stopped off at the Blue Ox to have a few beers and try and get control of myself. The beer didn't help and when I got home I was still furious. I took a swing at Angie. She was able to duck out of the way, grab her purse, and run out the door to her car. She drove off and spent the night at a friend's house."

I kept an eye on Carolyn to see her reaction to her parents' *True Confessions* episode, but she didn't seem disturbed by it. I guessed she had heard the story at least once before.

Carolyn's Mom interjected, "Several weeks before, my friend, Sue, told me if Carl ever hurt me again I should get out of the house. She offered to let me stay with her, and I even stashed a few of my clothes and a little money at her place in case I needed to get out of the house in a hurry. She lived in Randle so I drove over to her house. We parked my car in the garage so Carl couldn't see it and I spent the weekend with her. She told me I should leave Carl for good and I was a fool if I expected him to change. I rationalized to her that he didn't mean to hurt me, and he was always sorry afterward. She didn't buy it and countered saying his being sorry wouldn't help me if I was dead."

Carl explained how he felt when Angie walked out, "I really did love Angie, and I hated myself for hurting her; not just the physical harm but even more the emotional pain. I knew I was no good and thought about taking my new rifle up into the woods and ending it all. I had a little life insurance as a benefit through work and reasoned Angie would be better off with a little money and without a no-good husband who would probably terrorize her or hurt her again.

"I needed help but didn't know where to get it. Then I remembered Zeke telling me if I ever wanted help he knew someone who could help me. I was at the end of my rope and didn't have anything to lose so I went see Zeke. To this day I don't know why I did. I drove over to his place — it's your place now — got out and walked up to his door. Part of me wanted him to not be home, and part of me hoped he really did know someone who could help me. I knocked lightly on his door half hoping he wouldn't hear me. I waited a bit and then turned around and headed back to my truck, but just before I opened the cab door, Zeke opened his door and hollered out to me, 'Hey, Carl come on back. I was in the bathroom and couldn't get to the door right away.'

"He motioned me inside, and he and I went into his living room, where each of us sat in a recliner. After nervously rubbing my hands together for a few seconds, I blurted out, 'Angie up and left me.' I took a swing at her. The good news is that I missed. The bad news is she got in her car and took off. I don't have any idea where she is or if she ever plans to come back. You told me if I wanted help you know someone who can help me. I guess I need help. Can you put me in touch with your friend, the one who can help me?

"Zeke said, 'Carl, I was thinking of me. Although given the episode when I smashed your nose, I don't expect I have any credibility with you or with Angie. Still, I think I can help you if you'll give me a chance.'

"No offense, but I am pretty sure I need more help than you can give me; professional help.

"Zeke continued, 'You might be right. I'm no professional counselor; not even a semi-professional. But sometimes people need a friend they can lean on more than they need a professional counselor; someone they can turn to when they feel the pressure starting to build; someone they can turn to before they do the very thing they don't want to do.'

"So you want me to call you next time I start getting mad, but before I lose control. Is that it?

"He said, 'That's part of it, but there needs to be a lot more. I want to be your friend and do things friends do. You know, like hunt and fish. Stuff like that. I hear you're a pretty good fly fisherman, and I'd appreciate it if you would teach me how. I'd also like to learn to hunt. It seems like every guy here in Packwood knows how to do those things, except me.'

"I asked him, 'Do you really think just being friends will help me not hit Angie again?' I was pretty skeptical, but willing to try almost anything.

"He replied, 'I think it just might. I sure hope so because if you hit her again I could be out another thousand bucks and your nose may never be the same. One thing though, most guys never open up to their buddies. They hunt and fish, watch sports, have a few beers, but never discuss their problems and other important things. I would like us to develop the type of friendship where we can be honest about our problems. That can only happen over time, and it can only happen if we promise to keep the things we tell each other confidential. What do you think?'

"I told him, 'I don't know. It sounds a little girly. You know – sharing our inner secrets with each other. I don't know if I'll ever be ready to bare my soul.'

"Zeke laughed. 'It does sound weird, I admit. But then again we have been opening up for the last ten minutes. You came to me and admitted your problem. That is the first step. And you have seen me at my worst. Can you teach me how to fish tomorrow?'

"I asked him, 'You have any gear?'

"He laughed again. 'No, and for some reason I'm a little short on money to buy it.'"

Carl continued, "I told him I had extra gear and would pick him up at six o'clock in the morning. That's how our friendship began."

Angie caught my eye, "Zeke had a rare ability to cut through superficial chit chat and lead conversations into deep water. He put people at ease by giving his complete attention to whoever he was talking with. That's an unusual trait, especially in a man. Before long, Carl got comfortable talking about what he was thinking and what he was feeling. He began opening up his feelings to me, too. I think it's what helped him overcome his anger outbursts. It was like he got mad because he was keeping everything packed down so deep inside. Once he quit keeping things inside him, he didn't boil over any more, and I started trusting him again."

I started to worry that I was wearing out my welcome, and stood up saying, "I probably should get going so you folks can get back to the things you need to do."

Angie motioned me to sit back down and said, "I was hoping you could stay for lunch. I thought we could each make our own sandwiches. David, I would like to hear about your family. Zeke didn't talk much about it."

We took a break from our conversation and went into the kitchen where Angie set out an array of meats and cheeses, lettuce, pickles, and tomatoes, several types of bread, and more condiments than anyone could put on a single sandwich. I made myself a Dagwood so tall I could hardly squeeze it into my mouth. The others made sandwiches of more modest proportions. We filled any empty spots on our plates with potato salad, poured ourselves iced tea and went back to our chairs in the living room. I told them what I knew about Zeke and our family including the blow up at the country club. Then I asked them, "None of my family knew my grandmother kept in touch with Zeke, but apparently she did. What do you know about that?"

Angie swallowed the bite she was chewing and said, "EZ's mother came to visit him a couple of times a year; sometimes more and sometimes less, but twice a year seems like the average. She was a very classy lady and always dressed nicer than we're used to seeing around here. She usually flew into Seattle and rented a full sized Cadillac to drive to Packwood. Cadillacs aren't common around here either. Most of the times she was here we would invite Zeke and her over for dinner so we got acquainted with her."

Angie took a sip of tea. "She didn't say much about Zeke's Dad, and she never mentioned Zeke's brother. We wouldn't

130

have even known he had a brother if she wasn't bragging about you. Every time she visited, she brought pictures of you and updated us about what you were doing at the time. We saw pictures of your high school graduation and your college graduation. She was awfully proud that you went to that big name school in Massachusetts."

I was a little self-conscious about all of the talk about me and interrupted her, "My grandmother and grandfather were quite well off. Did Zeke ever say anything about Grandma giving him money?"

Carl replied, "Zeke didn't talk about it much, but I think she might have because it seemed like he gave quite a bit of money away to people who needed it. One time, I asked him how he managed to pay his bills and give so much money away. He told me his mother occasionally gave him money, but he only took it because he didn't want to hurt her feelings. He said the Klein family money was tainted and he didn't want any of it for himself."

I asked Carl, "Did he say anything about the Klein family money being cursed?"

"Not exactly. He didn't say the money itself was cursed. I specifically remember he said, 'The money is a curse to the Klein family.'"

"I don't understand the difference; the money being cursed or the money being a curse. Either way, it sounds like he thinks the money was big trouble. Personally, I haven't thought of it that way. In fact, I am glad to have my share of the Klein money."

"I hear what you're saying, but Zeke, he said the money had become the yard stick the Klein clan used to evaluate nearly any decision they made. Any decision resulting in more money was good, and any decision resulting in less money was bad. People took second place. Relationships took a back seat. Doing the right thing sometimes got rationalized away."

"I have to admit everything else being equal, I think more money is a good thing, and less money is a bad thing."

"I don't think Zeke thought everything else was equal, and I don't think he thought much of the idea that money should be the measuring stick of our lives, the way we determine our value, the motivation we use to select our friends, or the place where we find security."

"I would have liked to have had the opportunity to discuss the topic with Zeke, but I doubt he could have won me over to his point of view."

"Don't be too sure. Zeke was persuasive, very persuasive. Don't get me wrong. Zeke wasn't against money, but he was against the love of money. He told me more than once that the love of money is the cause of all kinds of evil, and I can't dispute his position."

On one hand I was glad to learn as much as I could about Zeke, but on the other hand it sounded like the Andersons thought Zeke was a prime candidate for canonization into sainthood. I took a slow sip of my tea, cleared my throat, and raised a question that had been brewing in my mind since talking with Carolyn at the Mountain Coffee Shop. "It is clear you all thought a lot of Zeke, and I'm not saying you shouldn't. Everyone I have talked to, except for Bert and Ernie – or whatever their names are, make Zeke sound like some sort of superstar Christian. Maybe he was, and I tend to trust your opinions more than Bert and Ernie's."

"Burt and Herb," Carolyn corrected.

"Okay; Burt and Herb. I trust your opinions more than theirs, but if all this born again Christianity and conversion stuff is real, why are the Zekes so rare in this world? Most Christians I've met are nothing like you describe Zeke. So many are self-righteous, judgmental… asses."

A hint of a smile flitted across Carl's face, but I couldn't tell what he was thinking until he responded, "I hope I can answer without sounding like an ass myself." Carolyn and Angie both laughed a little tee-hee laugh. Carl's eyebrows furrowed in thought, and he said, "Seriously, I find it difficult to defend the way many Christians act, and I include myself in that group. You asked a difficult question; one I sometimes ask myself when I wonder why I'm not more like Jesus.

Carl looked me in the eye, "Have you ever heard anyone refer to Jesus as their Lord and Savior?"

"Yeah. I have heard the phrase, but I don't know much about it."

"Well, I think, too often, Christians embrace Jesus the Savior, but reject Jesus the Lord. We like Jesus the Savior because He saves us from our sins and promises us eternal life. He gives us a free ticket to heaven. People too often grasp the truth of God's unconditional love, but don't respond to His love by surrendering their own selfish desires for His will. The absurd thing is, while we say we are saved only by the grace of God and not because we have earned God's favor with our good behavior, we often act as if we have earned our salvation by our actions, by doing things like smiling, saying nice things, not getting drunk, and not cursing. We obviously can come across like we think we're better than others, and non-

Christians are rightly turned off by our arrogance. Then when they see us mess up they think we're all a bunch of hypocrites."

Carl took another bite and chewed it slowly enough to give him time to collect his thoughts. "But that is just the beginning. It gets worse. Many of us ignore the notion of Jesus being the Lord because it really means Jesus is my Master. In truth, we want to be our own masters, our own bosses. Instead of loving our neighbors as ourselves we love ourselves and want to have more stuff than our neighbors. Some Christians, like Zeke, really do let Jesus be their master and as a result really do love their neighbors. Others, like me, are awfully inconsistent, and I fear we are a discredit to Jesus."

Although Carl wasn't pressuring me, all the Lord and Savior mumbo jumbo made me more than a little uncomfortable. As he looked at me, I felt like I needed to say something in response. "I kind of get what you're saying. However, I still think there are too many hypocritical asses passing judgment on others."

"I agree. Although there aren't enough Zekes, there are lots of imperfect Christians who have moments of truly loving their neighbors. It certainly isn't as black and white as it might seem."

"I suppose not, but the asses overshadow the saints."

"Maybe so. But keep in mind that our selfish natures don't change quickly. Maturation is never fast. It is made up of a series of miniscule, often unnoticeable changes. No one who sees their child every day notices how much the kid grows every day, but the child does. Spiritual growth is sometimes less visible because we can't see it with our eyes, but when it happens, it's real, and I think it's miraculous."

I had more than met my annual quota of religious talk in the prior twenty minutes and moved the conversation on to a safer subject. "Carl, it sounds like you taught Zeke to hunt."

"Yeah, and he took right to it. We started out using rifles but after bagging our animals on the first day of the season three years in a row, Zeke insisted we switch to archery. He thought it would be much more of a challenge because we would need to sneak up to within thirty or forty yards of our prey."

"Did Zeke kill those three deer mounted on his wall with a rifle or with a bow?"

"He killed all three of them with a bow, but only two of them are deer. The big one in the middle is a bull elk."

"I have heard of elk, but never have seen one. What is the difference between deer and elk?"

"'Bout five hundred pounds. A large buck black-tail deer in this area might get close to two hundred pounds, while a bull elk can reach seven hundred."

"Do elk have a shaggy mane and a light tan colored rump?"

"Yep. Besides the size difference, the rump coloring is the easiest way to tell them apart from a deer."

The penny dropped in my mind. Gigantor wasn't a deer on steroids after all. "Now that you say it I realize I have seen some elk; close up, while I was out running this morning."

"They are amazing animals, aren't they?"

"Amazing and a bit scary. I got between a bull and his ladies. He didn't seem very happy."

"As a rule they won't hurt you. The biggest danger is hitting one while driving at night. They can come right through the windshield and crush you. Watch out for them when you drive at night."

"I'll be sure to drive carefully."

While Carl and I were discussing elk, Angie had disappeared into the kitchen. Just as we finished talking, she appeared carrying a plate of chocolate chip cookies. I had been planning to take off, but the cookies enticed me to stay awhile longer.

After swallowing the first bite, I returned the subject of Zeke, "I may be coming back up to spend time at Zeke's place over the next several weekends. I need to decide what to do with all of his stuff. But first, I need to get a better handle on what all is there and then decide how to get rid of it. Carl, is there anything of his you would want to have?"

"There isn't anything of his I need. However, I would like to have his archery equipment, at least one of his bows. They're both in better shape than mine. Besides, they have sentimental value. We had so many good times hunting together. Using his bow would help keep those memories fresh in my mind. How much do you want for one of them?"

"I have no idea what it is worth. What do you think?"

"Probably a couple of hundred dollars."

"Why don't I just give it to you and then I won't feel bad if I impose on any more of your time asking questions about Zeke. Deal?"

"Deal."

"You can just go over and get it? You have a set of keys don't you?"

136

"Yeah. I'll do that. I have a key to his gun safe, too."

I stood up and took a step towards the door. "Thanks again for lunch. I need to get back to Vancouver for the consulting project I am working on. I hope to come back to spend more time looking through Zeke's stuff in a week or maybe two."

Angie said, "Be sure and drop by whenever you are up this way. We'd be hurt if you didn't."

"One more thing, Angie. It looks like someone recently spent a lot of time housecleaning at Zeke's. Was it you?"

"Yes, but don't think anything of it. I wanted to make sure you were able to see it in its best light."

"You didn't need to do that, but I really appreciate it."

I shook hands with Carl and Carolyn, but Angie wouldn't settle for anything less than a big motherly hug.

As I was walking out the door, Carl said, "By the way, once in passing Zeke mentioned a floor safe. You might want to see if you can find it, but I don't know where it would be."

Although I would have liked to spend Saturday night in Packwood and use Sunday to take a closer look through Zeke's stuff and especially to hunt for the floor safe, I felt a responsibility to Joan to get back to the mole hunt. I told Carl, "I'll look for the safe when I come back next weekend."

Thirteen

I relaxed and took in the scenery on the two and a half hour drive from Packwood back to Braxter. I saw two small elk herds grazing in fields alongside the highway, but none were near enough to be a threat of me running into them or of them running into me. I was glad to have met the Andersons even though I felt like a city slicker for not knowing the difference between elk and deer and because I overdressed in business casual shirt instead of logger denim or hunter camo. But it's not like we have a lot of deer, elk, or loggers in Boston. I also wished I had enough time at Zeke's to explore his safe. I put that item at the top of my to-do list for the next trip.

I pulled into Braxter and parked in the front row of the nearly deserted parking lot. Joan had promised to instruct the security staff to allow me to take my personal devices in and out of the building, but just in case they didn't get the memo I took my cell phone and tablet out of my briefcase and slid them under the passenger seat. I took my laptop with me because I planned to use it. If the security guard wouldn't let me take it in I could store it in a locker.

Daylight had faded to dusk, and the overhead lights had already come on, mottling the pavement I walked across on my way to Braxter's main doors. My entrance into the building roused the security guard from a cat nap. I showed him my badge and asked him if I had been cleared to carry my laptop in and out of the building. After rubbing his eyes, he pecked on his keyboard and gazed at his monitor before informing me the clearance came through yesterday afternoon. He motioned me past the checkpoint, and I continued on to the Kilroy security station where I performed the authentication incantation allowing me to proceed past the second level of security.

Eight high-speed, two-terabyte USB drives awaited me in my cube's storage drawer. I unpacked them and installed the copying software from my laptop to each of them. After labelling each drive and noting which drive was going to connect to which person's computer, I connected the first drive to Joan's laptop and fired up the copying software. I did the same thing to Greg, her admin's computer. I hadn't explicitly told Joan I would copy all of her files, but she was likely smart enough to at least suspect I would. Even with high speed drives I expected the copy procedure take two or three hours on each computer, depending on the size and speed of their hard drives. I was especially eager to copy the files from Harold, the firmware engineer's laptop because his defensive behavior on Friday put me on high alert. After connecting a drive to Harold's machine and starting the copy process, I connected the fourth drive to Theron's computer and then used the remaining drives to copy files from the software engineers' computers.

Technically, I should have copied from one computer at a time while remaining present to monitor the entire process from start to finish. My continued presence would have enabled me to attest that the chain of custody for the data I copied was intact, and the data could not have been compromised by anyone. However, it was more important to move quickly and copy multiple drives at once. I had to cross my fingers and hope that if I was fortunate enough to catch a perp there would be other evidence to support criminal proceedings. The important thing was to stop the leak, if it existed, as soon as possible.

I went back to my cube to kill a few hours reading some of the security specifications I hadn't yet read. The silence in the building on a Saturday night was unsettling so I inserted my ear buds and cranked up some tunes I had stored on my laptop. Joe Bonamassa's guitar riffs eased the boredom of reading the specs. I was concentrating on a particularly detailed section of Braxter's incident response procedure when my chair suddenly spun 180° around so fast that I fell out of it onto my hands and knees. I looked up and saw Harold's furious eyes staring down at me. He was wearing the same rumpled clothes he had worn Friday. It didn't look like he had gone home at all. He sneered and tossed the hard drive that had been copying files from his computer onto my desk. Without saying a word, turned and strode back towards his cube. I stood up, grabbed the drive off of my desk and trotted to catch up with him. I put my hand on his shoulder and pulled him around. I stuck my face about eight inches from his and snarled, "Hold it right there!"

He turned away from me and kept walking towards his cube. I reached for my cell phone to call Joan, but then my empty pocket reminded me I stupidly left it in my car. I took off, this time running after Harold to make sure he couldn't compromise his computer. I pushed him aside and beat him to his cube by a second and turned to block his way to his computer. "Sorry, Harold, this area is off limits until I finish. Go home. Now!"

I held my hands in front of me and started taking slow, deep breaths to prepare myself for the probable fight. I had studied taekwondo for three years in my teens and hoped I could summon enough technique to defend myself. Harold's clenched fists trembled, and his flared nostrils signaled an aggressive intent. Just when I thought he was about to take a swing, he took half a step back and exhaled and then finally spoke, "Alright. I'm going to leave, but don't think this is over. This is your last day at Braxter. After I tell Joan what you're up to, you'll be lucky to get a job cleaning toilets at the circus."

I wished he had taken a swing because I wanted an excuse to kick his nerdy ass. Instead I resorted to sophomoric insults, "You're the jerk making the career limiting move. Joan told me to tell her if anyone didn't cooperate. She authorized me to analyze everyone's hard drives. I'm going to call her tonight and tell her how cooperative you have been. By tomorrow, it's going to suck being you. But then I'm sure it sucks everyday so what's the difference?"

Harold gave me the finger and walked towards the exit.

I hollered after him, "You're right about me looking for a leak, and you're now number one on my list. Best case, I prove it's you, I'm the hero and you go to jail. Worst case, I can't find the leak, I just move on to my next client and you and everyone else on Kilroy will be looking for new jobs. Either way, I win, and you lose."

I plugged the drive back into his computer and restarted the copy process from scratch. I didn't want to give him the opportunity to come back and interfere, but I took the chance to get my computer and ear buds from my cube so I could get back to reading the specs while supervising the copying. Charging $275/hour just to babysit Harold's disk copy was outside my ethical comfort zone, besides it would have been too boring sitting there doing nothing, even more boring than reading the specs.

I tried to read, but the adrenaline from my encounter with Harold had wired me up too much. I thought about the altercation and tried to rationalize my reaction. Why had I been so hard on Harold? Why did I let him drag me into to an invective outburst? The only good news was we didn't resort to physical blows, although if he would have taken the first swing I would have welcomed the slugfest.

After contemplating my disturbing behavior without coming to any conclusion, I realized I needed to copy as many disks as possible before Harold alerted everyone I was copying their hard drives, even if it meant I had to pull an all-nighter and then work all day Sunday. The hard drives Joan procured for me had much more capacity than I had expected, and the Braxter computers were several years old so their hard drives were small by current standards. I calculated I would be able to put the content from three computers on each drive. I planned to finish with Harold's drive and then get the other drives and then copy from more computers. Harold's copy job was almost complete when a shadow fell across my laptop screen. I quickly spun around and steeled myself for an attack. Harold stood staring down at his feet, his hunched shoulders sagging. "Daniel, I came back to apologize. I shouldn't have gone off like that. I know you are only doing your job."

"It's David, not Daniel, and yes, I am just doing my job." I stood up and planted my feet far enough apart to give me a solid stance.

Harold held an open palm up and said, "Look. I'm sorry. Okay?"

"Is what okay? Stealing top-secret information? That's not okay. Interfering with my work? That's not okay either. What is it you want to be okay?"

"I just want to tell you I was out of line. I was wrong."

"Okay. You were wrong. I already knew that."

Harold looked up at me and muttered, "Cut me a little slack here? I don't want to... I can't lose my job."

"That's up to Joan, not me."

He rocked in place and added, "I'm under tons of pressure. I've got to deliver my code by Monday, and it's got to be top quality. I haven't been home since Thursday because I am double and triple checking everything. My last code release had two critical bugs, and Joan wrote me up. Ron's team caught them, and it's a good thing because they would have caused the whole Kilroy system to fail."

I scowled at him and said, "Maybe you need to focus more on your own job and less on mine."

"I know my code didn't have those defects in it when I checked it in. Somebody changed it."

"Maybe... Or maybe you are losing it. Who knows?"

"I know. I can picture the code I wrote, and it was correct. Problem is I can't prove it."

I softened my tone. "Do you really think somebody changed the code after you wrote it?"

"Somebody must've."

"Okay. Let's say someone did sabotage your code... I'm not saying they did or that I believe you, but let's say someone did. How could they do it?"

"Remember the software control system I told you about? It's new. We didn't have it during the last release. Almost anyone could have stolen a copy of my code, sabotaged it, and then copied the bad code back onto the server."

"Sounds unlikely. I'm going to need more proof than your guesses."

Harold's eyes started to water, and he continued to rock back and forth from one foot to another. "Please don't tell Joan about tonight."

"No promises. I'll think about it, but I'm going to do whatever I think is best for Braxter." Harold nodded as I continued, "You're not the only one under a lot of pressure. If you're really sorry, I need you to keep quiet about me copying everyone's disks. You can't tell anyone. If anyone finds out, I'll know you were the leak. And then I'll tell Joan about tonight. Deal?"

"The secret's safe. I won't tell anyone."

"Okay. Now go home and get some sleep. I've got to get back to work."

Harold nodded and slowly walked down the aisle. The disk copy had completed by the time he left so I disconnected the drive and went to collect the other four drives I hoped were ready for me to connect to other computers. Three out of four were ready so I hooked them up to the computers used by three people on Ron's QA team. I didn't add any more to the drive that stored data from Harold's computer because I didn't want to let it out of my sight. I realized I had been present during the entire copy operation, and I could testify that no one could have possibly compromised the data from his computer. If Harold proved to be the mole, and if his computer contained evidence of maleficence, the data I had copied onto the hard drive would be defensible evidence.

I circled back to the one drive which was still copying when I checked it earlier. It had finished so I hooked it up to Mike's computer in IT and started copying his drive. I then attached the drive containing the files from Harold's computer to my laptop and fired up my analysis software. I told the software to search for any hidden or partially deleted files. Then I directed the software to find all of Harold's emails having attachments and that he had sent to anyone outside of Braxter.

While the files were copying from Mike's computer, I thought of a way I could test Harold's story about his firmware being sabotaged. Stealing specifications was bad enough, but sabotage was a whole new problem. If Harold had told me the truth, then the risk to Braxter's reputation and financial health went through the roof. If there was evidence, beyond Harold's claim, then I needed to let Joan know, and she would probably need to notify the DoD.

Telling myself I could finish the copying on Sunday, I waited for the current batch of copying to complete and paused the analysis of Harold's files. I packed my laptop and the eight hard drives into my briefcase and called it a night. I drove to the hotel I had stayed at before my trip to Packwood and parked in a well-lit spot under a light. I pulled my cell phone and tablet from under the seat and crammed them along with the drive from Harold's computer into my crowded briefcase. I got out of the car and went around to the trunk where I hid the other seven drives as best as I could under the carpet covering the space saving spare tire. I didn't have a totally secure place to keep the drives so the trunk would need to suffice until I could purchase a large, hard sided briefcase.

*****

I awoke to streams of sunlight poking through the narrow gap between the drapes in my hotel room. I rolled over and went back to sleep for more than an hour, and because I rarely have the chance to sleep in, getting an extra hour felt like a regal luxury. I put on a pair of jeans and a tee shirt and set out on foot to find the nearest coffee shop; anywhere I could relax with a morning paper and be lazy for an hour or two. I walked about a half mile before I found a promising bakery. I stepped through the door to see if they served coffee and Danish, and instantly the sweet aromas of fresh baking wrapped around me and pulled me into the line of people waiting to order. I bought a marionberry muffin, a fruit cup and a large coffee. I took my breakfast to an open table where someone had left their copy of the Sunday Oregonian.

The paper included a sale flyer for a luggage store in Portland. I walked back to my car in the hotel parking lot, got in and drove across the river into downtown Portland. Because of the early hour I found a parking spot right outside the luggage store. I wanted a metal sided briefcase and looked at several before buying a locking five inch aluminum attaché for nearly $500. I returned to my car and moved the hard drives from under the trunk's carpet into my new briefcase. As I drove to Braxter I wondered if the metal sided case would make the hard drives more secure or less secure. Something about the expensive case screamed, "Steal me. Steal me."

I cleared the security checkpoints and resumed copying the hard drives. I estimated that with any luck I could almost finish by the end of the day. It all depended upon the capacity of the source drives. I read specs and copied, and read more specs and copied some more. It was not my favorite way to spend

146

the bulk of my Sunday. I called it quits at six in the evening, although I still needed to copy two more disks. I planned to copy them on Monday evening.

FOURTEEN

After sleeping only three hours, I was awakened by the sounds of horns blaring, tires skidding, and then a loud crash; the clamor of a car wreck. I hoped no one was injured and rolled and was almost back to sleep when I heard blaring sound of sirens coming closer. As soon as the sirens stopped, flashing red lights strobed through my closed drapes. I reluctantly got up and peeked out the window to see a car that had T-boned a minivan and then went back to bed. I lay in bed for fifteen minutes unsuccessfully willing myself back to sleep. I gave up at two forty five and realized if I went to Braxter I could copy the rest of the drives before anyone arrived for work. That would save me the trouble of working late another night.

I arrived at Braxter at three thirty and started copying contents from the remaining computers. I figured I would be finished by six thirty and could take the drives back out to my car and stow them in the trunk with nobody the wiser. I dozed off in my chair for a couple of hours while the disks were being copied so the time passed quickly, and I felt moderately rested for the coming day. As soon as the copying finished, I gathered the disks into my briefcase and took them out to my trunk. It was early and I hadn't eaten so I drove to a one of a kind café in downtown Vancouver for breakfast and coffee, lots of coffee.

When I arrived back at my cube at seven fifteen, I saw a note from Harold asking me to come to his cube right away. I picked up the specification for secure software development practices and walked down the hall to his area. He must have taken my advice the night before to go home because he was wearing a fresh white shirt and his hair was recently washed. He looked up and started to motion me to sit down in the side chair beside his desk, but then stood up and said, "Let's go get a cup of coffee." The last thing I needed or wanted was more coffee, but realized it wouldn't hurt me to go along with Harold. Besides, I needed to talk with him before he had an opportunity to talk with his coworkers. I nodded and we walked down to the cafeteria. He insisted on paying for my coffee and walked over to a table in the deserted back corner. He sat with his back to the walls and I sat across from him and asked, "Harold, what's on your mind?"

He leaned toward me and asked, "Did you tell Joan about last night?"

"No, and I'm leaning against it, but I wanted to talk with you first; ask you a few questions. That okay?"

He leaned back. "Sure."

"Tell me again about the changes you allege someone made to your code."

"They changed the data format the software uses to encode the GPS location. Kilroy uses a classified data format which communicates very precise locations. The code was changed to use a less precise, civilian format, and the change also offset the actual location by a random distance that could be anywhere from 5 meters to 15 meters from the actual location. The changed code appeared to work, unless you carefully compared the reported location to the actual location."

"And you are certain you didn't code it wrong?"

149

"Like I said last night, I can picture the code. It wasn't what I wrote."

I silenced my skepticism. "Photographic memory. Right?"

"Technically it is called eidetic memory."

I put the document I had brought with me on the table and turned it so he could read the cover. "You told me you used to read specifications on your lunch hour. Do you remember reading this specification for secure software development?"

He looked at it closely and nodded, "I read it."

I picked the document up and without letting Harold see the content. I thumbed to a page near the middle. "I'm going to pick a section at random and start reading it to you. I want to see if you can tell me what comes after what I read."

"What page are you on?"

"Twenty-six."

Without waiting for me to start reading, he started reciting the text at the top of page twenty-six, "Resource owners and resource custodians must ensure secure coding practices, including security training and reviews, are incorporated into each phase of the software development life cycle."

I held up my hand for him to stop. "I'm impressed. You didn't miss a word."

He smirked at me and said, "Do you need to hear more?"

"I'm convinced." I was beginning to believe Harold was telling the truth about the code changes being made by someone else because he was certainly telling the truth about remembering everything he had read. Besides, his direct and guileless manner caused him to say whatever came into his mind, without filtering, and made me think he would be a lousy liar.

He leaned back toward me. "Are you going to tell Joan?"

"No. I think you're being straight with me about someone else sabotaging your code. Who else have you told about your suspicion?"

"I tried to tell Ron, and Joan, too. But I don't think they believed me."

I leaned back in my chair and said, "For the time being, let's keep it just between the two of us. I don't want to tip anyone off."

Harold nodded his agreement, and I continued, "Harold, here is the deal. Don't tell anyone about me copying the hard disks, and I won't tell Joan about last night."

"Deal. By the way, let me know if I can help you with your investigation."

I nodded and said, "Let's get back to work."

I returned to my cube, but just as I started to plan the next steps in my investigation, my phone vibrated with a text message from Joan. "My office. Now!"

I was getting tired of her early morning chain yanking, but hurried to her office anyway. I didn't immediately enter because she was talking with two somber looking men who wore dark business suits and ties. Joan motioned me to come in, and I stepped off to the side near her conference table because I didn't want to interrupt. One of the men turned to me. He was about six feet, six inches tall, with broad, imposing, if not intimidating, shoulders. I guessed his age at forty five, but he looked as fit as a twenty five year old. His full head of blonde hair was cut in a flat-top that screamed "military" even though he wasn't in uniform. The other man, a wimp by comparison, was noticeably shorter, thinner, and younger, maybe thirty five years old. He had lost some of his brown hair, but wore what remained just like the big guy. Flat top number one asked Joan, "It this Klein?"

Joan said, "David, we have unexpected visitors from the Army's Defense Security Service." Pointing toward the older man she said, "David, this is Mr. Gerald Gross, Director of Contractor Security. Mr. Gross, this is David Klein." She pointed to the other man and said, "David, this is Mr. Samuel Tinker. He's been performing quarterly on-site inspections of our security for the past year." I looked each of them in the eyes and shook their hands. Both had firm handshakes and returned my direct looks. They were all business.

Gross took a half step towards me, close enough that I considered taking a step back, but I didn't want to yield any ground and appear to be intimidated. He said, "General Matthews is very concerned about security here at Braxter. He called the Defense Security Service in to conduct our own security audit; with our own people. Our full on-site team will be here later today. Klein, you are off the job. Tinker will escort you out of the building."

Gross' demeanor didn't leave room for discussion, but I wasn't about to leave without pushing back. I said, "I'm already well into the audit. I can show your team what I've done, and then we can work together to quickly wrap things up. I'm sure you don't want to lose any time."

Gross replied, "I appreciate the offer, but it won't be necessary. My team works alone."

Joan shrugged her shoulders as if to say there was nothing she could do. She gave me a wink that Gross and Tinker couldn't see and said, "David, this is out of my hands. I'll call you shortly to make arrangements for paying you for the time you've spent."

I nodded as Tinker put his hand on my shoulder and firmly turned me toward the door. I told him I didn't need his help and I needed to get a few personal things from my cube. I was out in the parking lot and climbing into the Altima by eight. I put the keys in the ignition, but didn't start the car. I had been totally blind-sided, and it looked like Joan had been, too. General Matthews must have called Defense Security Services right after talking with Joan the week before. He never gave me a chance. I had mixed feelings about the whole mess. It was going to take me at least a few weeks to line up a new consulting assignment and I would have an income gap. That was the downside. But on the positive side, I would have more time to finish my business with Zeke's estate in Packwood.

I couldn't see any upside in this for Joan though. She was sure to be the big loser if the DSS boys pinned anything on Braxter. I wouldn't expect the Braxter brass to step up and shield her from the blame because they all have their own careers to protect. Maybe Harold was right all along about me being brought in to be the scapegoat. If he was, Joan might be able to protect her position by blaming me. Either way, I was out, but I needed to get in touch with Joan. She didn't know about the eight hard drives in my trunk, each loaded with potential evidence. If Harold ratted on me before I notified Braxter, I could be in pretty deep myself if Braxter or DSS accused me of stealing critical evidence. I made a mental note to tell Joan about the hard drives when she called me about my last invoice.

I started the car and as I left the parking lot I saw a dark blue Ford Taurus follow me out of the lot. It caught my attention because all of the other cars were arriving, and only the two of us were leaving. My imagination ran off wondering if I was being followed. As I drove back to my hotel, I kept looking in my rear view mirrors. There were always one or two cars between us, but the Taurus stayed behind me. I thought about making a few sudden turns to see if he was really following me, but didn't because if I was really being followed I didn't want to let the tail know I was on to him.

When I pulled into my hotel, the Taurus drove slowly by. I was only going to need fifteen or twenty minutes to pack my bags and check out, but I didn't want to give anyone a chance to break into my trunk and steal the hard drives. Instead of pulling into the hotel parking lot I pulled into the loading zone at the hotel entrance. The sign warned me cars left for more than five minutes were subject to towing, but I didn't care. I needed to leave the car in plain view. The bellman opened my door and asked if I was checking in. I told him I was checking out. I handed him a twenty and told him I shouldn't need longer than twenty minutes. I knew he would keep an eye on my car.

Twenty minutes later I had checked out and was back at the front entrance. My car appeared to be in order so I tipped the bellman another twenty. It was an excessive tip, but I wanted him to remember me in case I needed it later on. The safest option for me was to stay close by Braxter until I heard from Joan so I could return the disks, but I didn't like the idea of hanging out until she found time to call. Plus, I didn't know how long Gross and Tinker would keep her busy. I started the car and headed for I-5. I hadn't traveled more than two blocks when I passed the dark blue Taurus parked on a side street. I got a quick look at the driver, and saw his hair was a little too long for him to be a Fed, unless he was undercover. He slowly pulled out and stayed a tenth of a mile or so behind me.

I didn't want to let him know I was on to him, but I didn't want him to follow me to Packwood either. Maybe I was being paranoid but I started wondering if he had stuck a tracking device to my car while it was parked at Braxter. So instead of getting onto I-5 I headed to the car rental return lot at the Portland airport. The lot entry was restricted to rental cars so he couldn't follow me into it. I hoped he would think I was leaving Portland. Instead, I moved the drives from the trunk into my new briefcase, grabbed my suitcase and my soft-sided brief case, and headed from the Hertz lot to the adjacent Avis counter, without entering the airport terminal. I thought about turning my cell phone off so nobody could use it to track my location, but I needed to be available if Joan called. I rented a Malibu from Avis and headed to I-5 while paying close attention to my rear view mirror.

I didn't notice anybody following me on I-5, although if someone was following me it would have been difficult for me to be sure. I drove about sixty-five miles north to Highway 12 and headed east. Nobody followed me off of the exit, but just to be safe I pulled into the gas station at the intersection of I-5 and Highway 12 and kept an eye out for the blue Taurus. After ten minutes of fruitless watching, I got back on the road.

My phone rang, and I saw it was Joan. I quickly attached my headset to my ear and answered. "Hey, Joan."

155

"David, I've only got a few minutes before I need to get back to the goons. Sorry about this morning. Gross and Tinker met me at the security checkpoint and escorted me to my office. They blindsided me. I know Matthews is behind this. I tried to convince them to keep you on because I trust you more than I trust them. They refused and ordered me to text you to come to my office."

"Joan, I don't like it either, but don't worry about it. You've got bigger problems than worrying about me. I'll be fine." I knew I would be doing enough worrying about me and Klein InfoSec Associates and didn't need any help from Joan.

"Thanks for understanding, but I hate the way they treated you. I told them we were going to pay you for two months. I know it's is only half of what you were expecting, but it is the least we can do. Maybe you can take a vacation on Braxter."

At the moment it sounded very appealing. "Maybe I will."

"If you ever need a reference, let me know. I'll say good things about you."

"Joan, have you talked with Harold today?"

"No. Should I have?"

"No. I was just wondering. Listen, I may need a little help from you to keep me out of trouble with the feds. Last night and early this morning I copied everyone's hard disks. The copies were in my car so I still have them with me. If Gross and Tinker find out they could charge me with theft. I am on my way up to my late uncle's place in Packwood, but I can turn around and have them back to you in less than ninety minutes. What should I do?"

She didn't answer for a few seconds and then said, "Are you willing to postpone your vacation in a few days?"

"What do you have in mind?"

"I'd like you to search the hard drives and report anything suspicious to me, and only to me."

I thought for a bit and responded, "I want to help, and I am willing to spend the time, but if this goes south I could end up in prison – for a long time."

"How do you figure?"

"I didn't have written authorization to make those copies, and I certainly don't have authorization to have taken them off of Braxter's premises. I could be accused of espionage."

"I see. What if I gave you written authorization?"

"Then I would be covered, but if Gross finds a copy of the authorization he is probably going to come down on you hard. It protects me, but it's risky for you."

"Fine." Joan paused a second before adding, "Then there won't be any paper trail. After I hang up, I am going to call you back. Don't answer your phone, and I'll leave a message authorizing you to have the drives in your possession and to analyze them. As long as you don't delete the message you'll be in the clear."

"Works for me." I hesitated and then said, "Joan, one more thing. Harold knows I made the copies. He promised to keep quiet about it, but if he talks we're going to be in deep with the DSS."

"I need some time to think about how to handle him. Give me a day or two. I've got to get back to Gross. Remember, don't answer your phone."

A minute later my phone rang again. I saw it was Joan but didn't answer. I gave her a few minutes to leave the exculpatory message and then called my voicemail and listened to the recording. Joan identified herself and then instructed me to keep the copies I had made and analyze them off-site from Braxter in an effort to discover suspicious behavior. I ended the call and realized I would be very busy while in Packwood.

I headed east on Highway 12. Twenty miles from Zeke's I entered the broad Cowlitz River valley surrounded by countless mountains. When I first entered the valley, it was several miles wide, but it gradually narrowed with each mile I drove, and the mountains seemed taller as they sandwiched the road. Packwood affected me much differently than Boston. I loved Boston on an intellectual level. I loved it for its history, its academia, its restaurants, and its ethnic neighborhoods; things closely intertwined with people, but I didn't love it for its land. I didn't think of the land underneath the city of Boston any more than I thought of the foundation under a house. To me, Boston land was invisible.

I was attracted to Packwood, not on an intellectual level but on some form of primal level, and I was attracted to the land, the rugged forests, the mountains, and the wildlife. Such an attraction was new to me. I didn't know if it was an adolescent crush, a passing infatuation, or something deeper. I hadn't resolved the issue before entering Packwood. My stomach was growling so I pulled the Malibu into a space in front of Duffy's Grill and went in for lunch. I sat in one of the dozen or so tables in the front part of the building. The menu offered about ten burger varieties; beef, elk, and bison, with and without cheese, bacon, eggs, and mushrooms. I almost opted for the elk burger hoping my consumption would reduce the size of the local herd, but ordered a club sandwich with soup and a diet cola instead. I walked around the rest of the establishment while waiting for my sandwich. Duffy's had something for everyone; the front area, where I sat, catered primarily to families and light drinkers. A long wooden bar backed by a huge mirror, additional tables, and four video poker machines filled the "no minors" section in the rear. I returned to my table to eat my tasty sandwich and homemade chicken noodle soup.

Next, I stopped by the local grocery store to buy a few staples to get me through dinner and breakfast the next day. The small store carried a surprisingly large assortment. I bought a small filet of fresh salmon, a package of brown rice, and the usual coffee, milk, bread, and breakfast cereal. I only bought enough for a couple of days because I didn't know how long I would be staying or how long I could bear to eat my own cooking.

I drove up to Zeke's and parked the Malibu in the carport. I realized that once I programmed my analysis software to search the hard drives, it was going to take hours to process each drive. Since I wasn't at Braxter, I couldn't spend the time reading specifications or interviewing any of the Braxter team. As a result, I could spend the time enjoying Zeke's place and looking for his floor safe.

FIFTEEN

I lugged my two briefcases and my suitcase toward the house, but stopped half way. The aroma of cedar trees once again filled me with contentment as I inhaled a slow, deep breath to completely fill my lungs with its essence. I walked slowly over to the nearest cedar tree and reached up to the lowest branch which bowed downward before reaching skyward. I pulled the end of the limb down toward me and broke off a light green sprig of new growth and rubbed it between my palms to release more of the fragrance into the air and to leave an aromatic residue on my hands.

As I lingered outside craning my neck to look up to the treetops more than 150 feet above, an appreciation for Zeke's idyllic place took root in me; a secluded home in the woods, a cedar shake roof, a wood stove, and no traffic, no air pollution, no noise pollution, no light pollution; nothing to interrupt or distract from a tranquil life. It was alluring in its contrast to weeks of travel and weekends in Boston, but I wondered if I would go stir crazy after a few months in the same serene place. The old adage saying the grass is always greener on the other side of the fence warned me that what is great as a change is not always great as a steady diet. I hoped working on the Braxter project while at Zeke's place would provide a good opportunity for me to learn if the reality would match the allure.

I covered my nose with both open palms and took another cedar whiff and then grabbed my bags and went into the house. The inside temperature was uncomfortably cool due to the trees shading the house from direct sunlight. I opened the drapes to let in the ambient light and then set up my computer to resume running the analysis software on the files copied from Harold's computer. Finally, I started looking for the safe. I assumed it was built into the floor on the ground level so its bulk could be hidden between floor joists in the crawlspace under the house. I could have looked for the entrance to the crawlspace, crawled underneath the house, and then searched for the safe suspended from the floor above. However, the near certainty of years of dirt and countless spider webs encouraged me to look for the safe from inside the house. Diving into the crawlspace was my last resort.

I looked in all of the closets on the first floor but didn't see any evidence of a safe. I entered the living room and immediately thought the safe could be hidden under the bearskin rug. I pulled it aside and studied the hardwood floor beneath it. The sunlight coming through the living room window at an acute angle outlined a faint square about sixteen inches by sixteen inches. The square looked like it might be a removable floor section that could hide the door to the safe. But, try as I might, I couldn't remove it. The gap between the square and the floor was only a tiny slit; not even wide enough to insert a narrow knife blade. I pushed on each edge and each corner hoping to raise the opposite side, but couldn't budge it. I thought of using one of Zeke's hunting knives to pry it up but discarded the idea because I didn't want to damage the beautiful floor. I gave up and left the floor under the bearskin rug alone for the time being so I could rule out the safe being in other parts of the floor.

I found a floor-to-ceiling closet located just off the kitchen and opened its two bi-fold doors to discover Zeke's laundry. His washer and dryer covered the entire floor space, leaving no room for a floor safe, unless it was underneath one of the appliances, which was unlikely. A wooden shelf above the washer and dryer spanned the width of the closet. It held a box of detergent and a bottle of bleach, but most of the space was taken up with an assortment of common household tools – adjustable wrenches, screwdrivers, an electric drill and pliers. A suction cup tool like one I had seen glass workers use to carry panes of glass caught my eye. It appeared to be commercial grade and strong enough to hold a large pane of glass, or maybe even lift a section of floor. I took it into the living room and after a few minutes of fiddling, I figured out how to create suction strong enough to grab hold of the square on the floor. I squatted over it and pulled. After applying significant force I heard the ripping sound of Velcro tape as its hook and loop strips tore apart. I pulled a little harder, and the trap door came up, exposing a safe door that required both a physical key and a numeric code to unlock it.

I pulled Zeke's keys out of my pocket and looked for one matching the safe. I found the key and it turned in the lock, but I couldn't open the safe because I didn't know the correct code for the keypad. I replaced the access panel in the floor and went out to the car to get the papers Carolyn had given me hoping one of them mentioned the code. I scanned the papers but didn't find any mention of a safe or of a keypad code. I threw the papers back into the car, went back into the house, and slammed the door.

If Carl knew the code I was sure he would have told me, but he didn't sound like he knew very much about the safe, other than hearing Zeke mentioned it in passing. I was stumped and more than a little frustrated. It occurred to me that Grandma might know something about the safe. I had meant to call her, but had kept putting it off because we didn't have much in common. Normally I only called her on Mother's Day and on her birthday. Last year, I did my duty and called her on Mother's Day. We chatted about the weather, our health, and told each other what we had been doing. After five minutes of talking she asked me about some guy named Arnold. I asked her, "Who is Arnold? I don't think I know him." She replied that he was my brother. Only then did we realize I had called the wrong number and was speaking with someone else's grandma. I hung up to call *my* Grandma and essentially repeated the prior conversation sans Arnold.

Chuckling to myself about chatting with the wrong grandma, I looked her up in my phone's address book and called. She answered on the third ring and immediately said, "I hear your Dad told you about Zeke. What do you think about having a long lost uncle?"

I raised my voice more than I should have. "It makes me mad. I'm upset that nobody told me about him. I don't see why it needed to be a deep, dark family secret. I am in Packwood sorting through Zeke's things and trying to learn something about him, since none of my relatives saw fit to tell me anything about him. Why didn't you tell me; if not before Grandpa died, you should have told me after?"

"I should have, but I was used to keeping my contact with Zeke a secret. I was more comfortable hiding it. It was almost like I was having a clandestine affair. I also thought it was up to Zeke to contact you. I was a little surprised he didn't, because I know he wanted to see you again."

"What do you mean 'see me again?' I never met him." It seemed the more I learned about Zeke the more I found things had been hidden from me.

"Yes, you did once. Do you remember when you were seven or eight? I took you down to Disney World for a long weekend?"

"Sure, I had a blast." I remembered reveling in my doting grandmother's attention and eating whatever junk food I wanted.

"Do you remember when we ran into a man, and I said he used to be my neighbor. He spent the entire afternoon with us?"

"Yeah. I thought it was quite a coincidence."

"It was no coincidence. That was Zeke, and he and I planned for him to meet us there. He took you on rides while I waited. You and he had so much fun. After we left Disney World he took us out to dinner so he could spend a little more time with you before he returned to Washington."

I was starting to get irate. "You took advantage of my trust and lied to me. Why didn't you just tell me the truth?"

"David, I'm terribly sorry. I couldn't take the chance that your grandfather would find out. At least that's what I told myself. He would've divorced me, and I didn't want to start life all over, even though I knew I could easily get a very generous divorce settlement. Call me old fashioned, but I married for better or worse. Losing my son was the worse, and I didn't want to also lose my husband. Our relationship was never the same after the disownment. I tried to block out the pain and love Samuel completely, but was never able to. I couldn't bear to go back to the country club. …We used to dance there once a month, but after that horrendous night, I never danced with your grandfather again. Our marriage went from being one of love to being one of convenience. I hated the wall that grew

164

between us, but the thing I hated most was he didn't seem to be at all bothered by it. My love once overflowed for your grandfather, but it hardened into cold resentment and then crumbled into indifference. The only good thing was the distance between us gave me opportunity to travel and see Zeke on the sly."

"None of it makes sense. It sounds to me like someone should have had the guts to stand up to Grandpa. Dad didn't do it because he didn't want to lose his trust fund, and I still don't understand why you didn't do it. Maybe you were too concerned about the money, too."

"It wasn't just the money. It was the house. I love the house, especially the garden. I couldn't bear to lose it, and I was afraid Samuel would have put up a big fight to keep it; just to spite me. And Clara next door was my best friend. I would have been terribly lonely without her nearby. But I was wrong because I was lonely anyway, very lonely."

Even after Grandma explained why she didn't tell me about Zeke I wasn't satisfied and didn't understand why people let their fears destroy relationship. "Grandma, I didn't call to give you a hard time. I'm sorry if it sounds like that's what I am doing. I called because, as I said, I am going through Zeke's things and found a safe, and I need a code to open it. I can't find it anywhere. Do you know where he might have kept it?"

"Yes. The last time I visited Zeke before he died, he told me about the safe and if you called asking about a code I was to tell you it was the month and day you were born. It is 1227."

"Thanks. I'll try it. What else did he tell you to pass on to me?"

"Only that he wished he would have contacted you on your twenty-first birthday and invited you to come and visit with him."

"I would have liked that. At least I think I would of. It sounds like he was a little too religious for me, though."

"You would have liked him a lot. Yes, his religion was important to him, very important. But he didn't preach it as much as he lived it; he wouldn't have made you uncomfortable. Zeke became my favorite person, but don't tell your father."

"I need to go and try the code, but I promise to call you again sometime soon."

"Bye for now. I love you."

"Love you, too."

I grabbed the glass carrier and hurried over to stick it back on to the access panel in the floor. I was able to pull the floor piece loose much faster this time. I twisted the key, entered the code, and turned the lever. It was too dark to see what was inside so I reached inside and pulled out a small stack of old, musty envelopes that smelled like cheddar cheese molding in the back of a refrigerator. I thumbed through them and saw all five were addressed to Aaron Klein at an address in Berlin, Deutschland, which I recognized as Berlin, Germany. I pulled one page from its envelope and found a handwritten letter written in German. I put it back into its envelope and checked the other letters to see if any were in English. None were so I set the stack aside and reached back into the safe.

I brushed my hand across the bottom and discovered a book lying flat. As I slowly pulled it out, the malodorous aroma of dusty mildew combined with the pungent smell of the musty letters. I felt like I was snooping in a cave hiding buried Klein secrets. I ran my fingers gently across the book's faded brown cover. The worn cloth and the dog-eared corners spoke of frequent handling over many years. The title, *Hauptbuch*, imprinted on the front cover in gold letters didn't mean anything to me. I slowly folded back the cover to expose the first page and saw what looked like accounting entries. Page after page of numbers and German writing penned in blue ink by a calligraphic hand implied the book was some kind of ledger. The word, *Jahrezahl*, was at the top of a column that looked like dates, the earliest being 1936. I flipped to the last page which was dated *Januar* 15, 1941. *Aufwand* and *Ertrag* were at the top of two columns of numbers, big numbers. I assumed DM referred to Deutschmarks, but I had no idea what a Deutschmark would have been worth in the late thirties. All of the numbers were large; at least one hundred thousand DMs. It looked like somebody, presumably my great, great grandfather, Aaron, was dealing with big bucks.

I reached back into the safe to be sure I had everything and touched something that was about the size of a half book of matches. I pulled it out to discover it was a 4 gigabyte USB memory stick. I needed to plug it into my laptop to discover what was on it. Two minutes later I was sitting in Zeke's recliner, the USB drive plugged into the port. I paused the analysis software and scanned the USB drive. I saw a folder named *documents* and a Microsoft Excel spreadsheet named *Hauptbuch.xlsx.* I opened the spreadsheet first, hoping it had information about the unintelligible ledger book. It was my lucky day. I compared the spreadsheet layout to the Hauptbuch book, and saw Zeke had painstakingly translated the German text into English and input all of the numbers into the spreadsheet. Zeke also made a note saying he had converted German Marks to US Dollars, based on the 1940 exchange rate. Clearly Zeke had been a bean counter because he really knew his way around Excel. He had also entered each year's transactions on a separate page with subtotals and average markups for each year, and had created a summary page complete with line graphs showing the trends and annual averages for each asset type. I imagined him sitting at his desk keying data from the old ledger into the spreadsheet, then entering the formulas to add the columns, and finally inserting the charts.

The graphs clearly showed that old Aaron had mastered the knack of buying art, jewelry, and precious metals low and selling them high. Although the transaction size started to decrease notably in early 1940, he managed to sell nearly all of the art and much of the jewelry for nearly four times what he paid for it. He sold precious metals for an average of twice what he had paid. Although a lower markup than he got for the art and jewelry, a two times markup was incomprehensibly high because the price of precious metals is public, and the bid and ask price spread is normally less than 1%. I couldn't guess how Aaron could turn such a high profit.

During the four plus years recorded in the spreadsheet, Aaron netted just over five million dollars' worth of diamonds– in 1940 dollars, which would be worth more than eighty-million in current dollars. Zeke's spreadsheet didn't say why Aaron kept the loot in diamonds and not in currency, leaving me to guess. I knew Aaron and his family relocated to the United States in the early 1941 so I surmised Deutschmarks were worthless outside of Germany, while diamonds were the most compact way for Aaron to transport his wealth with him. I wondered how heavy his family's suitcases were. They would have been much heavier if loaded with gold.

After studying the spreadsheet, I turned my attention to the other files in the *documents* folder on Zeke's USB drive. The other files were all text documents. Five of the files had names sounding like names of German people. I grabbed the musty envelopes and compared the names on the letters to the file names. Bingo! Zeke had somehow translated the letters into English. The first letter was a heart wrenching plea from Herr Braun for Aaron to offer the Braun family a fair price for their valuables so they could afford to take their grandparents with them as they fled Germany. Apparently the price Aaron offered to pay was well below what Braun thought it should be and was insufficient to both bribe the officials to get travel documents and pay for transportation for Braun's extended family. The letter ended with a denouncement of Aaron and his unscrupulous business practices. The other four letters chronicled similar complaints from other families. The mystery of the Klein family fortune began to look less cryptic.

The final document on the drive was a letter from Zeke to me describing what he had learned about Aaron's business dealings in the late 1930s and early 1940s.

David, you obviously were able to get into the safe and find my memory stick. I didn't think you would have much trouble with it. If you did, you might want to reconsider your vocation. I hid this information in the safe because what you are about to read isn't very complimentary to the Klein clan. I don't think anyone would benefit if it became public knowledge.

Several years ago, Mother went into the attic and discovered a box containing the ledger and letters which are now stored in my safe. She

169

couldn't read them, but mentioned them to me. She planned to toss them out, but I asked her to ship them to me. Part of me wishes she would have trashed them, but part of me is thankful to know the truth; Klein pockets were lined with diamonds while Dachau was lined with unsuspecting refugees on the way to their unthinkable end.

You may find it ironic, as I did, that I got interested in the Klein family history only after I was disowned by my own family. I researched Jewish history in Germany, especially in Berlin, and was able to trace our history back to 1922. I possibly could have traced the family further back, but I lost interest after discovering enough shameful history to make me want to change my name to Smith.

Jews lived in northern Germany since the thirteenth century, when they migrated there to escape religious persecution in southern Germany. I had always assumed Jewish persecution in Germany started with the Nazis, but it started much earlier. Almost immediately persecution began after the northern migration to Berlin; first with small things. For example, merchants were forbidden from selling wool to Jews. In the ensuing years Jews were blamed for starting the Black Plague, which made them the focus of widespread vindictiveness; many had their houses burned, and they were expelled from Berlin. I tell you this so you will understand that our ancestors' collective psyche could have easily expected and therefore tolerated persecution, even as it terrorized them.

The ebb and flow of persecution in Berlin continued for several hundred years. In the sixteenth century, Jews were again expelled from Berlin, this time the government confiscated their property. However, the Jews once more returned to Berlin in the eighteenth century, when about a thousand Jews crowded into a ghetto. I can't understand why they returned; maybe Berlin with its history of persecution was better than other places, although I have difficulty imagining it.

In spite of being forced to pay a multitude of unfair taxes many of the Jews prospered as merchants and bankers. Their wealth became the source

170

of envy and additional contempt. I picked up the Klein family trail as Berlin's Jewish population continued to grow into the twentieth century.

In 1922, my great grandfather, Aaron Klein, lived in the Mitte district of Berlin. He started out working as a jeweler in his father in-law's store but soon opened his own shop, and then another. In the early 30s he expanded into art galleries and sold art to the same prosperous clientele who bought his jewelry. His business provided the opportunity for him to develop acquaintances with non-Jewish business leaders and government officials. Aaron wasn't the only Jew to prosper, and 1930 found more than one hundred and fifty-thousand Jews living in Berlin.

The short-lived prosperity turned to uncertainty and then to anxiety and then to dread, after the Nazis rise to power in 1933. Jewish social and economic status began to erode. Even though Jews were restricted to attending Jewish schools and their houses and shops were vandalized, many Jews hoped the persecution would start to abate. Aaron wasn't so optimistic. He cultivated his relationships with government officials, relationships he used to obtain false papers and travel documents; all of which he sold for a substantial fee.

Wealthy Jews, herded into cramped ghettos, sold their belongings to Aaron in exchange for travel documents allowing them to flee Germany. Of course, Aaron used some of the money to bribe officials, but he apparently kept a significant portion for himself. The Jews resented his friendship with their oppressors, but many realized he could provide an alternative to relocation at forced labor camps. As the subjugation increased, government officials expected higher and higher compensation for providing travel documents.

Aaron saw the writing on the wall. According to the ledger, he had been caching diamonds in preparation for his own family's exodus. He fled with his wife and one son in January of 1941 for New York. He used the diamonds to bankroll his son, my grandfather, who opened a wholesale diamond business and, over the next ten years, converted his diamonds to *the cash he used to finance his first retail jewelry store in the United States. One store grew into two, and two into four. By 1950, my grandfather had ten stores that he sold to a large chain and walked away a multimillionaire. He retired a very wealthy man who lived well below his means. Grandpa died in 1955 when the car he was driving slid into a ditch and flipped. He left all of his wealth to my father who shrewdly invested the family fortune in the stock market.*

My father loved the pleasures the family wealth afforded him; membership at the right club, an estate in the neighborhood where the most successful Jews lived, and expensive cars. His wealth provided him with exalted status within the Jewish community, status inextricably tied to his wealth and every bit as important to him as his wealth. He disowned me because I threatened his status, and he tried to use wealth as the lever to force me back in line.

I believe he was enslaved to thinking life was all about money, and enough money could solve every problem, could remove every difficulty.

Please don't let the Klein money enslave you, too.

Uncle Zeke

Zeke's evidence that great, great grandfather had lined his own pockets at the expense of lives he could have saved sickened me, but I couldn't see anything I could do about it in the present. More than seventy years had passed, all of the émigrés Aaron provided papers for were probably dead, and the details, except for what Zeke had hidden in his safe, were most likely lost. Aaron's ledger didn't include any names, only cryptic codes to identify his clients so it would be nearly impossible to make reparations to them or to their descendants.

I imagined a vivid black and white scene of a hopeful émigré, Herr Braun, coming into Aaron's jewelry store, lowering his voice to a whisper and asking to have a word in private with Aaron. Without speaking, Aaron put his hand on the man's shoulder and walked him behind the counter into a cramped office; a spartanly furnished office crowded with an old wooden desk, a matching side chair, a tottering coat rack and a wastebasket. Aaron remained standing because he always kept such meetings short and didn't want his visitor to feel comfortable.

The man, dressed in a tailored suit that, although once striking, now had frayed sleeves and worn elbows, said, "I have been told you can get papers for travel."

"It has become very difficult. Impossible."

The man's skin tightened on his bony cheeks and he rubbed his hand over his cracked lips. "I have money. I can pay."

"Money is no good. No one wants the Deutschmark."

The man's eyes darkened. "I have some things. Things I planned to take to New York."

"I wish you the best, but what you ask is impossible. It's very risky; too risky."

The man's eyes brightened a little. "But there might be a way?"

"It's very expensive. The officials demand more and more each time. It's nothing but extortion."

The man looked down toward his scuffed black shoes and said, "My things are valuable."

"It's hopeless… What things?"

"A pearl necklace, several gold rings, some loose diamonds, a couple of kilos of gold, and some silver,"

"How many people?"

"Six. My wife, two children and my wife's two parents."

"Too many people; not enough money. If you sold all of your things for papers you wouldn't have any money left to pay for your passage. Bring your things here tonight at seven. Come to the back door and knock three times. I will see."

The man left with a faint glimmer of hope in his eyes, but mostly with fear and despair. How could he tell his wife her parents would be left behind for the Nazis? Leaving them would break her heart. Would she ever agree to leave without them? He decided not to tell her about the meeting unless Aaron told him there was a way for at least the four of them to get out.

Later the same evening while his wife was tending to the children, the man quietly went into the small bedroom he and his wife shared with their two children and her parents, slid a cardboard box out from underneath the bed, extracted their remaining valuables, and wrapped them in four of his wife's scarfs. He stuffed the scarfs into the pockets of his overcoat. At seven sharp he knocked three times on the shop's back door. Aaron opened the door and then ushered the man down a dark hallway and back into the office. The man took the scarfs from his pockets and carefully unwrapped what remained of his family's assets. Aaron deliberately scrutinized each item, paying special heed to the diamonds, which he carefully examined with his loupe, turning them over to see each facet. He slowly shook his head back and forth. He looked up at the man and said, "It's not enough even for four. The papers and tickets are so expensive. As I said – it's extortion."

The man said, "There must be a way. Just yesterday our neighbors were taken away. We must leave before they come for us." The man tightened his shoulders and rubbed his clammy hands together.

"Maybe I can call in a favor with one of the officials to get papers. You would barely have enough left for passage to New York. Leave your things and come back with your family tomorrow. Only four, No more."

The man left knowing he was very fortunate to get a chance to start over with his wife and children. His wife would surely understand there was no other way.

The next night the man and his wife whose eyes were red and swollen and their two children whose eyes showed fear and confusion, all having said goodbye to his wife's parents, came to the door to pick up their papers and train tickets from Berlin to Amsterdam. The woman's untrimmed hair and wrinkled clothes could not hide her erect posture and proper manners. Aaron pulled the man aside to describe the itinerary and give the man his family's papers and tickets. They would be on their own to get third-class tickets for a steamer to take them to New York.

I was confident my imagination was not far from the foul truth, and the foul truth sickened me. But what could I do? I couldn't unring the bell, I couldn't bring the dead back to life. The only sensible course was to move on and leave the shame behind and to recognize I would never fully know or understand Aaron's times or his reasons.

Sixteen

I was about to write the additional searches I needed to analyze the files on the Braxter hard drives when a knock at the door offered a reprieve from the drudgery. I opened the door to find my neighbor, Carl, standing on the porch smiling. He said, "Hey, David. It *is* you. I saw an unfamiliar car in the driveway and thought I'd better check it out. Sorry to bother you, but I didn't want anybody messing around the place."

"No problem. My plans changed, or I should say, my plans were changed for me. My client is using someone else for the next phase of the audit. I still have a little work to do, but it won't take much of my time. I can do it remotely so I came up here to work and look through Zeke's stuff."

"Okay. Sorry if I bothered you. It's just that I didn't recognize the car."

"No bother." Not telling him I changed cars to lose the tail, I said, "Glad you checked. I swapped the other rental for this one."

Carl stepped back away from the door. "I'll let you get back to it. I just wanted to make sure no one was here that shouldn't be."

"Thanks. I appreciate your concern. Do you have a few minutes to come in? I'd like to hear some more about Zeke."

Carl hesitated. "This isn't the best time. I promised Angie I'd wash the outside of the windows before dinner, and I have several more to go."

"Maybe another time?" I didn't want to sound pushy, but it sounded like Carl knew Zeke better than anyone else.

"How 'bout you come hiking with me tomorrow? August is a great time to get out on the mountains and scout things for the early elk season. I was planning to hike up to the old Tatoosh fire lookout. You can come with me, and it'll give us a good chance to talk. Plus, Tatoosh was one of Zeke's favorite treks."

I didn't want to miss the chance to learn more about Zeke, and liked the idea of exploring the area. "Sounds like fun. What gear do I need?"

"That could be a problem. We could run into some snow patches on the trail so you'll need good boots and trekking poles. Zeke had all the gear you will need, but his boots probably won't fit you."

"Snow in August?"

"It's likely, but it'll only be here and there."

"I saw all sorts of hiking gear in Zeke's closet. I already looked at his boots, and we're the same size. I'm sure I can find everything I need. What else?"

"You'll need a day pack to carry a little food and water. We'll be gone most of the day so bring at least two bottles of water. We can get some on the way, but not for a while. You might want to wear camo if Zeke's will fit you. I plan to take my camera. If we can sneak up on some animals I might be able to take some good photos."

I thought about all the gear I saw upstairs. "There's plenty of camo in Zeke's closet. I'll find something. What time do you want to leave?"

"Why don't I come by at six? …If it's not too early. That will put us on the trail before seven so we can do most of the climbing before the day gets hot."

"I'll be ready. See you then."

Carl nodded and turned to walk back to his place, and I went up to Zeke's spare room to make sure he had everything I needed for the hike. I put his boots on and planned to wear them for the evening to make sure they didn't cramp my feet. I tried on a camo tee shirt and convertible pants having legs I could unzip and take off just above the knee to convert them into shorts, and I set a day pack and two indestructible Nalgene water bottles aside. I made a couple of peanut butter and jelly sandwiches and set them next to two apples in the refrigerator so they would be ready for the morning.

I had often thought about hiking, but rarely got around to actually doing it. Julie and I occasionally took short hikes in the Ipswich River Wildlife Sanctuary, north of Boston, and we always enjoyed seeing an occasional deer or river otter. I was hoping a strenuous hike with Carl would help me get out of the emotional fog that had settled on me after I read Zeke's account of Aaron and his misdeeds; a fog that threatened to enshroud me in an apathetic gloom.

After gathering Zeke's hiking gear, I sat back down at my computer to write the searches I should have written before analyzing Harold's files. One of the tricks bad guys can use to hide files which are not supposed to be stored on their computers is to change the filename and extension to something innocuous. A miscreant might try to hide a sensitive document named *specification.docx* by renaming it *vacation.jpg* to make the document containing proprietary information appear like an innocuous vacation picture. My analysis software had the ability to examine files and determine if the actual file content matched the filename extension. I wrote a search to identify any files whose names didn't match their content and another search to identify email messages including file attachments that were sent to anyone outside of Braxter. I knew most files sent to people outside of Braxter would be harmless, so I wrote another search to highlight any attachments containing the words *Kilroy, specification, GPS, positioning,* and the like. The analysis software was designed to run on multiple powerful server computers harnessed together to share the processing load. However, I had only my laptop so the processing jobs that should have run in several hours were likely to take overnight or longer. I fired off the analysis because I wanted to take a closer look at Harold's file and went into the kitchen to bake some meatloaf and a potato for dinner.

After eating, I took a walk to test out Zeke's boots and explore his eight acres that abutted the national forest. I chanced across a game trail leading south from the house toward the forest and followed it up an extremely steep but short hill. The climb was so steep my heels didn't touch the ground, and my shirt was soon soaked with sweat. After reaching the crest, the path opened into a relatively flat area, and I followed it as it turned left through a continuous carpet of green moss sprinkled with ferns, salal and Oregon grape bushes. Everything was green except for the huge brown tree trunks, some four feet in diameter.

Even though I was within a half mile of Zeke's house, I had an eerie feeling like I was intruding on someone's secret place; a secluded, private sanctuary. I stopped for several minutes and looked around for animals and listened for any that might be moving about. I heard several birds and saw two chipmunks scurry up a nearby tree. One chased the other, and they both spiraled up the tree as they climbed. They went up, back down, and then up again before running the length of one of the topmost branches and leaping onto a branch of another tree. They circled the tree a couple of times and then jumped to another tree and kept leap frogging one another until I couldn't see them any longer.

I continued walking and stepped over several small downed fir trees and at one point climbed over a larger fir blocking the path. The downed tree was only about two feet in diameter, but its snapped off branch stubs held it up off of the path like centipede legs. The trunk was too high for me to step over and too low to crawl under, forcing me to pull myself up and over. The path began a gradual descent, and I heard the sound of rushing water. The descent steepened, and the trail soon took me to the side of a tumbling creek where the air was noticeably cooler. The creek whooshed through a canyon and down a steep, narrow chute carved out of solid rock. I walked up to the water's edge and stood in the mist for a few minutes and let the spray cool me.

A vertical cliff on the far edge of the creek rose straight up for at least a hundred feet, and the rock wall acted as an orchestra shell, reflecting the creek's noise back towards me at an amplified volume. The reverberating roar overshadowed the sound of the chirping birds. I stepped back about twenty feet from the creek where the roar was much quieter and sat down on the moss covered ground to savor the peaceful surroundings. It truly was a private sanctuary, a world of variegated green hues. Sunlight knifed through the tall fir trees, filtered through vine maple leaves waving in the breeze, and lit up shiny fern fronds. The spindly vine maple branches slowly rose and fell as if they were bowing in adulation. It was the perfect place to relax and rid my mind of Aaron's gloomy memories.

I lay back on the moss carpet and closed my eyes. Flickering shadows of fluttering branches hypnotically danced across my closed eyelids and lulled me into a half-awake, half-asleep trance-like state where I heard the towering fir and hemlock trees quietly recite poetry as their branches swayed back and forth in the gentle breeze. I heard the sound of their words, and I felt the rhythm of the verse, but I couldn't understand the language; a beautiful language, more melodic than any music I had ever heard.

I must have fallen asleep; for how long I don't know. It could have been for a few seconds or for ten minutes, or more. I awoke slowly and strained to listen to the trees just in case I hadn't been dreaming, but only heard the slight breeze ruffling leaves and branches. Human brains amaze me, but the psychology course I took in college provided more questions than answers. The left-brain; right-brain theory especially intrigued me, and I came away from the course thinking the analytical side of my brain dwarfed the creative side. Specifics and detail appealed to me, and math and science courses never presented a serious challenge. But creativity and seeing the big picture; that's a completely different story. I imagined the right side of my brain as half of a scrawny walnut shell barely attached the left side of my brain, leaving me bankrupt in terms of insight, feeling, and gut-knowing. I admit my mental image is lame; I rest my case about having little imagination.

By the time I headed back to Zeke's, the temperature had cooled and the sun was barely visible above the hill to the west.

It was still more than an hour before sunset, but shadows were beginning to darken the canyon.

*****

The alarm on my phone jolted me awake at five ten the next morning, and although the room was beginning to get light I struggled to remember where I was. My memory gradually came into focus, and I swung my feet out of bed and pulled on the camo clothes. I went down to the kitchen, ate a quick bowl of frosted wheat cereal, and packed my lunch and water into the day pack. I checked the analysis software, hoping to find evidence of Harold's wrongdoing, but his files were clean. I fired up the next analysis job on Karl Matson's files so the job could run while I hiked.

I was ready ten minutes early so rather than waiting for Carl I walked down the driveway to his place. Angie was sitting in a rocker on the front porch sipping a steaming cup of coffee. She waved me over to a matching rocker and told me Carl would be out in a few minutes. I sat down and she told me that Carl had been planning the hike up to Tatoosh for three weeks and was pleased I was able to go with him.

Just then Carl walked out onto the porch with his gear and took it over to his old Ford pickup. Angie said, "It looks like he's raring to go."

I followed Carl to the truck and said, "Good morning, Carl. Will these clouds burn off?"

"Good morning to you, too. Yes, they'll be gone in a few hours. It may be cool for a bit, but we'll generate enough of our own heat hiking. You'll be warm enough even in a tee shirt."

I reached over the pickup's side and tossed my pack into the bed before climbing into the cab and buckling myself in on the long bench seat. Carl climbed in and gently put his pack on the space between us. "My camera's in it," he said by way of explanation. I thought it must be a large camera because his pack was almost twice the size of mine.

Before starting the truck, Carl explained we could hike the Tatoosh trail from the north end or from the south end. He suggested we leave from the north end where we would climb for about three miles and then go about three mostly flat miles, climb up to the site of the old lookout and then return. He thought starting on the north was more scenic. I asked, "If we take two vehicles could we leave one at the south trailhead and then drive to the north end, hike north to south, and then go pick up the other vehicle?"

Carl wrinkled his nose in thought and replied, "We could but the forest service roads would be hard on your rental."

"What if I drive Zeke's pickup?"

"Sounds like a plan."

Carl started the truck and drove me back to Zeke's. I dashed into the house and returned with the keys to Zeke's four wheel drive Toyota. I hopped in and turned the key. The engine coughed a couple of times before catching, but then fired up. I revved it up a couple of times then backed it out and caught up with Carl who had already turned his truck around. We drove to the edge of town and turned right to cross over the Cowlitz River and then turned right again and drove through a community of dozens of houses. After three or four miles we emerged onto a pothole-ridden unpaved road. It soon began to climb, and I followed Carl as he swerved from one side to the other in a vain attempt to dodge potholes. Carl knew which way to take at each fork in the road and soon we were pulling off to a wide spot at the south trailhead. Carl reached out of his open window and pointed to where he wanted me to park. I got out of the Toyota, locked it, and climbed into Carl's truck.

Carl wheeled his Ford around and we headed back down the same rutty road. We went through the housing community but instead of heading toward town we turned right and headed the other way. After about four miles, he turned off on another unpaved forest service road. This road started out just as bad as the other but soon got worse. Carl explained that since the scarce spotted owl curtailed logging, the forest service didn't have the budget to maintain the roads. We swerved and bounced, and bounced and swerved for four or five miles, each mile seeming like five. He pointed to a small sign designating the north trailhead and wrestled his truck around on the narrow road until it was pointing the other way. He pulled it off the road toward the forest, barely giving me enough room to open my door. I climbed out and reached for my pack which was no longer behind the cab. It had bounced back to the tailgate but didn't look any worse for it. I walked back to get it and swung it on to my back.

Carl reached into his glove box and pulled out a black semi-automatic pistol and holster. He strapped the holster onto his belt and inserted the pistol. Then he strapped on his pack and pulled a pair of telescoping trekking poles from the truck bed. He lengthened them to the proper height and then went over to a wooden box attached to the trailhead sign where he pulled out a permit tag and an old pencil. He entered the required information, tore off the original and stuffed it into a slot, and then asked me to turn around so he could tie the duplicate onto my pack.

He pointed the tip of one of his poles toward the trailhead and started walking up the wooded trail. I followed about ten feet behind him as we hiked into the dense forest. Low clouds hung just above the tree tops and secreted a fine mist. Depending on how high we climbed, I realized we could soon be hiking in the fog, and it would obscure the mountains I had hoped to see. The trail started climbing immediately, but after about a half mile it got serious as it wound us back and forth along a series of switchbacks. Carl was right; we easily generated enough heat to keep warm. Sweat soaked my shirt, and I had to make a conscious effort to walk fast enough to keep up with Carl. I guessed he was somewhere between 55 and 65 years old, and most likely in his early sixties. His ability to motor up such a steep trail impressed me, and I hoped I could trek along like him when I got to be his age. In fact, I hoped I would be able to do it at my current age.

I had hoped to talk with Carl about Zeke while hiking. However, both of us were breathing too hard for conversation. Instead, I tried to peer out through the trees to see how much climbing was ahead of us. We were hiking on a hillside that followed the left side of a valley up to a higher altitude. I occasionally glimpsed the far side of the valley to my right. Green trees crowded into each other like Celtic fans going to a playoff game. Trees grew everywhere the sunlight reached the forest floor. We made our way through the switchbacks and, as the trail straightened out, came into an area of less dense tree cover and entered into the fog. Dew-covered bushes crowded the trail from both sides. The trees on the steep downhill side of the trail were young enough that their tops were only 15 feet or so higher than the trail. The glistening dew drops hanging from their branches refracted the light like a crystal chandelier.

My pant legs soon dripped with dew. At first, the dampness posed only a minor inconvenience, but within twenty minutes the water soaked through my pant legs and drenched my socks, and then the water ran down my socks into my boots. Zeke's waterproof boots promised to keep water from the outside from penetrating into the boot, and I could certainly attest to their ability to keep water already inside the boot from penetrating to the outside. My feet audibly squished and squashed with each step, and I pictured my toes looking wrinkled like they get while taking a long hot bath, a bath that became more attractive by the step. I looked up at Carl's pants to see how he was faring. I hadn't noticed earlier but he was wearing a pair of camo-colored waterproof gaiters keeping him dry from the knees on down. Funny that he didn't mention gaiters the night before when I asked him about gear. He probably wasn't used to hiking with a newbie and didn't think of mentioning them. At least I was willing to give him the benefit of the doubt.

The good news was Carl guessed right about the clouds burning off. We came into a clearing where I could see both up to where we were heading and down into the valley we had hiked through. Looking back down the trail, I saw we had gained a lot of altitude, and looking up the trail, I could see we were going to gain plenty more. We were almost above the tree line, and it looked like the trail was going to take us into a beautiful sub-alpine meadow. We came to a fork in the trail, and immediately after we took the left fork, Carl nodded toward a downed tree lying alongside the trail. "Let's take a break here." I agreed, and we plopped down on the log. I ate half of my first sandwich and chugged most of the water from my first bottle. Then I removed my boots and socks and wrung about a half cup of water out of each one. I wished I had brought a spare pair of socks; another thing to remember for next time.

Carl pointed up the trail and then swept his hand from left to right. "If you look carefully you'll see the trail running through the meadow a couple hundred feet below the ridge line." I nodded, and he continued, "I like to take it slow from here. No sense rushing through the pretty part, especially since it is so much work to get here." I was glad to hear the pace was about to slacken. Running had given me a strong fitness base, but it hadn't prepared me for the ninety minutes of relentless climbing.

Carl stood and said, "There is a stream just a ways down this side trail. Let's head over and refill our water bottles."

I followed and watched him pull out a pump-action water filter. He moved the pump's lever up and down and said, "This stream is probably one hundred percent pure, but it's possible a deer made a deposit in it this morning. It's best to play it safe so I filter it just to be careful."

He filled our bottles, stowed his filter, and we walked back to the main trail. Carl said, "Going up the trail from the north trailhead like we did the trail gains more than a half mile of elevation in three miles. We only have a few hundred more feet to climb and then it is more or less flat until we start back down the south side."

I asked, "Did you and Zeke hike this trail often?"

"We did it every year for the past twelve years; except for 2011 when we got so much snow the trail didn't clear. This was one of Zeke's favorite hikes; this and the Goat Rocks loop. He said he saw God's handiwork in every wild flower, in every tree, and in each one of the animals we saw."

"So I take it Zeke didn't believe in the science of evolution."

"He didn't, and I don't either."

I probably should have dropped the subject, but didn't because I was fairly sure Carl hadn't taken many college-level science courses. "It is pretty well documented as scientific fact. My biology prof said if you don't believe in evolution, then you believe in mythology."

Carl stopped in the middle of the trail, turned toward me, and said, "When it comes to evolution versus creation, I think people believe whichever one fits their world view; their religious view. We tend to believe the science that supports our position. Being a Christian, I am predisposed towards creationism. So was Zeke. And there is science to support it, too."

"It isn't a matter of world view for me. It's just science. I just accept the facts; facts like the fossil record, genetics, physics; hard facts."

Carl resumed walking, but at a slow enough pace that we could continue our conversation. "I didn't go to a mighty college like you did, but you shouldn't assume I'm ignorant just because I don't have a college education. I admit I'm no rocket scientist. But that doesn't mean I am stupid. I like to think of myself as a rocker scientist."

I questioned, "A rocker scientist?"

"Yep. All anyone needs to do is sit in their rocking chair and think about it with an open mind. Things will soon become clear enough."

"Sounds like sticking your head in the sand to me." Carl's folksy manner amused me.

Carl chuckled. "So you believe life started out as a simple, one cell organism that divided into two and then into four and over time evolved into a more and more diverse and complex organisms. And the process went on until we got to where we are today. Is that more or less correct?"

"More or less, but a bit of an over simplification."

"Well, me and my rocker, we have a couple of problems with that. Take the engine in my Ford pickup for example. It is made up of lots of different parts; engine block, valves, crankshaft, camshaft, pistons, and more. Heck, the carburetor alone has enough parts that most people couldn't put one together if their life depended on it."

"Where are you going with this?"

"Each part needs the other part. Unless every part is made perfectly and assembled perfectly, the engine won't run. Compare that to your eye. Your eye is made up of an iris, rods, cones, a retina, nearby tear ducts and lots of parts that I don't know much about. Your eye needs an optic nerve and the optic nerve needs a part of the brain to interpret the signals. Each part needs the other part, and unless every part works perfectly you can't see. Evolution says eyes developed gradually over millions and millions of years. Even if the first eye was simple it would need multiple parts to be able to see. If any one part was missing, the other parts wouldn't do any good. In fact, the other parts would probably be a liability, a weakness

189

causing whoever had one to be vulnerable, to be killed off. Thinking it all happened by chance is preposterous. I can't even begin to understand how animals could go from having one eye to having two."

I countered. "Given enough time it's certainly possible."

"David, you're polishing a turd."

"Say what?"

"Polishing a turd. No matter how much time you take to make it shiny, no matter how much mustard and relish you slather on it, no matter how many onions you add to it, no matter how perfectly the bun is baked, it's never going to be a kosher dog, and when you bite into it, it's going to taste like shit."

I couldn't help but laugh. "Carl, you crack me up, but you haven't convinced me. In fact, I think you are *off* your rocker."

Carl and I both chuckled as we continued along the trail. It struck me as unusual that he and I could have such opposing beliefs but not let them become a reason to get mad at the other. We walked through the meadow and then Carl stopped and asked me to turn around. Mount Rainier rose above the craggy lesser mountains like a giant among mortals. It stood majestically as if to say, "Look at me. None of these other mountains can compare to my grandeur." I had never seen a view so breathtaking, the mountain's white snow contrasted with the lush green foliage growing on the sides of the nearby ridges. I understood why this was one of Zeke's favorite hikes.

We turned back to continue our hike and soon were surrounded by an explosion of colorful wildflowers; blues, reds, oranges, whites, nearly every color imaginable. Carl

190

pointed to individual flowers and called each of them by name; western anemone with its blue tinged hairy, white petals. Tolmie's saxifrage whose white petals formed saucer shaped flowers. He informed me it was named after the first white man who attempted to climb Mount Rainier – at least the first recorded white man. Clumps of purple mountain heather and acres of purple lupine fluttered in the breeze.

The hills were alive with beauty. It reminded me of the scene from the Sound of Music that my babysitter made me watch countless times; the scene where Julie Andrews and the Von Trapp children are singing in the beautiful alpine meadow, except the Tatoosh view was better, plus it didn't have any of the annoying singing and prancing about.

I told Carl, "This is the most beautiful place I have ever been. It's incredible."

Carl commented, "I don't understand why such beautifully colored wildflowers are needed for evolution to work. I think they're completely unnecessary for evolutionary purposes. Do you think bees can see in color? I think God created all of these colorful flowers because He is so creative and because He wants us to enjoy them. David, being an evolutionist, why do you think flowers need to be so colorful?"

I had to admit I didn't know the answer to Carl's simple question, but made a mental note to do some research on the Internet when I got back to civilization. After about three miles of walking in the meadow and crossing a couple of snow patches, Carl pointed out a side trail we were going to take to reach the old Tatoosh lookout. My legs had relaxed while walking along the relative flat trail and complained loudly as we began our steep five hundred foot ascent to the lookout site, but it was worth the climb. Standing atop Tatoosh, we could see Mount Rainier to the north, Mount Adams to the south, and Mount St. Helens to the southwest. They each stood shoulders above hundreds of surrounding mountains each at least 8,000 feet tall. We sat down to eat our lunches and drink more water. I felt like I was sitting on top of the world.

After lunch, Carl took some pictures of the scenery. He told me he already had lots of pictures from this exact spot, but couldn't resist taking a few more. He said each picture was a little different because each day was unique. He put his camera back into his pack and then pulled out a blue metal urn closed with a screw top lid. He said, "These are Zeke's ashes. He asked me to spread them up here on top of Tatoosh, and I didn't think you would mind being here while I did it. We already had his service, so I am not going to say any words over his ashes. I'm just going to scatter them into the breeze."

"Actually, I'm honored to be here for this. I'm disappointed to have missed his service, so this is the next best thing." A mix of emotions hit me in the gut. Although I had never met Zeke, I truly missed him and grieved for him.

Carl walked over to the edge of the ridge just east of where the lookout once stood and waved the ashes. The breeze carried them for a few yards eastward over the edge and then they settled to the ground at least one hundred feet below us. He wiped his eyes and screwed the lid back on the urn. Without saying a word he put the urn back into his pack and put his pack on his back and started walking back down the trail. I put my pack on and followed after him. We rejoined the main trail and continued south until we entered a flat area Carl called Bum Springs. Carl pointed to the southeast and said, "There is a big field of wild huckleberries just over that rise. Let's sneak over and see if we can find any bears feasting on them. The breeze is blowing towards us so if we're real quiet we should be able to get close without them smelling us."

He took his camera out of his pack and pulled his pistol out of its holster. He said, "There's nothing like a Glock," as he pulled the slide back and jacked a shell into the chamber. Carl appeared confident that his pistol had enough wallop to stop a bear. I hoped he knew what he was doing.

We very quietly and very slowly walked over to the rise, and I copied Carl as he crouched down near to the ground. We crept over the hill being careful to keep behind bushes whenever possible. Carl, pointed to one of his ears, and I strained to listen. I heard noises I couldn't place, and I couldn't see what was making them. Carl skulked forward on hands and knees; moving only a foot or so before freezing for a couple of minutes. I copied him as best I could, keeping myself about five feet behind him. He slowly turned toward me and motioned for me to come up alongside of him on his right. He then nodded to his left, and I saw a big black bear ripping huckleberry branches off with his paws and cramming them into his mouth. Although he was only about thirty feet from us, he was unaware we were watching, and he sauntered from one bush to the next, cramming his face at each stop.

I had never seen a bear in the wild and was so mesmerized I almost didn't notice it when Carl motioned for me to look back to where the bear had been a minute earlier. Two small cubs were wrestling with each other in the grass. Carl pulled out his camera and started snapping photos. Every ten seconds or so he stole a look at Momma bear to make sure she was still oblivious to our presence. He must have snapped nearly fifty pictures of the playful cubs before Momma grunted and the cubs ran up to her side. We stayed put and the three bears sauntered away. Carl whispered telling me he thought he got some great shots and couldn't wait to get back and view them on his computer.

We slowly backed out the way we had come and rejoined the trail. It descended gradually for a mile or so and then became steeper with a seemingly endless series of switchbacks. After an hour, my legs had turned to mush, and I could hardly wait to get back to civilization. We stopped briefly to rest at an old log cabin, and Carl said we only had about another thirty minutes until we would be back to Zeke's truck. Thankfully, the trail got less steep so my legs quit complaining.

We arrived at the truck about when Carl said we would. In spite of being worn out I had a great day. I could see why Zeke loved Packwood, and I enjoyed being with Carl even though we didn't see eye to eye about evolution.

Carl unloaded his Glock and put his gear on the seat between us. He must have been as tired as I was because neither of us said a word during the drive back to Carl's truck. I climbed out of the Ford and then leaned back inside to shake Carl's hand. He smiled and thanked me for going with him. I thanked him for asking me to go along and asked him to let me know next time he wanted to go hiking. He said he would, and then he added, "Before you go, I have an important question for you to think about. You don't have to answer it now. What evidence is there that Jesus actually lived, died, and rose from the grave? It's an important question because if Jesus is alive, there is great hope for us all, but if He isn't, we have none."

I was glad that Carl wasn't expecting an answer because I didn't at all feel like diving into another deep discussion, but the answer was easy. No, Jesus didn't rise from the dead because no one who has been dead for three days has ever done that. It was preposterous. A far as hope goes… I could only hope I was right.

We drove away separately; Carl to his house, and me to Zeke's. I had never spent a day quite like that before.

Seventeen

As soon as I opened the door to Zeke's place, I heard a faint beeping sound, a sound I couldn't place, a sound so muted I couldn't determine where it was coming from. I walked toward the kitchen, and it grew slightly louder, but I still didn't recognize it. I followed it to my laptop but couldn't think why my laptop would be constantly beeping at me. I jiggled the mouse to clear the screen saver and saw a flashing message, "Anomaly Detected". The job I left scanning the hard disks' contents while Carl and I tackled Tatoosh had found something. Finally! I had a trail to follow.

I sat down to study the message. The software had analyzed the disk contents I had copied from Karl Matson, the second security guy's computer, and had identified a file in a *VacationPics* folder which was designated as a JPEG picture file but was actually a Word document. The folder contained 430 JPEG files, each about two and a half megabytes in size, as was the file that was actually a Word document. Word documents, even ones running a hundred or more pages, are typically much smaller than two and a half megabytes unless they contain diagrams or pictures. I opened the suspicious file named *IMG_0041_1.jpg* and discovered a document full of seemingly random words. At first glance, the entire document appeared to be unintelligible gibberish. However, I suspected Karl might have buried a few needles in the haystack.

I searched for key words that would indicate the document included some information about Kilroy. I quickly got multiple hits for *coordinate, GPS, location, transmitter, and RFID* which gave me a strong hunch that somehow Matson had buried specs in a million words of babble. The problem was to find a way to separate the wheat from the chaff. The document contained more than one-thousand pages so there was a lot of chaff, and although some words like the ones I had searched for were clearly wheat, many words could be either wheat or chaff. I assumed Matson had sent the file to someone, and whoever he sent it to must have possessed the secret decoder ring allowing him to extract the original specification.

Matson must have used a computer program to encode the spec, and I was going to need to write a computer program to decode it. I closed the file and reopened it using a debugging program to display the file's content in computer code rather than in human readable text. One of my college professors had forced me to write a small text analysis program, which I loathed at the time, but realized now it would be perfect for the task at hand. I sat at the table, still stinking from my hike, but unwilling to lose time even if only to take a shower and grab a bite to eat. After three hours of examining, scribbling possible solutions, and muttering obscenities, I got lucky.

I discovered the number of chaff words interspersed between the wheat words varied from zero to fifteen. I studied the machine representation of several wheat words and calculated the numeric value of the last four bits of the machine code; four bits that represented the numbers between zero and fifteen. I discovered the number represented by the last four bits was the number of chaff words randomly inserted before the next wheat word. I tested my theory by hand and in ten minutes was able to reconstruct most of one sentence from the Kilroy specification. I had broken Matson's code! I just needed to write a program to winnow the chaff automatically, but it was getting a little late for serious thinking. Showering and eating had become higher priorities.

I went into the bedroom and stripped off my sweaty clothes and tossed them into an empty clothes basket in the corner. I smiled in anticipation while walking over to the shower and ran the water until it was steaming hot and then stood under the water for several relaxing minutes. While summoning the energy to wash myself, I hoped Carl was equally worn out by our hike. After washing, I turned off the water, dried myself, and got dressed before going downstairs to the kitchen in hopes of finding leftovers to reheat or something quick and easy to fix. Finding neither I drove into town to reward myself with a burger at Duffy's Grill.

I made the drive in less than ten minutes and arrived just before nine o'clock. I was soon sitting on a stool at the bar in the back of the restaurant looking at a menu featuring burgers, fish and chips, and a few sandwiches. A plumpish waitress whose over-plucked eyebrows were colored with thick, black mascara, whose cheeks were plastered with a rosy blush, perhaps in a futile effort to fill in her crevased wrinkles, whose partially buttoned blouse was at least one size too small, walked over until she was standing behind the counter directly across from me. She waved her order pad and interrupted the flashback I was having of Theron's shirt stretched taut across his belly with, "What'll you have, Hon?"

I asked her for a tall Hefeweizen and a lumberjack burger and fries; not exactly health food, but I rationalized that the hike had put me into a serious calorie deficit. And who knows, maybe one day the experts will discover grease has miraculous health benefits. The waitress brought my beer, and I had just squeezed juice from the lemon wedge into it when I looked at the mirror directly across from me and saw Bert or Ernie— I couldn't remember which one it was – entering the bar and walking toward the empty stool next to mine. I didn't want to hear any more about Zeke's superiority complex. I wished I could make myself invisible. Where were my headphones when I needed them? My hopes were futile, and I felt a hand on my shoulder and heard a voice saying, "Hey, David. Remember me – Herb from the coffee shop? How ya doin?"

I swiveled my stool to face him. He was wearing a couple of days' stubble and the same Coors cap he wore at the coffee shop. "Hi, Herb. I'm fine. A little worn out. Carl and I hiked up to Tatoosh today, and *up* is the key word. How are you?"

"I'm still smarting from the blasting Carolyn gave me the other day. Maybe I was a little out of line by not respecting Zeke's memory and all."

"It seems people either loved him or hated him. I haven't met any undecideds yet."

The waitress brought my burger. Herb ordered a Coors, pointed to my plate and said, "Rita, I'll have the same".

Herb cleared his throat and looked down at his hands. "I was thinking about paying back the bail money I owed Zeke. Would you take twenty five dollars a month for two years? You'd earn a little interest for all the time I didn't pay."

I took a bite of my burger and slowly chewed it, letting Herb's request hang in the air before swallowing and asking, "How much time has passed since he loaned you the money?"

"Least five or six years, maybe more."

I took another bite and chewed it even more slowly and then said, "Herb, if Zeke had wanted you to repay that money I think he would have let you know. Let's just forget about it."

He raised his eyebrows and replied, "You sure? I don't want Carolyn coming after me with a law suit. She'd crucify me in court."

I smiled at the thought of Carolyn ripping Herb a new one on the witness stand, "Yes, she would. But, if it'll make you feel better maybe we can agree on an equitable trade. I know you think Zeke was a self-righteous ass, so I don't want to hear you rehash any of your gripes. But, if you can tell something amusing about Zeke, I'll call it square. If you can make me laugh, I'll even tell Carolyn to cut you some slack."

Ms. Buxom interrupted us by bringing Herb his Coors. She bent over to flash her splotchy cleavage at Herb. My eyes took the high road and noticed the gray roots peeking out of the part in her hair. Herb's eyes were occupied elsewhere. She winked at him and said, "Here you go, Hon." Herb smiled and thanked her.

Herb took a deep swig and then started to chuckle. He said, "I know just the story. Dave Emerald told it to me. Actually, he told it to almost everyone he met for two weeks after it happened, and Dave was the best story teller around. I heard him tell it three times myself. He used to run Packwood Auto Repair, but it went out of business just after the mill closed down. He moved to Eatonville to live with his sister."

Herb poked a couple of my fries into his mouth, and started to tell the story, "I'll act like I'm Dave and tell it how he told it… While I was tuning up Mary Beth's Corolla, I looked out and seen Charlie Garrison pull his old pickup into the parking spot in front of the garage. Charlie was talking with someone in the passenger seat, but I couldn't see who it was. I kept an eye on them while I was removing the old spark plugs. After a couple of minutes, the passenger got out, and Charlie drove off; his truck belched blue smoke like it always did. He didn't have enough money for me to do a ring job on it. The passenger was Zeke Klein. I recognized him because I had met him a couple of months earlier when he was teaching *Intro to Computers* at the library. He seemed like a pretty smart fella.

"Zeke came into the shop and stood at the front of the Corolla. So I said, 'Hey Zeke, how come you're on foot. Nothing wrong with that new truck of yours is there?' Zeke took off his nearly new Stihl cap, looked at his feet, and quietly said, 'Yeah, I seem to have overloaded it. It's broken down on the side of the highway about ten miles east of here, just below Forest Service Road 45. Is there any chance you could take your tow truck up there and haul it to the Dodge dealer in Centralia? That's where I bought it.'

"I told Zeke I could help him as soon as I finished the tune-up. I warned him the tow was going to be pricey. I charge two dollars and twenty five cents a mile when traveling and three dollars and seventy-five cents when I'm towing. The trip to Centralia was going to cost about five hundred bucks so I asked Zeke why he didn't let me fix it in my shop."

Herb paused while Rita delivered his burger and fries. He took another swig and pushed a couple more fries into his mouth before continuing telling the story from Dave's point of view, "Zeke fidgeted with his cap and shuffled from one foot to the other and finally mumbled, 'I don't know if you can fix it. In fact, I am not sure it can be fixed at all. The frame is bent; bent pretty bad. You can't straighten a frame, can you?'

"Zeke had my full attention so I asked him if he rolled it.

"Zeke sighed and answered, 'No, I didn't roll it. Do you want the thirty second explanation or the whole painful story?'

"I knew I could listen while installing the four new plugs, wires, and points so I told Zeke I had plenty of time. Zeke told me if everyone else in Packwood could cut their own firewood, he could too. So he bought a new Stihl chainsaw and all the accessories and paid his ten bucks for the woodcutting permit. The saw worked great, at least at first, but that's another story. Anyway, Zeke drove way up 45 and found a couple of recently blown-down alders not far from Cortright Creek. He cut the trees up into rounds until his saw froze up. Zeke was such a city slicker he didn't even know he needed to mix oil with the gas to keep the engine lubricated. He destroyed a brand new saw in less than a day."

I held up my hand and told Herb, "I'm not laughing yet. In fact, you're starting to piss me off. If you want to square the five hundred dollars you'd best be getting to the funny part."

Herb said, "I think the whole thing's hilarious." Herb forgot he was telling the story from Dave's point of view. He continued with the story in the second person, "Dave swears he heard Zeke say, "Shit." under his breath. Wish I could have heard it. Anyway, Zeke told Dave he cut so much wood he had to stack it all the way up to the top of the cab to load it all. The fool didn't even know that a pickup truck load of wet alder could weigh up to five thousand pounds. He started driving down the forest service road to the highway, but felt his brakes getting mushy. He had the sense to pull over for a few minutes to let them cool. He took off again, but had to pull over another time or two to cool his brakes."

Herb took a minute to finish his beer and eat two bites of his burger. Then he motioned for Rita to get him another Coors. He resumed the story that so far hadn't amused me in the slightest. "Zeke finally made it to the highway and figured he was home free. He got the truck up to fifty five miles an hour, but didn't remember about the sunken grade at milepost 142, and the sudden dip was hidden in a shady spot so he didn't see it until it was too late. He told Dave when he hit the second lip, the front of truck nearly went airborne. Then it came down real hard and the springs bottomed out. The whole frame gave way. It must have made an awful scraping sound on the pavement before grinding to a stop. The frame bent into a vee; the cab and bed were shoved together, and the frame between the axles was dragging on the road. He was lucky he didn't kill himself or someone else. So much for saving a few bucks on heating oil."

Herb noticed I was fiddling with the coaster that Rita had put under my now empty glass. He said, "Here comes the funniest part."

I turned towards him, and he said, "While he was parked alongside the highway Shepherd, the Lewis County Mountie pulled over and chewed him out for having an overweight load. He told Zeke he had endangered all sorts of innocent people and then gave him a one hundred dollar ticket for excessive weight. He didn't even offer to call a tow truck before getting into his cruiser and taking off."

Herb looked over at me as he laughed and said, "Isn't that hilarious? He ruined his new truck and ruined his new saw and got a one hundred dollar ticket; all in one day!"

Herb finally finished the monologue only he found funny. I wished I hadn't told him I would cut him slack if he told me an amusing story because I wasn't amused. Not even a little. I was pissed that he thought Zeke's misfortune was so funny. I don't think he noticed I didn't even crack a smile throughout the entire story.

"Herb, that's enough. I don't need to hear anymore. You're off the hook. I've got to get going. See you later."

Herb ordered another beer so I could tell he was going to be ogling Rita a while longer. I had planned to have a second beer, but getting away from Herb had become the higher priority. I left a twenty on the counter, excused myself and went outside, but rather than going home, I went around back to Duffy's outdoor beer garden; I was pretty sure Herb was going to stay where Rita could flirt with him. I found a deserted table in the back corner and sat facing away from the few other patrons. It was breezy and quite dark, but a propane heater behind me took the chill out of the air. Shortly, a waitress came by to take my order. She smiled nicely and didn't call me 'Hon;' two things in her favor. I ordered another Hefeweizen and sat back to relax and forget about Herb.

Without me consciously thinking about them, questions quietly settled in my mind like the morning dew settles on rose petals; questions about truth, questions about deception, and most importantly, can we really know truth from deception? I wondered how often we don't even recognize when we are lying to ourselves. We can be so blind to our underlying motives, doing whatever makes us feel good at the moment and rationalizing our actions with lofty sounding motives. I'll bet old Aaron told himself he was taking huge risks smuggling Jews out of Germany, and the obscene amount of money he made was more than justified by the risks he took. After all, wasn't he helping his countrymen get to freedom?

And Herb. Herb probably had an inferiority complex that, without his awareness, drove him to debase others, especially others who had their act together and treated others well; others like Zeke.

And me? How can I really know? I can only see myself through a distorted lens that is me. I consistently avoid looking into the dark abyss of my unvarnished heart because there is a chance, however small, I will see a monster staring back at me. I don't think so, but I wondered if Julie had seen it.

I nursed my beer and turned my thoughts back to the program I needed to write to confirm Matson really had buried a confidential specification in his document of gibberish. With that thought, I walked to my car and drove back to Zeke's to get some sleep. The program could wait until tomorrow.

Eighteen

After returning home from Duffy's I was beat. I opened several windows to cool the house, then stripped off my pants and shirt and fell into bed as tired as I had ever been. I started thinking about the program I still needed to write, but fell asleep before giving it more than two minutes of bleary thought. When I started to wake up the following morning, I lay in bed; my eyes still closed, and inhaled the wonderful aroma of the cedar trees the breeze wafted into my room. The light filtering through the undulating tree branches flickered across my eyelids coaxing me to open them. Instead, I rolled over to turn my back to the window and catch a few more winks.

Unfortunately my mind fully awoke before my body fell back to sleep, and I started thinking about how great it would feel to outsmart Gross and Tinker, the pretentious feds, and rub their noses in their incompetence and inability to find the leak. I could taste the pleasure of finding conclusive evidence, a smoking gun, which would prove Karl Matson had sold military secrets. He could easily be looking at twenty-plus years in prison, and it served him right. However, I did feel a twinge of sorrow for his wife and new baby and wondered if she knew of her husband's illegal escapades. I also felt sorry for Joan because Braxter would almost certainly make her the scapegoat, unless of course, she could hang it on me.

I'm not a proficient programmer but I eventually get the result I need, albeit with a healthy dose of trial and error. This program was no exception. I wrote and debugged the code all morning, but by lunch time it was separating the wheat from the chaff, and I could read the Kilroy related content buried within the gibberish. I extracted the complete detailed functional specification for Kilroy's transmitters, enough information for the bad guys to continuously reprogram the transmitters to not broadcast their location. With the information from the spec, the transmitters could essentially be jammed, or worse, to broadcast inaccurate information. Either way, the command and control software would be in the dark, and the military personnel would be flying blind.

I needed to tell Joan about Matson's file and discuss what it could mean, so I texted her that I needed to meet with her face-to-face and asked her to name the place and time. She replied in less than five minutes, "Toutle River rest area. MP 54 on I-5 North in ninety minutes. Blue Cadillac CTS". I confirmed the time and place and then printed out the recovered document on Zeke's printer. Before leaving, I took the precaution of stashing the eight hard drives into Zeke's floor safe and of putting my laptop in my shiny new case and taking it with me.

I arrived ten minutes early at the rest area and pulled into the section on the right designated for cars without trailers. I parked near the entrance so I could spot Joan when she arrived. A few minutes later her CTS passed me, and she parked at the far end of the rest area. I was just backing out to catch up with her when I was shocked to see the same dark blue Taurus that had followed me in Vancouver enter the rest area. I texted Joan, "You've been followed. Go to the restroom then exit to the left toward the truck area. I'll pick you up."

I carefully backed out of the car area and down the entrance road so I could turn into the truck parking area. My illegal maneuver only incurred the horn-blasting wrath of one truck driver. I pulled over to the curb by the restroom and waited a minute until Joan came out. She jumped in my car, and we took off north on I-5. I watched my rear view mirror but didn't see the Taurus pull out after me.

I glanced at her and said, "He must have followed you from work. Didn't you check your mirrors?"

Joan looked back over her shoulder and asked, "Who?"

I shrugged my shoulders. "I'm not sure. I saw someone tail me from Braxter back to my hotel when I went there to check out on Monday. Instead of leading him to Packwood, I went to the airport and swapped rental cars and lost him. He must have followed you instead. Didn't you notice the dark blue Taurus behind you?"

"No, but I have been just a little preoccupied. Why would someone follow me?"

"Someone needs to know how close we are to discovering the leak; someone with a lot to lose; someone with deep pockets."

"Why?"

Continuing my thought, I said, "Someone who will do whatever it takes to stop us if we get too close."

Joan's eyes blinked rapidly, "What are you saying?"

I responded, "There's a lot at stake here, and stealing Kilroy secrets is very important to someone. Anyone who threatens to get in his way is at risk."

"But taking us out would only increase the scrutiny."

"Unless it was made to look like an accident.

Joan lowered her voice to a near whisper, "Or unless they just needed to buy time to get everything they need."

We both paused. Joan's face turned ashen, and mine probably did too. She covered her face with her hands and started to sob. "Rick left me for a younger woman. At least he waited until the boys were out of high school. It's just a matter of time before Braxter fires me, and now someone may want to kill me."

In spite of hating melodrama, I held her hand to comfort her, and after a couple of minutes, I asked, "What do we do about it? I think you should tell Gross."

"Tell him what? That you are still on the job, and you have copies of all of the hard drives? He'll have me fired on the spot."

"Tell him you think you are being followed. Hopefully, he'll have someone keep an eye on you."

I joked as I pulled over at the next exit and parked in at a mini-mart, "The tail is likely to crap his pants when he finally figures out you're not in the restroom with a bad case of constipation."

"Not funny. What's going on?"

"I needed to talk with you in person in case your phone is tapped. Karl Matson emailed a supposed vacation picture to an email address I can't track. But it wasn't a vacation picture; it was an obfuscated Kilroy specification. I found the leak."

Joan shook her head and started crying again as she said, "No. It's not Karl. He wouldn't do anything like that. I'd trust him with my life. He's a straight arrow. Besides, whenever he plays poker with the other guys he's always the big loser, every time. He couldn't bluff his way out of a paper bag. It's not Karl."

"Joan, wake up! It's Karl. His hard drive proves it."

"I don't believe it."

I slapped my hand onto the dashboard. "Joan, I said wake up."

"Have you analyzed all of the other drives?"

I exhaled a deep breath. "Not yet. It is going to take several more days; certainly through the end of the week."

"I don't want us to jump to any conclusions about Karl until you're finished."

I felt my jaw muscles tighten. "Okay. I'll keep looking, but you can't deny Matson looks suspicious."

She ran her hands through her hair and said, "You're right. By the way, Karl's new baby has pneumonia. Karl was camped out at the hospital the last few days and may be there for the rest of week."

I asked, "What else is happening at Braxter?"

"Gross and Tinker's minions arrived, full of bluster; seven of them in total. All wearing short hair and dark suits. They commandeered every conference room and didn't just interview my people; they interrogated them. Endless questions about work, family, finances, and vacations. Then they pulled out each person's phone records and credit card history and demanded each entry be explained.

"They went easy on me; only five hours. They grilled Harold for ten straight hours with only one lunch break and two bathroom breaks; Tinker was with him every step of the way. Harold is about to quit, and if he does we'll get penalized for missing our delivery dates and probably lose the contract. That's what Matthews wants. I'll be blacklisted."

"Will you quit whining. You're not the only one with skin in the game. My business was poised to expand to the next level, but this disaster could kill it."

Joan dabbed her eyes with a tissue from her purse. "Now who's whining?"

"What else happened?"

Joan reported, "Ron inserted the Easter eggs into the footers of all the specs, and the flat tops don't know anything about them.

I thought for a moment and said, "Are they analyzing everyone's hard drives yet?"

"Not yet."

"They will. It's standard procedure, and the feds always do everything by the book. Did Theron enable the detailed logging I asked for?"

Joan nodded. "Yup."

"What about the backup log storage server?"

"He did that too."

"Can you make me a copy of both the primary and backup log files? It may take a couple of hard disks."

"I can have Theron do it."

"Make sure he encrypts them, and don't let the feds know I have them.

"Can you pick them up?"

"Too risky. Overnight them to me general delivery to the Packwood post office. I'll pick them up and get started analyzing them as soon as I'm done with the other hard drives."

"I'll overnight them tomorrow."

I knew we needed to take every precaution and said, "You need to assume the feds have tapped your phone. I don't want you to use it to communicate with me; no calling and no texting. You need to do two things. First, stop at Target or Best Buy or wherever and purchase a prepaid phone, a smart phone. Use cash and don't give them your correct name or address. Second, download one of those apps that gives you disposable phone numbers."

Joan wrinkled her forehead and asked, "A disposable phone number?"

"It's designed for chicks who don't want to give their real phone number to guys they meet in bars, guys who may turn out to be creeps. The app lets the chick give out a disposable number that gets forwarded to her primary number. If the guy turns out to be a serial chainsaw molester who doesn't floss at least once each day, she can trash the number so he can't reach her."

"And I need one because I'm going to start trolling in singles bars?"

I laughed. "You need one because I'm getting paranoid. If they tap my phone and monitor who I am communicating with, they won't be able to trace it to you. The combination prepaid phone and disposable number should throw them off the trail."

212

"It sounds like you need to get one too."

"You're right. I'll stop by Centralia on the way back to Packwood."

"How will I know your number?"

"Send me your disposable number with the hard drives you're sending. After I get it, I'll text you my disposable number. By the way, keep your prepaid phone turned off while you're at Braxter. They may be scanning for personal phones. But be sure to turn it on and check for messages every evening."

"You really are paranoid."

"Now we need to get you back to your car without letting the tail see me."

I hid in the back seat and had Joan drive south on I-5 past the rest area and turned around at the next exit. She drove back to the rest area and pulled into the truck section, keeping an eye out for the Taurus. She parked my car while I kept my head down and reported she didn't see the Taurus. Our plan was for her to get into her Caddy, drive north a few exits and then turn around and head back to Vancouver.

After ten minutes, I got behind the wheel of my Malibu and took a short detour to the Walmart in Centralia to buy myself a prepaid phone. I stopped by their ATM to withdraw five hundred dollars, the maximum amount the machine would let me take in one day. I bought a clunky, refurbished Android phone for eighty-nine dollars and 1,500 minutes with unlimited texting for an additional thirty bucks. I got back on the road and headed to Packwood, keeping a close eye on my mirrors.

NINETEEN

A note tacked to the front door greeted me when I arrived back at Zeke's place. It was from Angie inviting me to come over for dinner at six that evening. I put the note in my pocket and went into the house, pulled the eight hard drives out of the floor safe, and fired up the next disk analysis job. Once I was sure the job was running, I walked over to the Andersons to let Angie know I would be happy to join them for dinner. A doe and her spotted fawn pranced across the driveway about 40 feet in front of me, oblivious to my presence. I knocked on the door, but nobody answered so I scratched "I'll be here at six" on Angie's note and inserted it between their front door and the door jam.

When I got back home, I double checked the analysis job then checked my email. I had received a report from Pat Hoard, the PI who was watching Julie. It detailed all of her activities for the prior five days. During the week she drove to the CPA office, arriving by eight as regular as clockwork. She left by five thirty and arrived at her roommate's by six fifteen. She was staying in a house rented by Laura Gumbo, a name I recognized as a college roommate of Julie's. Pat provided the address and a photo of the place. He also included five photos of Julie going out to dinner with a guy who Pat couldn't identify. I recognized him immediately. He was Julie's younger brother. No problem there.

It didn't look like Julie had found anyone else. Still, seeing the close-up, color pictures of her took the air out of me, as if I had forgotten how to inhale. I fell into Zeke's chair by the wood stove, cast back in time. I could see her vibrant brown eyes light up when she smiled. I could smell her freshly washed hair. I could hear her chuckle when I cracked a witty one-liner. But, I couldn't reach out to her. She was only near in my wistful thoughts. It hadn't been two weeks since we had coffee together, and although I tried not to think about her, she was always just a thought away, a thought triggered by the sight of lovers holding hands, the scent of gardenias, or the sound of The Avett Brothers singing the Ballad of Love and Hate. The two weeks felt like two months; January and February when it seems like spring will never return.

It was three thirty my time, which made it six thirty in Boston. I picked up my phone and texted her, "It's been ages. Can I call you?" She immediately replied, "Give me an hour." I jumped up from the chair and walked into the kitchen and then back into the living room. An eternal hour. I grabbed my iPad and sat back down in Zeke's chair to read more of my Clancy novel. I checked my watch every five minutes and squirmed like a two year old at a portrait session.

I picked up my phone at four thirty five, scrolled through my contacts, mostly business contacts I planned to farm, and found Julie. I pressed "call" hoping I would sound relaxed, but afraid she would sense my desperation born of not knowing if I could cope with losing her, cope with the harsh silence of living alone.

She picked up on the fourth ring. Words nearly frozen in my throat, I managed to say, "Julie, I've really missed you. What've you been doing?"

"Going to work then going home. Nothing exciting. I'm spending time with Laura. I'm staying in her extra room. We took the train down to New York City for the weekend to catch The Jersey Boys on Saturday. We wanted tickets for the evening show, but had to settle for the afternoon one. It was terrific. Better than I expected."

I wished I could have taken her. "Sounds great."

"Laura just got engaged, and I'm going to be one of her bridesmaids. We spent one evening shopping for dresses. It was fun, but I won't bore you with the details. What've you been up to?"

Julie's voice was wonderful. I couldn't hear enough of it. "How's everything at work?"

Julie continued, "Fine. It's the slow season so I'm catching up on some back burner projects; updating audit procedures and report templates. The rumor is that the partner committee is meeting in three weeks to select two new partners. Three of us are being considered, but I have the inside track because my accounts have increased the firm's billings more than twenty-five percent in the last year. The partnership committee wants new partners who will grow their coffers. What have you been doing?"

I wanted to be back with Julie so much I felt like proposing then and there. I didn't. It would have been insane. Impulsive emotions can't be trusted for important decisions like marriage.

I replied, "My life is going full speed in two or three directions at once. The day after you moved out I learned I had an uncle, my Dad's brother, who had been disowned from the family. Zeke, my uncle, recently died and left his estate to me. He lived in rural Washington, and right now I'm at his place trying to figure out what to do with the pieces. I can tell you all about it once I get my brain wrapped around it all. "

"You'd never even heard of him?"

"No. He was the Klein family's banished black sheep, an exiled pariah."

"How's work?"

"Crazy. Volatile. I was counting on this assignment to take my business to the next level, but instead it may kill it. I'm looking for a parachute. The client's a DoD contractor with a huge security leak. Everyone's running for cover and looking for someone to blame it on. The DoD kicked me out so they could do things their own inept way and then pile the blame on me. But I am doing a little of the work on the side, maybe I can pile the fault back on them."

"You'll land on your feet. You always do."

"Maybe not. Things are different. The deck is really stacked against me."

"It would only be a temporary setback. You'll bounce back."

I appreciated her encouragement, but wasn't sure it was justified. "Maybe. This whole Zeke thing is making me rethink some things; reconsider what's really important. I'm getting to know Zeke's neighbors. Their lives are simple, but very content. They're born-again Christians. You know religion puts me off, but I feel okay with them. I can't explain it."

"Don't make any crazy decisions."

"No way! Hey, speaking of crazy, what would you think of taking a few days off and coming out to Washington for some hiking around Mt. Rainier? It's incredible, and it's high on my 'to do' list. You can stay in a hotel, and I'll stay at Zeke's. Strictly platonic."

Julie paused as if checking her mental calendar. "Maybe I could. I have lots of comp time and could easily take some time off next week, but I couldn't leave here until Monday morning because I promised Laura I would go shopping with her on the weekend."

"I'll pay for everything. You'll love Mount Rainier. Google it."

"I'll let you know one way or the other early tomorrow morning."

"Okay. Julie, thanks for the chance to catch up."

We disconnected, and although we had talked for only a few minutes, I was floating. No other woman could put such a spell on me. I had read somewhere that you shouldn't settle for marrying a person you could live with, rather you should only marry a person you couldn't live without. I was thinking I may not be able to live without Julie. I was going to be very disappointed if she didn't come out to Washington.

*****

At a few minutes before six I checked on the analysis software. It had finished so I hooked the last two drives up to my computer, and after I was sure the analysis program was running correctly, I headed over to the Anderson's for dinner. Angie met me at the door and led me into the living room where Carl sat looking at his laptop. He motioned me over and said, "Look at the pictures of the bears we saw up on Tatoosh." The first picture of the sow was zoomed in so her face filled the entire screen. Her menacing, lower canine teeth look fierce. I was thankful she didn't smell us, see us, or hear us. I made a mental note to take Zeke's pistol with me on all future hikes. Carl's best pictures showed the two young cubs

218

wrestling with each other. The photos were fantastic, and I asked him for copies so I could email them to Julie and Dad.

I sat down in the chair next to Carl's, and as he handed me a photo album said, "These are pictures taken over the years of Zeke and me doing guy stuff." All of the pictures were of Zeke out in the woods and mountains, pictures Carl had apparently taken to chronical their activities and their friendship. Carl relaxed in his chair while I perused the pictures. Some I had already seen at Zeke's, but most were new. Carl's pictures portrayed Zeke as a man's man who loved to ski, hike, hunt, and fish. One picture showed him on the summit of Mt. Rainier and several showed him cross country skiing and snow shoeing. I would have loved to have hung out with Zeke, hiking in the summer, skiing in the winter, even hunting in the fall; like a favorite nephew. Unfortunately, my family's duplicity stole my opportunity.

Angie asked us to come to the table where a Caesar salad awaited us, a pot roast cooked with potatoes, carrots, and onions sizzled in a glass pan, and warm, freshly baked bread filled the room with its aroma. Just like Mom tried to make; just once. I nearly chipped a tooth on her crust. Carl prayed, and we started eating and I realized I hadn't eaten a delicious home cooked meal like the one in front of me since Julie and I visited her parents in May. After I swallowed the last bite, Carl told me the roast was from the elk Zeke took last fall with his bow. "After Zeke died, we cleaned out his freezer so nothing would be wasted. Brought everything over here. We'll take it back now that you're here."

"Keep it. I'm temporary, and my cooking wouldn't do it justice."

I helped Angie clear the table and the three of us went to sit in the living room to have blueberry pie. I said, "Since you two have been married quite a while and get along so well, I have a question for you if it isn't too personal. How did you make your marriage work?"

Carl replied, "I've never been asked a question like that before. I'm not sure where to start."

I winked at him. "Where would your rocking chair start?"

Carl laughed and said, "It isn't any single thing. Our marriage is a hobos' pot luck stew. Neither one of us brought much into it, but we put in everything we had, we let it simmer, and we eat it together." Carl nodded a couple of almost imperceptible nods to himself and continued, "You put in everything you have; you take out less than you put in."

Angie smiled, shook her head and said, "Carl's idea of romance is what keeps Hallmark in business. I agree it isn't just one thing. It's a combination of long days at work so the other person has what they need and loving smiles and tender caresses and overlooked wrongs and healed wounds and an occasional Hallmark card. Flowers probably wouldn't hurt, but how would I know?"

Carl said, "The Bible says 'the two will become one' and over time our individual identities have become our identity. We're still two different people, but every time I make a decision I think of how it'll affect Angie."

Angie nodded and said, "I'm the same way."

Carl added, "Angie, she's seen me at my worst, more than once, but somehow she loves me. She's the only one in the world who would love me like she does, and it makes me want the best for her, to treat her the best way I can."

Angie said, "It's true. You see the success with the failure, and the confidence with the fear, and the compassion with the selfishness. It's all in each of us. We can't pretend it isn't. But you've got to choose to think about the good and nurture it, in spite of the not so good."

She smiled at Carl who continued, "I know non-Christians can have great marriages, and I know Christians can have bad ones, but we wouldn't have made it without Jesus gently nudging me to admit it when I screwed up and then to ask Angie to forgive me. Over the years, He has changed me from the inside out. It's a slow process, like a glacier carving a valley, but it is happening. I'm not a slave to my anger anymore."

I asked Angie, "How did you know for certain that Carl was the right one for you?"

Angie said, "I didn't. You couldn't know for certain. You've got to commit to making it work for better or for worse."

Carl added, "You never know up front. Deciding who to marry is like deciding to get a tattoo. You'd better plan to love it for a long time, even after it gets saggy and baggy."

Angie cringed, shook her head in mock disgust, and threw her wadded up paper napkin at Carl. As it landed lamely at his feet she said, "I hope your saggy butt likes sleeping on the couch."

We all laughed, and I said, "The dinner was fantastic, and I appreciate your thoughts about marriage, but I really need to get back and make sure my analysis job is still running."

Carl asked me, "Before you go, would you be interested in a one night backpacking trip up to Goat Lake? It was one of Zeke's favorites."

"How tough is it compared to the Tatoosh hike we took?"

"It has about the same amount of climbing, but each day has less distance than Tatoosh. The total is thirteen miles; the uphill half on the first day and the downhill half on the second. The mountain lake, a small tarn, is at the highest point of the hike."

"Sure. I can handle that. When do you want to do it?"

"What about leaving the day after tomorrow? Angie, she's leaving tomorrow to spend a few days with her sister in Yakima, and I'd rather not be home by myself."

"What do I need to bring?"

"I snore so we should each take our own tent. You'll need water bottles, a sleeping bag, sleeping pad, warm clothes – we'll be at six-thousand feet so the evening may be cool – food, and toiletries, toilet paper is essential. You should be able to find everything, except food, in Zeke's stuff."

"Can I buy freeze dried food in town?"

"Yes, at the Outdoor Store. I'll bring my camp stove and water filter."

"When should I be ready?"

"Let's leave in the morning to get the climbing out of the way before it gets hot. How's eight o'clock?"

"I'll be ready."

I shook Carl's hand and returned Angie's hug before walking home. Ten minutes later I had confirmed the analysis job was still cranking and estimated it to finish by the next morning. I sat down to read, but put my book down after a few pages and reflected on what Carl and Angie had said about marriage.

I wanted what Carl and Angie had; a simple life, a comfortable home – maybe even in the woods, and each other. Until that point in my life, marriage had only been an ephemeral cloud in the distant horizon, not a storm cloud, but a wispy cirrus cloud refracting a spectrum of brilliant orange hues ignited by sunrises and sunsets. Now the cloud was no longer on the distant horizon. Winds were blowing it closer, so close I might soon be forced to decide if I should duck for cover while it blew over, or not.

I had begun to realize how significantly marriage would change my life. My relationship with Julie couldn't stay the same but just have a new label. It would certainly need to change. I could understand what Carl had said. If Julie and I got married, it would be us, not Julie and David. The two must become one. I wondered what would happen to Klein InfoSec Associates if I cut back on my travel and quit spending weekends writing reports. Would it survive? The problem was I wasn't sure that the upside of being married would compensate for the downside of risking my firm.

TWENTY

The smell of the nearby cedar trees again wafted through the open bedroom window, and golden sunbeams knifed diagonally through the trees as I awoke on Thursday morning. I rolled out of bed and went down to the kitchen still wearing the PE shorts and tee shirt I slept in. While the coffee was brewing I checked the progress of my search program and saw it had completed its analysis of the eighth and last disk. Finally. I spent two hours drinking coffee and scrutinizing the results but didn't find anything suspicious, nothing to incriminate anyone other than Karl, who in spite of Joan's protests, was certainly the culprit.

It was too early for the package from Joan to have arrived so I put on my running gear for a run to explore a few of the game trails I had seen on the hill up from Zeke's house. Just to be safe I took my iPhone to track my route and make sure I could find my way back. Still within sight of Zeke's house I picked up a faintly visible trail covered with fir needles and small hemlock cones half the size of my little toe. Once I thought I had lost the trail as it disappeared into the encroaching Oregon grape and salal, but it soon reappeared. I jogged along for about a mile until the trail became an old one lane road that saplings had partially reclaimed and ran on it until it intersected a narrow lane gravel road. Surprisingly my sense of direction seemed intact so I turned right expecting the gravel road to lead me down to the highway, which it did. I headed up the highway to the turnoff taking me back to Zeke's.

After sitting in one of the porch chairs for twenty minutes to cool off, I took a quick shower and then went into the kitchen and stared at the eight hard disks I had searched. They were sitting on Zeke's kitchen table, stacked side by side like books on a desk. Seven had revealed nothing interesting, one was Matson's, and the evidence it stored was going to restore my reputation. I wanted to leave room in the crowded floor safe for the two disks that Joan had hopefully sent so I took the other eight disks up to Zeke's "sports room" and stowed them in his gun safe. Before closing and locking the safe I removed Zeke's semi-automatic pistol, loaded magazine and holster to carry on the hike.

My cell phone told me it was after ten o'clock so I drove the Malibu to Packwood's post office to retrieve my package. The clerk said it had just arrived via FedEx. I took it back to Zeke's and ripped it open to find two hard disks and a note from Joan giving me her disposable phone number. I texted her so she would have my disposable number. Ten minutes later, my prepaid phone chirped, informing me I had a text from Joan. She had sent the 128-character encryption key I needed to enter allowing me to read the log data off of the disks.

I had instructed Theron to enable detailed logging on every computer used by the entire Kilroy team. In addition to logging the exact time when someone signed into or out of their computer, the detailed logging made a record every time someone opened a file to read it, every time someone edited a file, and most importantly, every time someone copied a file from one location to another. I was most interested in knowing specifically when someone copied a file to an external storage device, such as a USB hard drive or memory stick. USB memory sticks are ubiquitously available and can be built into key chains, bracelets, pens, and even Calvin Klein – no relation – sun glasses, making them easy to smuggle data past Braxter's security checkpoints.

I had also asked Theron to record the log events on two separate log servers. The first was Braxter's primary log server, the one that Kilroy shared with corporate security. I didn't trust the primary server because any enterprising member of Braxter's corporate security team could bypass the server's access controls and delete any log events they wanted to make disappear. The second log server was the secret one that only Joan, Theron, and I were privy to. It was much less likely anyone would erase records from it.

Having copies of both log servers, I needed to compare them to find any suspicious activity. I sat down at the kitchen table to write a program to detect whenever a file was copied onto removable storage and to detect any discrepancies among the two log servers. The program was so simple I had it working perfectly by the end of the afternoon. I started it up and timed its performance over a fifteen minute period. The little status lights on my laptop and on the two external hard drives flashed on and off indicating a high level of activity. At the rate it was going, I expected it to complete the analysis by early the next morning.

I went upstairs to gather all the things I would need the next morning for the backpacking trip. I opened the closet door to Zeke's storehouse of outdoor gear and found two equipment lists laminated in plastic; one for backpacking and one for bow hunting. The items on each list were organized under headings such as packs, shelter, kitchen, safety, clothing, and footwear; where gaiters were listed. I grabbed the largest pack and loaded it with a tent, sleeping bag, sleeping pad, and everything else I thought I might need. The batteries for the miniature flashlight and for the handheld GPS unit were good so I started to put them into one of the pack's external pockets, but the pocket wasn't empty. In it I found a small digital camera, apparently forgotten by Zeke.

I took everything downstairs and put the backpacking gear by the front door. I removed the memory card from the camera and inserted it into the SD slot on my laptop to see Zeke's pictures. I felt like an eavesdropper looking over Zeke's shoulder as he snapped the photos. I saw pictures of Carolyn Anderson graduating from law school – dated two years earlier, pictures of a trip Zeke and Carl took to Glacier National Park where they saw bighorn sheep and grizzly bears and rugged mountains, pictures of Zeke baptizing people in a river, and pictures of a hunting trip from the fall, presumably the trip where Zeke took the elk whose leftovers were in the refrigerator. I put the memory card back into the camera and put the camera into the backpack hoping we would see vistas and scenery I could show off to Julie.

The only thing I didn't find in Zeke's closet was food, which I needed to purchase in town. I hopped in the Malibu and headed for the Outdoor Store. The store had a little bit of nearly everything, including several freeze-dried dinner entrees. I opted for lasagna with beef and also bought a large package of trail mix and a couple of packages of instant oatmeal. I was ready to survive in the wilderness.

Ten minutes later I was home and had stuffed the food into the pack. I texted Joan, "Can you talk?"

Fifteen minutes later she called me. I immediately asked her, "What's the latest?"

"You were right. The feds just performed forensic analysis on everybody's hard disk, looking for documents where they shouldn't have been, and they found three unauthorized specs on Karl Matson's computer."

"Three?"

"Yes, this morning. Two U.S. Marshalls showed up while Karl was working in his cube. One handcuffed him while the other read him his rights and told him that he was a suspect under the Espionage Act and would likely to go to prison for more than thirty-five years. Karl was in a state of shock. He begged me to do something and kept looking at me, his eyes pleading for help. It was awful, just awful. The desperate expression on his face is still haunting me. They're going to hold him without bail up at Fort Lewis. No visitors."

The cool evening air sent a shiver through me. "He knew the risks."

"I still don't believe it."

"After they interrogate him, he'll confess, especially if his lawyer can negotiate a reduced sentence. What else?"

"Harold filed a harassment claim against Braxter and quit. He almost quit earlier, after his interrogation, but I was able to talk him down off the ledge. Having his hard disk searched was the straw that broke the camel's back. He completely lost it."

My altercation with Harold came to mind and I said, "I can imagine."

"David, he let it slip that you had already copied the hard disks. Gross flew into my office and demanded to know why I hadn't told him. I explained I didn't think it mattered because he didn't trust your work. He asked for the copies, and I told him that you still had them, that I had authorized you to have them."

I interrupted, "We're both toast. He'll fire you and blacklist me."

"He asked where you were, and I told him that I didn't know for sure – somewhere in Washington."

"They'll find me. When did you tell them?"

"Just a couple of hours ago."

"It won't take them long to ferret out the link between me and my uncle. They'll be on my doorstep by tomorrow afternoon. Thankfully, I won't be here."

"The next Kilroy release is in a shambles. It'll take months for a replacement to come up to speed on Harold's firmware. We'll miss our deadline, and Matthews knows it. He's sending the army in next week to take over the project and undoubtedly give it to another contractor; Calkins, no doubt."

"Did you tell Gross you were being followed?"

"Yeah, but I'm not sure he believed me. Said he'd have Tinker check into it, but I haven't heard anything more about it."

"I need you to stonewall them a little longer. Give me time to compare the two log servers. It'll take a couple of days." I wanted to buy an extra two days not only from the feds, but also from Joan. "Keep telling them you don't know where I am, and don't tell them we've talked."

"Fine. When will you contact me next?"

"Two or three days. Hang in there. It won't be long."

As we hung up, my mind was racing a million miles an hour. Maybe I should cancel my hike with Carl and wait for them to show up. Maybe I should dig a deep hole out in the forest and bury all of the hard drives and tell the feds I destroyed them. Maybe I should just go hiking and let the feds enjoy a day in Packwood wondering where I was. Bingo.

I had a late dinner of the reheated leftovers Angie had sent home with me and drank a beer I found tucked into the back corner of the fridge. After eating, I looked in on the log analysis job and was astounded to find multiple events from the past week that had been removed from the primary server, but were recorded on the secret server. But it wasn't what I expected. Instead of files being copied from a computer to a removable storage device, two files had been copied from a removable device to a computer, Matson's computer. That explained why Joan said the feds had found three files on his computer. They found the one I already knew about, plus the two new ones. Maybe Joan was right about Matson. I couldn't see how he could copy files to his computer and how he could do it if he was with his wife and baby at the hospital.

I wanted to lock up my laptop and the two external drives it was analyzing, but I needed to let the job finish in case it revealed additional anomalies. I went to bed and set my alarm for six thirty the next morning so I would have time to tidy up and make it look like I hadn't been to Zeke's. Why make it easy for the feds?

I hardly slept at all and finally got out of bed fifteen minutes before the alarm was set to wake me, put on Zeke's boots and camo clothing, and ate a large bowl of cereal. The analysis job had completed just an hour earlier. I disconnected the two hard drives and stashed them, along with my prepaid phone, in the floor safe. Next, I packed all of my clothes and toiletries into my suitcase and locked it in the trunk of the Malibu. I collected all of the garbage and the food from the refrigerator into a plastic trash bag, strapped on Zeke's holstered pistol and drove into town where I tossed the trash into the dumpster behind the grocery store.

When I got back to Zeke's I just had time to take my laptop upstairs and lock it in the gun safe. I reached into my pocket for the key, but couldn't find it. I ran downstairs and anxiously looked all over. It was already eight o'clock, and I didn't want to be late for our hike, but more importantly I didn't want to hang around until the feds arrived. I gave up looking for the keys and picked up the loaded backpack and my laptop and tossed them into the rental's back seat. At the last minute, I realized that I should set tripwires on the front and back doors to tell me if anyone had opened the doors. I grabbed two fir needles and inserted one between the front door and the door jam and did the same on the back door. Anyone opening the door would disturb the needles and warn me that they had entered the house.

Carl was sitting in one of the chairs on the porch with his gear leaning against a post. He wore his hiking boots, green convertible pants, camo tee shirt, and a camo baseball cap. His pistol was in the holster attached to his belt. I thought that with a few more guns and some face paint we could both look like commandos. I offered to drive us to the trail head, explaining that we might as well take my rental car since I was paying for it whether I used it or not. Carl loaded his pack into the back seat, and I feigned surprise at finding my laptop there, and said, "Can I leave my laptop at your place? It will save us the time of taking it back to Zeke's." Carl nodded and took it into the house, and we left for the trailhead. I had just turned onto the highway heading west when a dark Suburban with government plates passed us heading east. I watched in the rear view mirror as it turned off the highway and up the road to Zeke's. I was surprised that they had moved so fast and made a mental note not to underestimate them again.

TWENTY-ONE

We drove west on Highway 12 for six miles before turning onto the forest service road that rattled the rental car for fifteen miles until we reached the Berry Patch trailhead. I parked the car and immediately saw the *Northwest Forest Pass Required* sign. Carl undoubtedly noticing my frown said, "Don't worry. I bought a lifetime pass when I turned 62. He pulled it out of his wallet and put it on the dashboard. I put the cars keys into a zippered pocket on my pants for safe keeping and found the key to Zeke's gun safe wedged into the corner of the pocket. It must have worked its way off the key ring.

I snapped Zeke's gaiters on over my boots and lower legs while Carl registered us and tied our permit onto his backpack. We strapped our packs on and headed up the trail to Goat Lake. The trail reminded me of the Tatoosh trail as it immediately dove into thick woods and started climbing. However, the Berry Patch trail wasn't crowded by dew soaked salal and Oregon grape. It was no wonder Carl didn't snap on his gaiters. We hiked for an hour before gaining enough altitude to see occasional views through breaks in the trees. After another hour we emerged from the forest and saw the narrow trail snaking ahead of us as it hugged the side of a valley carpeted with wild flowers. In the distance, the trail crawled through a narrow gap in the rocks along Jordan Creek, where the crystal clear water charged down to the valley below. The view was fantastic.

We stopped in the Jordan valley to rest and eat a few handfuls of trail mix. I was in wild flower heaven, just like the Tatoosh hike. After our brief break we climbed up the valley and over a lip that opened into an upper valley splotched with snow fields. We trudged up three switchbacks to reach a ridge separating the Jordan Creek valley from the Goat Creek valley. After crossing the ridge, we walked along the narrow trail traversing the uphill side of the Goat Creek valley and shortly arrived at Goat Lake. Carl suggested we set up our tents on one of the several flat spots near the lake. I dropped my pack and slowly turned around in a full circle completely unable to absorb all of the surrounding beauty.

Carl set up his tent and laid his sleeping pad and bag inside it. I did the same and wondered if I would get bored looking at the scenery for the entire afternoon and evening. I sat down to take off my gaiters and boots and rest my feet. I told Carl I could hardly believe the lake could be completely frozen over in August. He explained that more than seventy five feet of snowfall inundated the area each winter, and winter started in October and lasted as late as May. I sat on the ground and leaned against a log to look at the tall hillsides surrounding the lake on three sides and rising too steeply to climb without mountain climbing equipment. Carl said "When the sun goes behind the hills in the early evening, the goats will stroll out from the small copses scattered across the tops of the surrounding hills. You'll be amazed to see them traverse the steep slopes.

I had just closed my eyes for a quick nap when Carl said, "The goats won't be out for hours. Let's take a side trip up to Hawkeye Point."

"Where's Hawkeye Point?"

"You're looking at it," he said pointing up to the hill standing a thousand feet above the left side of the lake.

I reached for my boots and said, "Sure."

He opened up a nylon sack and said, "Put all of your food in this. We need to hang it from one of those tree branches."

"Bears?"

"Worse. Chipmunks. They'll gnaw through your tent or through your pack to get at your trail mix."

I laughed as I imagined the damage Alvin, Theodore, and Simon could do. Using a rope that was too thin for a chipmunk to shinny up or down he suspended the stuffed food bag from a high limb, and we set out for Hawkeye Point. We walked back on the trail we had just come in on for a half mile and then turned off and started some serious climbing that soon had me panting for breath. Carl even stopped a time or two to catch his wind. The last two-hundred yards were as steep as a stairway, but the thin air made it feel even steeper.

From atop Hawkeye Point we could see for miles in any direction. Mt. Rainier to the north, Mt. Adams and Mt. Hood to the south, Mt. St. Helens to the southwest. I was blown away. Carl said, "Zeke, he loved Hawkeye Point. We slept up here a few years ago. It was too windy for tents so we stacked some rocks on the windward side and tried to nestle down below them in our sleeping bags. After the sun went down the wind really kicked up. It attacked us with one assault after the other. The wind would calm down for a few minutes, long enough for us to hope the storm had stopped, but then we would hear the next salvo coming from far off in the distance like a freight train rumbling down the tracks. It got louder and louder and then would hit us like a locomotive. I shivered as my sleeping bag flapped like a flag in a gale. Neither of us got any sleep. Zeke loved it. The next morning Zeke said, 'That was great, wasn't it? Nothing like sleeping outside.' He was serious, too."

Carl and I walked back to camp and ate our dinners and waited for dusk and for the goats to come out. We leaned back against a log, side by side. Carl had a distant look in his eyes and he started telling me the story he must have been seeing clearly in his mind's eye.

He said, "I miss Zeke every day. After I took him fishing the first time, we started having breakfast once a week, just to talk. Mostly it was guy talk about fishing and hunting. I got him started hunting and within five years he was the best hunter in Packwood. He spent hours in the woods studying deer and elk, learning to track them, learning to get real close without their notice. He always got his deer and elk, every year.

"Often at breakfast we talked about important things. Zeke would talk about faith, and I occasionally would talk about family. After I quit losing my temper at Angie, she and I decided to have kids. We tried for over a year before she got pregnant. We were both super happy, but decided not to tell anyone until she started showing. Angie, she bought a crib and bassinet, and she started stockpiling diapers, baby shampoo, baby powder, and baby wipes. The miscarriage broke her heart. Mine, too.

"She was afraid to try again, but eventually I coaxed her into it. After several months she got pregnant, but this time she didn't let herself get so excited. We were both afraid to hope very much, but with each day, hope grew all by itself. It happened again; this time early in the third month. Angie, she spent four days in the dark bedroom, crying. She said it was her fault, that God must be punishing her. I hugged her and rubbed her back and told her it wasn't so. On the fifth morning she came into the kitchen and told me if I wanted kids we should adopt. I knew she couldn't take losing another one so I agreed. She got dressed and went to work and tried to act like nothing happened. She told Zeke she had been out with the flu.

"I'd never talked with anyone about our trouble, until I eventually talked with Zeke about it. He said he would pray for us to have a child. Angie and I started saving up to adopt a baby. We saved for two years and almost had enough, but in spite of not trying, we got pregnant again. This time we just waited for it to happen again, but it didn't. We were so happy to be spending the adoption money on our own baby. By the end of the third month, Angie couldn't hide it anymore. By the end of the fifth month, we were starting to hope. By the end of the seventh month, we cleaned out the spare room. By the end of the ninth month, Angie had quit work to be a stay at home mom. A week later, Carolyn was born.

"But she was blue and stayed blue. The doctors rushed her to the infant ICU where they found a severe ventricular septal defect, a large hole in her tiny heart. We didn't even get to hold her before they took her into the operating room for open heart surgery. The surgery only took three hours, but every minute seemed like hours. After he closed her up, the surgeon told us the operation had gone perfectly, and he expected her to make a full recovery, to live a normal life. Angie and I hugged each other and cried with happiness. They kept Carolyn in the hospital for a week to make sure her little body healed up right. When we brought her home we couldn't stop staring at her and making sure she was still breathing. One of us looked in on her every hour throughout the night for the first three weeks. We couldn't have been happier.

"Then we got the hospital bill. Our insurance through the mill was cut rate, and our part of the bill was $198,000. Carolyn was worth every penny, but we didn't have that kind of money. Angie called Zeke hoping her job was still available. It was, so she asked him to hold it for her. That week at breakfast Zeke asked me why Angie wanted her job back. I told him about the medical bill we couldn't pay. Zeke told me he was the primary contact for the mill's health insurance plan and he would look into it. Three days later we got a letter from the insurance company informing us they had misclassified the procedure and would pay eighty percent of the bill. Two days later we got a letter from the hospital telling us that the twenty percent we owed had been dismissed.

"The next week I asked Zeke what he said to the insurance company to convince them to cover it, and he said, 'It just took a little persuasion with their General Counsel. I threatened to sue them and take the mill's business to their competitor.'

"I told him that the hospital forgave the $39,600 we owed, and he asked me if Angie still wanted her old job. I told him I was sure she didn't. Angie loved being a stay-at-home mom with Carolyn. Seven years later, Carolyn fell off her bike and broke her arm. We took her to the emergency room and while we were checking her in, the lady at the desk printed out our payment history. It showed that someone had paid the hospital $500 each month until all $39,600 was paid off. I know it was Zeke. Nobody had ever stuck up for me like that before. If Zeke was your friend, your back was covered. Every time. I really miss him."

We waited quietly for the goats, and I realized that I, too, really missed him.

The goats didn't make an appearance that evening, so as soon as it got dark we crawled into our tents and I slept like a rock. The next morning, I put on my fleece and crawled out of the tent. The eastern sky had just begun to glow. I sat and watched the sun quietly peek over the ridge of the valley and then shine its light on the top of the western ridge, gradually working its way down the slope as if methodically searching for a hiding fugitive. When I stood up and turned around I saw twenty-one goats grazing less than fifty yards from our tents. Several noticed me but were more interested in eating than in keeping an eye on me. I quietly woke Carl and asked him to get up and bring his camera. He took dozens of pictures as the goats meandered up the hillside and eventually disappeared over a rise. We ate breakfast and quickly broke camp so we could hike back to the car in the cool of the morning. I was anxious to get back to Zeke's and see what the feds had done.

TWENTY-TWO

We stopped in town for burgers before going to our homes. I checked my cell phone for messages and was elated to see an email from Julie saying she could fly out of Boston early Monday morning and needed to be back on Friday morning for an important meeting. She asked me to book the tickets and pick her up at the airport.

I dropped Carl off at his place and remembered to pick up my laptop. I turned the car around and slowly headed over to Zeke's while looking for any sign of feds hanging around. I didn't see their Suburban and hoped they had just taken a quick look, concluded I had never been there, and left to look for me elsewhere. I parked near the front door, picked up my laptop and pack, and slowly walked toward the porch, looking for anything amiss. When I reached the door, I knelt down, and the missing fir needle tripwire warned me someone had opened the door and probably entered the house. I set the pack down but hung onto the laptop and circled the house looking for fresh foot prints by the windows. I didn't find any additional tell-tale signs of their uninvited presence.

Before going into the house, I searched the carport that stood across the driveway and directly across from the front of the house, and I found a motion triggered camera aimed at Zeke's front door. It looked like the type of camera hunters set up on game trails to discover what animals are in the area. If I was correct, the camera would take a picture every time someone entered or left Zeke's house by the front door. It was a battery powered unit attached to the backside of the carport's front fascia board. I only discovered it because whoever had drilled the hole for the lens to see the front door through the fascia board hadn't cleaned up all of the wood shavings that had fallen onto the gravel below. The unit didn't have an antenna to broadcast the pictures so I knew the feds would need to send a junior flattop to periodically check the batteries and swap out the memory card.

Ideas multiplied inside my mind like paparazzi at a celebrity wedding. Should I wire up 110 volts to the camera and zap the poor sap they sent to check on it, or should I hide it and take pictures of whoever came to check on it, or should I copy Bigfoot pictures onto its memory card? I rejected those ideas as being infantile and removed the memory card and inserted it into my laptop. I also removed the batteries and installed them backwards so whoever installed the camera would look like an incompetent galoot to the big boys. Although not as much fun as 110 volts, it had the advantage of not letting them be certain I was on to them.

I unlocked the front door and brought the backpack inside, keeping in mind that if one camera was hidden outside it was likely that one, or more, were hidden inside, along with hidden microphones and a network recorder to track all of my internet activity. After two days hiking, I was dying for a shower and fresh clothes so I fetched my suitcase from the trunk of the rental car and took it upstairs and showered.

If the feds did plant cameras in the house, I didn't want them to suspect I was on to them so I tried to act casual as I went downstairs to grab the pack and hauled it back upstairs to put all the gear back into the closet and to return the pistol to the gun safe. I opened the safe and immediately noticed the eight hard drives were missing. Because the feds found the drives they wouldn't have any doubt I had been squirreled up at Zeke's. They were definitely on to me and were probably a lot smarter than I had been giving them credit for. I figured they took the disks to make copies and would return them as quickly as possible, hoping I wouldn't notice they were missing. I took the pistol back out of the safe in fear the feds would confiscate it when they returned the drives.

I needed to retrieve my prepaid phone from the floor safe so I could tell Joan about the missing log events and the two additional files on Karl's disk. I also wanted to ask her what was going on at Braxter. Hopefully the feds hadn't found the floor safe. The problem was I had to assume their cameras would record me when I opened it, and I didn't want them to know it existed. I developed a plan and drove to Packwood's community library to use its wireless internet access.

The community library sat just off of Highway 12. I pulled into its small, gravel parking area and was able to connect my laptop to their internet without leaving my car. I navigated to a travel site and booked Julie's flights, purchasing a first class ticket that would get her into Portland by one in the afternoon on Monday and a first class return ticket leaving from Seattle on Thursday at two in the afternoon. I emailed her itinerary to her and confirmed I would meet her flight on Monday. Next, I used my PC-based messaging app to text Joan that I would call her at eleven that night. I had nearly finished reading *The Hunt for Red October* so I went inside and checked out *Clear and Present Danger* to occupy me while waiting for Julie. They didn't require local identification, and I didn't bother telling them I lived in Boston.

I returned to the house to read my book and to hopefully bore to death whoever was watching me. At six that evening I remembered I had thrown all of the food away so I called the pizza place in town to order a family-size veggie take-and-bake pizza. I turned the oven to 425° and dashed off to pick up my dinner and stop by the grocery store for a six pack of beer. When I returned back to Zeke's, I baked the pizza, ate, and sat in Zeke's rocker, reading until dark. I pretended to get ready for bed at ten fifteen but after turning out every light I quietly took a heavy brown blanket, a small flashlight, and the key to the floor safe downstairs and put them on the floor near the floor safe. I then slowly crawled to the closet to get the glass carrier I needed to pull up the floor panel and access the safe. I crawled back to the floor safe and pulled the blanket completely over me to deaden any sound and block any stray light. I turned on the flashlight and attached the glass carrier's suction cups to the removable floor section and pulled it up very slowly to minimize the Velcro's tearing sound. I opened the safe, checked to make sure the two disks from the log servers were there and removed my prepaid phone and then closed the safe back up and replaced the floor panel. I quietly put the glass carrier, flashlight and blanket away and crawled out the back door and circled around behind the house until I came to the driveway. I skulked down the driveway to get away from any microphones in the house. By then it was eleven so I called Joan. She answered on the first ring.

I sat down on a moss covered rock and said, "I finished comparing the two different log servers. There's strange stuff going on… very strange. Last week, someone copied two specs to Karl Matson's disk. When I analyzed Matson's disk early in the week, there was only one, but recently two more were added. That's why Gross told you they found three. The strangest thing is I think the two new files were copied when Karl was out while his baby was at the hospital. If it's true, then Karl couldn't have copied the files himself. You may be right about him. Someone may be setting him up."

I could picture Joan smiling as she agreed, "I never thought Karl would do anything like that."

"There's more. They found out where I'm staying. I discovered one surveillance camera, but there are probably more. They broke into the house so I've got to assume my phones are tapped, and the feds are snooping on all of my internet activity. Plus, they picked the lock on a safe and took the copies of everyone's disks. It's not likely they will compare my copies to their copies, but if they do they may find that Karl's disk originally had only one spec."

"What makes you sure it was the feds? What about the guy who followed us?

"I saw the feds drive up in a dark Suburban with government plates so I just assumed they're the ones who stole the disks."

"It could have been the guy who followed us."

I scratched my head and admitted, "I suppose you're right." *Good point, Joan.*

"Maybe you should set up your own surveillance cameras." *Another good point, Joan.*

"Maybe I will. What's happening at Braxter?"

"The feds intercepted copies of the three specs that were on Karl's disk, and now they're threatening to sue Braxter. They claim we're negligent because our information security program didn't meet the due care standard."

"Can you get copies of the three documents?"

244

"Maybe. Why?"

"If they contain our Easter eggs we'll know which side leaked them. It's a long shot but it may not have been Braxter. Also, I need copies of the physical entry logs from the security stations. The two files were copied to Matson's disks by someone who was onsite in the middle of the night. I need to know who was there between one and three last Monday morning."

"I should be able to get that. The list can't be very long."

Staying ahead of the feds felt like a game of chess, and we needed to plan our next series of moves. "We have more information than the feds, and if we play our cards right you may be able to keep your job, and I may be able to keep my reputation."

"What are you thinking?"

"I haven't worked it all out yet, but for now don't tell them anything about the event log discrepancies. I hope we can use the information as a bargaining chip."

"It may already be too late, but it's worth a try. Let's talk tomorrow afternoon – say two in the afternoon."

"Agreed."

We hung up, and I walked back to the house, snuck inside, and went upstairs to bed – for real this time. Joan was right. I shouldn't have assumed the feds were the only trespassers. It was possible they broke into Zeke's, found nothing of interest, and then left. Maybe it was the real bad guys who stole the drives and set up the surveillance. *But how could they know I was staying at Zeke's?*

I finally fell asleep around three in the morning and woke up madder than a wet cat at seven. I grabbed both cell phones and my laptop and headed to the library to search the internet for the nearest place I could buy my own motion activated cameras. The Cabela's store near Olympia carried two models, each with infrared capability so they could take pictures in the dark. I hopped back in the Malibu for the two hour drive to Cabala's. Buying two of the lower priced cameras would use up more than three hundred dollars of my remaining cash, plus I needed money to buy gas. I hit an ATM near Olympia that I thought was far enough away from Packwood to be moderately safe to disguise my location, if they didn't already know it.

I got five-hundred cash, and after I paid for a tank of gas, bought two cameras, two 32 GB memory cards, and batteries. I barely had enough money left to pay for a fast food lunch to eat in the car while driving back to Zeke's.

The cameras were camo colored and had straps for easy attachment to a tree. I inserted the memory cards and batteries – being careful not to put them in backwards – and attached one to a tree that had good view of the front door and the other one high on a post on the porch, giving it a view of the carport and front yard.

The more I thought about the near certainty that someone had bugged Zeke's place the madder I got, mostly mad at myself for underestimating my adversaries. The feds have easy access to highly sophisticated surveillance equipment, much more sophisticated than the simple camera I had found in the carport. Their equipment would certainly transmit audio and video to a comfortable command center in real-time, probably using cellular technology like the OnStar system in my Malibu.

However, unless their equipment had large capacity batteries it would need an AC power source to recharge them, and that meant it would be connected to Zeke's power.

I examined Zeke's electrical panel but didn't find any extraneous wiring. Following that I embarked on a room by room search, removing every outlet cover, switch cover, and light fixture. I took the back off the toaster, microwave, clock, lamp, telephone, and every other appliance in my search for bugs. I found microphones in both phones and a miniature camera hidden in the table lamp beside Zeke's easy chair. Each of the devices was powered by a battery and was also connected to AC power to keep the batteries charged. I gathered the devices up and took them out to the carport where I laid them on Zeke's splitting block and pulverized them with his splitting maul. I must admit destroying them was therapeutic.

Not being certain I had found and destroyed all the bugs, I left the house and walked down the driveway before calling Joan on the prepaid phone. She didn't answer so I waited ten minutes before calling back. She answered right away, "Hi, David."

"Hi. What's up at Braxter?"

"Nothing new."

"I think you were right and it wasn't the feds who planted the camera. It was too low tech. However, I searched the place and found some bugs that weren't low tech. The feds must have planted them. I'm thinking two different folks paid me a visit, so I don't know who has the disks."

"I've got to tell Gross."

"Let's think this through."

"There's not much to think about. I authorized you to have the disks, but now you don't. They probably contain top-secret information, and we don't know who has them. It's my duty to report it, and I've got to do it ASAP. They're going to crucify you." I realized that it was no longer David and Joan against the feds; it was every man for himself.

"Yeah. You're right on both accounts. I want to talk to Gross face to face. I can get there by eight tomorrow morning. Can you schedule the meeting with him? Don't take 'no' for an answer."

"I'll try."

"See you then."

I set my alarm for five o'clock the next morning to give myself enough time to drive from Packwood to Vancouver and arrive just before eight.

Twenty-three

I woke up at four fifty eight, disabling the alarm on my phone just a minute before its chimes started their obnoxious ringing. I staggered to the bathroom and took a quick shower before pulling on a pair of khaki slacks and a blue oxford shirt and slipping on a pair of brown loafers. I skipped coffee and promised myself a quick stop at the first open gas station to buy a large cup and a donut or two. I fretted like a repeat offender at his sentencing hearing as I drove down to Braxter. The dark sky with its threatening rain matched my mood. It didn't look like the voicemail I saved of Joan authorizing me to take the disks was going to save my butt. Joan was right when she said she had authorized me to have the hard disks in my possession, but she didn't authorize me to lose them. I couldn't imagine what Gross would try to do to me, but I could imagine he would thoroughly enjoy doing it.

I briefly considered skipping out on the meeting. Although it was tempting, blowing the meeting off would just delay the inevitable and extend a morning of fretting into days of anxiety. I drove into Braxter's parking lot at a quarter to eight and was able to snag a spot near the front door because most people hadn't yet arrived. I opened the trunk to stow my laptop when I remembered that I hadn't looked at the memory card I removed from the camera planted behind the fascia board. I got back in the car to stay out of the light rain and took a quick look at the pictures before heading inside.

I signed in at the front desk, and the security guard called for Joan to escort me to the Braxter area. She arrived five minutes later and reservedly shook my hand. Her bloodshot eyes and sagging shoulders told me I wasn't the only one worrying. I asked her how I should expect Gross to react during the meeting. She bit her bottom lip and faintly shook her head back and forth as if to say, "I don't know, but it's going to get ugly." Joan, my former ally, had cut me lose, or worse, she had made me the scapegoat in an attempt to save her job. Without saying a word she made it clear I was on my own.

She led me into a no-frills conference room furnished with steel and Formica furniture that was common and perhaps even stylish in the sixties. Gross and Tinker were already seated on one side of the table, waiting. Joan took a seat at the head of the table, leaving me one of the two chairs facing Gross and Tinker. Before sitting down, I extended my hand across the table to the flattops, but neither stood up to shake it. Gross pointed toward a chair across from them, and I sat down, ready for the interrogation. I looked around for some water to soothe my dry mouth and saw six bottles of water on a side table. I walked over to get myself a bottle, purposely not offering one to any of the others. I silently returned to my seat and didn't say anything, hoping this was one of those situations when the first one to speak loses.

Tinker sat there like the lapdog he was and leaned back in his chair, his lips pressed to keep from smiling. It was obvious he was looking forward to watching Gross ream me out. Gross shook his head disgustedly, a vein throbbing visibly in his forehead, and snorted. "Ms. French told us you lost eight hard drives containing top-secret information. I can't belie –"

"Define lost."

"I can't believe that you were so careless to –"

I leaned towards Gross and put a clenched fist on the table in front of me. "Define lost."

"You had them in your possession, probably illegally; you failed to secure them properly which allowed someone to take them."

I said, "First, there is no possibility that they were in my possession illegally. I was hired by Braxter to perform a security audit and to determine if sensitive documents had been leaked, and if so, to determine who leaked them. I'm sure Ms. French can provide a copy of my contract. I copied information to the disks with Ms. French's full knowledge and authorization. She provided the disks I copied the data onto and authorized me to remove materials from the premises. I have a recording of her authorizing me specifically to analyze the disks off site, and I had already taken the disks off site by the time you so tactfully informed me that my services were no longer needed here at Braxter."

Gross waved me off and said, "It's immaterial that you were authorized to have the disks. You knew that they contained top-secret information, information protected under ITAR. Any competent security professional would know of his responsibility to safeguard the information. Obviously you didn't. In addition to a substantial fine, you're likely to do some time in a federal penitentiary. At a minimum you'll never get another dime from the DoD or any of its prime contractors."

I folded my hands in front of me mostly to calm myself but also to keep my middle fingers from popping up like they were both itching to do. I could barely suppress a smile. I nodded towards Tinker and said, "Maybe Tinker and I can get adjoining cells because breaking and entering and conducting an unlawful search are big no nos." Both Tinker and Gross swallowed in unison, and Gross said, "Unfounded slander will hardly help your case."

I looked Tinker in the eyes and said, "Show me the signed warrant authorizing you to search Ezekiel Klein's house."

Tinker found his voice and said, "I don't know what you're talking about!"

"Maybe the time stamped pictures the security camera took of you going through the front door while carrying a large box will refresh your memory."

Gross looked at Tinker as if begging him to say, "Tell me he's bluffing."

Still looking Tinker in the eye, I repeated, "Show me the signed warrant!" I turned toward Gross and said, "Those eight hard disks were locked in a fireproof gun safe. Tinker broke into my house, picked the lock on the safe, stashed the drives in the box he used to transport his hidden cameras and microphones into the house, and walked out the front door. I have pictures of that, too."

Tinker had a deer-in-the-headlights look, and Gross must have realized I wasn't bluffing. A flush spread across his cheeks. "Perhaps I've been a little hasty with my accusations."

Joan interjected, "Gerald, I told you David wouldn't be careless with the drives."

I glared at her and said, "Joan, just shut up and stay out of it. Friends like you, I don't need."

She replied, "David, don't be –"

Gross sneered at her and said, "Ms. French, please be quiet."

He looked back at me. "As I was saying, I may have been a little hasty and have momentarily lost sight of the fact that all of us have the same objective; we want to stop the leak and bring the perpetrators to justice."

"I want that, but I also want my business to be on the DoD's short list of preferred service providers."

"I can't promise that."

"Just keep it in mind because I think it's in your best interest to work with me. Joan told me you recently intercepted copies of three specs as they were being sent to an undetermined recipient. I need for us to take a look at them."

Tinker said, "That's not possible," but Gross gave him the evil eye and ordered him to go get them.

While Tinker was retrieving the files and a computer to view them Gross said, "I need those pictures you claim to have of Tinker."

"They're securely locked up; and not in the gun safe. Right now those pictures are the only thing standing between me and your threats, so I'll hang on to them."

Tinker returned with the computer and a memory stick containing the three files. He opened up the file explorer and I pointed to the file named *IMG_0041_1.jpg* and asked Tinker to open it with Word. He opened it to find nothing but the same gibberish I had found earlier. Tinker said, "I sent this file to our forensic lab in DC. They are working on it and promised to have it decoded in three weeks."

"I'll email the program I wrote to decode it. You'll have it by tomorrow. Now, please open the other two files."

Tinker opened them and smugly said, "These are the specs Matson had on his computer. They're our smoking gun."

"Let me take a closer look so I can see whose fingerprints are on your smoking gun. They may not be Matson's. I scrolled to the bottom of the first page of the document and clicked the mouse where the footer should have been. The fine line I knew to be the Easter egg was highlighted in blue. I winked at Joan and told Gross, "Last week, Braxter issued a new release of all of the Kilroy specs. We did this so the perp would believe he needed the latest specs because the earlier versions were obsolete. But we added a little something extra to each of the documents; an Easter egg to tell us who last had custodianship of the specs. The specs in Braxter's control were marked one way, and the specs that were sent to the Army were marked another way."

Tinker said, "It looks like the Easter egg in this document hatched into a chick and walked away."

I said, "It may look that way to you, but if you were an experienced Easter egg hunter you'd know to keep looking." I changed the highlighted line's font size from one point to 16 points, and it clearly said, *"Property of the US. Army – Do not copy."*

I grinned at Joan and continued my explanation, "This spec came from the Army, not from Braxter. If you want to examine all of the current Kilroy specs in the Army's possession you will find this footer on each and every one of them. If you examine the Kilroy specs on Braxter's servers you will find a different footer."

Joan leaned back in her chair, a smile slowly appearing on her face, a smile that quickly became a grin. Tears of relief ran down her cheeks.

Gross said, "Not so fast. This doesn't prove anything! We know that all of the specs, including the copies sent to the Army, originated here at Braxter. Can you prove that this spec came from the Army?"

"I think I can, but first I'm going to have my attorney write a statement that exonerates me from any wrong doing. Once you sign it, I'll show you all the proof I have."

Tinker looked as dejected as a top seed in a tennis tournament who had been ousted by an unknown. I loved it.

I turned to Gross and said, "Unless you have any more questions, I'm going to instruct my attorney to draft the exonerating statement and then take four well-earned days off." I turned to Joan and said, "Please escort me out."

As we walked to the front, Joan said, "David, I never doubted you. I knew you'd find a way to prove our innocence and our competence."

"Is that why you let me face the wolves alone?"

"I really didn't have a choice."

"We always have a choice."

She took my hand before I walked out past the turnstile and said, "I hope there aren't any hard feelings."

I let go of her hand, and looking back over my shoulder as I walked out said, "No hard feelings, but remember this isn't over yet. We still haven't caught the perp. If you trust me, I expect your full support; this time until the very end."

I made it back to the Malibu by eight-forty-five and drove to Portland to kill two or three hours before going to the airport to pick up Julie.

TWENTY-FOUR

After parking my car on the fifth floor of a Smart Park lot, I used United Airline's app to confirm Julie's ETA and then walked to the Pioneer Place Mall to shop. I wanted to surprise Julie with something nice and looked at several chic handbags and a beautiful necklace, but thought they were too personal for the current state of our relationship. I wandered into a store specializing in products from the Northwest and bought her a bright red Pendleton Rainier National Park blanket as a nice souvenir of our upcoming trip to the park. The clerk carefully folded it and placed it into a plastic tote bag.

I left the mall to roam the surrounding area and happened into a wine shop dedicated to Oregon wines. I bought two different Pinot Noirs and a cork screw, in case Zeke didn't have one. I carefully cocooned the wine bottles in the blanket for the walk back my car. Twenty-five minutes later I was in at the airport terminal, eagerly watching for Julie.

I spotted her in the distance as she briskly walked from her arrival gate toward the main terminal. Her ponytail swayed back and forth and her trim figure exuded energy; my pulse quickened. She looked up and I waved my hand high above the other travelers. Her face lit up fueling hope that she had missed me. As soon as she passed through the security gate, I took her roller board and gave her a discreet hug and savored her perfume. She wore my favorite fragrance; a very promising sign.

Julie thanked me for the first class tickets as we walked over the sky bridge to the parking garage, and she told me about her conversation with the sixty-five year old lady who sat next to her on the flight from Chicago to Portland. "She lost her husband, whom she described as a bloated couch potato, three years earlier. They were both sixty-two and overweight at the time. Lois, that's her name, set a goal to lose sixty-five pounds and get in good enough shape to climb Rainier by the time she was sixty-five. She joined a gym, hired a personal trainer and started working out five days a week. By the end of the first year, she had lost fifty pounds and could run three miles without stopping. By the end of the second year, she had lost seventy pounds and ran her first half marathon. Then she joined a trekking club near where she lived in North Carolina and started backpacking in the Great Smokey Mountains. Last spring she signed up with a Mount Rainier guide service to take a skills seminar and then climb the mountain. Now she is ready to do it. I want to be like her when I'm in my sixties."

"Wait until you meet Carl, Zeke's neighbor. He's in his sixties and can hike circles around me. I think you'll like him and Angie, his wife. If it's okay with you, I'll ask them to go hiking with us. They would be like having our own personal tour guides."

Being with Julie again was at the same time wonderful and awkward; awkward because my arms yearned to embrace her as before. We got into the car and headed out for Packwood, where I had reserved a roomy suite for her at the Butter Butte Lodge. Julie sat pensively for about ten minutes, watching the scenery, and then said, "I was thinking about the first time we met."

I recalled the cold February afternoon in Boston perfectly. Winchester Investments' Audit Committee was tired of incessant squabbling among each functional area's audit staff and ordered all of the stakeholders to attend what was essentially an attitude adjustment session. The mandatory meeting included multiple representatives from financial audit, regulatory compliance, HR compliance, and information security. Everyone else was seated at the conference room table when Julie entered, ten minutes late. The Audit Committee chairman had just finished chewing out Mr. Harris, the VP of HR, for being five minutes late. I expected him to give Julie her due earful, but she smiled and apologized for being late, saying the taxi driver had trouble with the snow. The chairman nodded and then opened the meeting. I hear cops give cute girls a break, too. Life can be so unfair.

Each went around the table and introduced ourselves and presented an overview of our audit responsibilities. Everyone in the room paid close attention to Julie's report on the financial controls. No one cared a whit about my report about the security audit.

I said, "During the big audit meeting at Winchester Investments?"

Julie replied, "Uh-huh. I didn't know the first thing about information security. You sounded like such a nerd."

"I thought you were a boring bean counter; kinda cute, but boring. However, I made a mental note to remember your name."

We both laughed.

I remembered how I had the foresight to reserve a cab to pick me up outside the Winchester lobby at five twenty, just after the meeting was scheduled to end. Julie hadn't made a reservation, and when she called for a cab the dispatcher told her it would be a two hour wait because of the snow. I overheard her ask the dispatcher if there was any way to get a cab sooner. When she frowned, I gallantly offered to share my cab. I think she knew it was a come on, but her only alternative was to wait two hours in the chilly lobby. She accepted my offer, and we chatted about the meeting as our cab crawled through downtown Boston. I asked for one of her business cards before she got out at her office. A week later, I worked up the nerve to call and ask her to meet for coffee. To my surprise she accepted.

Julie said, "Oh. I heard, unofficially of course, that they're making me a partner, the first female partner in two years."

"Congratulations! I'm not surprised."

"Thank you... I think... It's bitter sweet. I like the recognition – I've earned it, and the extra money will be nice. My annual bonus will double. But, I don't want to bury myself in a career, even one I love. There's more to life than work. At least I hope so."

I didn't know what to say. "It'll work out. Just give it time."

"Hey, tell me about this mysterious uncle. Zeke, is it?"

"Yep. Zeke. He was my Dad's older brother. Zeke went away to college at Berkeley and became a born-again Christian. He came home and dropped the bomb on my Jewish grandfather, who went nonlinear. Zeke didn't even spend the night. Grandpa disowned him on the spot and then dumped him right back at the airport. It cost Zeke millions. He was only two years away from gaining access to a huge trust fund – something north of three million – big bucks back then.

"Grandpa forbade Dad from ever contacting Zeke, and he never did. He tried to forget about Zeke, but always believed he had betrayed him. Grandpa also ordered Grandma not to contact Zeke, but she found ways to visit him without Grandpa's knowledge. They all kept Zeke a secret from me, so I never met him – except once when I was at Disney World with Grandma. Zeke pretended to be a friend of her's, and we spent the afternoon with him.

"Zeke didn't have any kids and somehow developed an affinity for me. Grandma filled him in on my life, and he even watched my MIT graduation from a distance. Zeke died a few months ago and left his estate to me. It isn't worth a lot, and may be more trouble than its worth. Since I was in the area, relatively speaking, I wanted to check it out and learn what I could about him.

"Carl and Angie were his neighbors for years, and Carl was Zeke's best friend. Carl's been willing to tell me what he can about Zeke so I've gotten to know them. Their daughter, Carolyn, was Zeke's attorney."

"To think I thought your family was perfect."

"Julie, this whole Zeke thing has shaken me up a bit, has gotten me thinking, and has changed my expectations."

"How so?"

"I haven't sorted it out, but I have started to feel very alone. It's more than you and me splitting up. I've got plenty of money, a growing business, challenging work, but no close friends, friends I would give an arm and a leg to help, friends I could open up with and talk about something besides the weather and sports."

"Did you ever have a friend like that?"

I quickly thought back about my school friends and roommates. There were plenty of friends, but all were friendships of convenience. As long as our interests aligned we had a good time. But if one of those friends needed something from me that wasn't convenient, I dodged him. A true friend wouldn't balk at an inconvenience.

"No, but until recently it didn't bother me. I thought it was normal."

Julie turned to look and me. "I hate to rub salt in an old wound, but traveling nearly every week isn't conducive to deep relationships, especially if you spend half the time you're at home writing reports."

"Yeah. I know, but at least I'm busy." I laughed, "Busy and friendless has got to be better than bored and friendless."

We sat silently for a few more miles. I don't think either one of us wanted to delve deeper into a philosophical conversation. I said, "Packwood doesn't have any first rate restaurants. I thought we could barbeque some steaks; maybe buy a salad and bake a couple of potatoes. How does that sound to you?"

"It sounds great, but I don't want to wait so long. I'm starving. Let's sample the local cuisine even if it is less than stellar."

We stopped at my regular watering hole, Duffy's Grill, for an early dinner; not so early for Julie because she was on east coast time, but early for me. However, I skipped lunch and was famished. Julie set her eye on a veggie burger, but changed her mind when I suggested she try the elk burger. While we waited for our meals I told her about my episode with Gigantor and his harem and explained that since then I was on a mission to eat as many elk as possible. "Just doing my part to keep the streets safe."

She chuckled. "I've been to Colorado and spent five days backpacking in the Rockies, but haven't been to Washington before. What's the plan for tomorrow and Wednesday?"

"Nothing firm, but I thought we could hike in the Park on both days. The weather forecast is primo, and Carl said the wild flowers are still out."

"Sounds like fun."

"Let's stop by Carl and Angie's to get their recommendation. If it's okay with you, we can invite them along for one of the days – probably tomorrow."

"Okay, but let's not stay too long. I'm beat."

I probably should have told the Andersons Julie was coming for a visit, but didn't because I wanted to save myself embarrassment if she changed her mind and cancelled at the last minute. We turned off the highway and drove up the driveway. When we got to the "Y" I pointed to Zeke's place. "My new estate is at the end of that driveway; the house and eight acres. I'd like to show it to you. Maybe tomorrow night, when you're not so tired."

We turned towards the Anderson's and headed down their driveway. Angie and Carl were sitting in their porch chairs, each drinking a glass of wine. They waved, and I parked the car. They stood up as Julie and I walked over to them. I said, "Carl, Angie, this is Julie, a good friend of mine from Boston. I invited her to come out and enjoy a few days exploring Mount Rainier."

Carl and Julie shook hands, and Angie gave Julie a hug. Angie invited us inside to sit and said, "We would offer you a glass of wine, but we just drank the last of it." I remembered the Pinot I stashed in the trunk and said, "I just happen to have a bottle in the trunk. Hang on. I'll get it." In the one minute it took to get the wine, Angie and Julie had started chatting about the blanket Angie was knitting. Carl and I went into the kitchen, where I opened the bottle and poured four glasses. We carried them to the living room and sat down.

I said, "I hate to interrupt your evening, but tomorrow and Wednesday, Julie and I want to explore Mount Rainier's highlights. I thought you could tell us the best places to go, and you're invited to join us."

Angie said, "Carl and I were just talking about hiking up to Shriner Peak. The huckleberries are ripe, and the bears will be feasting on them. Carl never has enough bear pictures. Why don't we spend the morning doing that, and then we can give you suggestions for some places to go in the afternoon if you have excess energy. The Grove of the Patriarchs is a must see."

Julie asked, "What's Shriner peak like?"

Carl replied, "It's about four miles uphill, but the payoff includes great views of Mt. Rainier and, hopefully, bear watching. Oh, and then four miles downhill. We can take it as slow as you like."

I knew Julie could handle the climb and was pleased when she said, "Sounds like a great idea."

We agreed to pick Carl and Angie up at eight to do the climbing in the morning. Carl said, "Firearms can't be used in the Park, and the rangers frown on people even carrying them, but I carry my Glock anyway. You can carry Zeke's pistol in your pack, but don't load the ammo clip into it. The rangers do more than issue a warning when they catch someone carrying a concealed, loaded weapon without a permit."

Julie frowned and said, "Do you really need guns?"

Carl replied, "I haven't yet, but if we accidentally get between a mad sow and her cubs I want to be able to make lots of noise."

We told Carl and Angie good night and agreed to pick them up the next morning. I took Julie to the lodge and helped her check in. She apologized for being a party pooper, but I told her not to worry. I wanted her to be well rested for our hiking.

TWENTY-FIVE

I left Zeke's place at five minutes before seven to meet Julie for breakfast before the hike. The beautiful morning enticed us to eat outside on the restaurant's deck. We were the only ones on the patio, I think because the sun hadn't yet taken the chill off of the early air. Our waiter was kind enough to wheel the patio heater to our table and ignite it. Julie seemed to enjoy the fresh air of the peaceful morning or maybe she sat quietly because she wasn't yet fully awake. I toyed with my omelet and let her experience the morning at her pace. After she finished eating her oatmeal and drinking a second cup of coffee, she asked me to wait for her in the lobby while she went to her room to freshen up.

When she returned, she pointed to her small daypack and said, "Snacks, water, and a new camera." As we were walking to the car, she spotted seven elk grazing in the next door neighbor's yard and stopped to take a few pictures. We pulled into the Anderson's just before eight, and they both came out, each carrying a day pack, and got in the car for the twenty minute drive to the trailhead. I pulled the car off of the highway and onto the shoulder, next to the sign marking the trail. Before starting out, we studied the large trail map on the sign. The trail initially ascended in a southerly direction, then circled the perimeter of Shriner Peak to the east before taking a 180° turn and heading back toward the western face of the mountain where multiple switchbacks zigged and zagged up the slope until the trail reached the abandoned fire lookout.

Angie apologized that she could only handle hiking four miles on a steep grade if she went slowly and rested every half hour or so. We all assured her we weren't in a hurry and asked her to set the pace; all following closely enough behind to be able to visit with one another. Angie and Julie passed the first two miles talking about their funny accounting experiences; Angie's as a bookkeeper at the mill, and Julie's as a public accountant. They say, "Busy hands make light work," but Angie seemed to discover that talkative lips could replace busy hands.

We soon found ourselves back on the west side of Shriner Peak with a fantastic view across a rugged valley far below us of Mt. Rainier. Carl suggested we take a slight detour to a nearby vista point and rest a while. In just a few minutes Angie announced she was ready to get back on the trail. We soon emerged from the woods onto the edge of a sloped meadow covered in what Angie said were huckleberries. I commented, "I thought huckleberries were red, not purple."

Carl's eyes were panning across the meadow as he said, "Some are, but up here most are Cascade huckleberries or Mountain huckleberries; both are blue or bluish purple. This clearing is loaded with both, and the bears love them." He pointed to two black spots in the distance. "Those are two bears eating berries." He pulled a pair of binoculars from his pack and focused on the bears before handing them to Julie, who watched the bears as they sauntered up the hill. Julie passed the glasses to me and whispered, "This is amazing. I feel like I'm on a safari."

I watched the bears with the glasses and saw them tear off branches with a swipe of their paws and cram the foliage into their chomping mouths. Not the daintiest eaters I had ever seen; they reminded me of Fred, one of my college roommates. Suddenly, Julie shrieked and pointed to a large bear that had just walked out from behind a tree not more than fifteen yards away. The bear looked at us, but didn't appear to be disturbed by our presence. Carl pulled his camera from his pack, and I pulled Zeke's pistol from mine. Julie and Angie tip toed over behind me, as Carl snapped pictures. The bear occasionally glanced our way, but was much more interested in stocking up for the winter than he was in us. We watched him amble and eat until he was far enough away for us to continue up the trail without getting too close. I put the pistol back in my pack, and Carl did the same with his camera.

We hadn't been in any danger, but I think we all experienced an adrenaline rush, which made the steep ascent to the old fire lookout seem easy. The lookout was closed, but we climbed the steps up to the walkway bordering the lookout's entire second floor. From there we saw fantastic views of Rainier and a large section of lesser Cascade Mountains. Julie said, "This is breathtaking. I had no idea."

Carl said, "Zeke, he and I camped up here a couple of times. We'd come up in the late afternoon to watch the sun setting behind the mountain and then see the sunrise the next morning."

As we continued to absorb the scenery, Angie mentioned to me, "By the way, when I was walking out to the highway on my way to check the mail earlier last week, I saw a car I didn't recognize driving up to Zeke's place. Were you expecting a visitor?"

Between the feds and whoever planted the cheapo camera I wasn't surprised Angie had noticed some activity. "No... Was it a man or woman?"

"A man, maybe thirty-five years old."

"What was he driving?"

She turned to Carl and asked, "What kind of car do the Perkin's have?"

He replied, "A Ford Taurus."

Angie looked back to me and said, "It was a blue Taurus."

Until Angie's comment about seeing a stranger at Zeke's, I had successfully blocked work from my mind and had given all of my attention to Julie, and I didn't want to blow the opportunity to reestablish our relationship. But since we all were hiking down the trail to the car without much talking, I let my mind return to the problems at Braxter. The fact that someone had added two files to Karl Matson's computer while he was out with his ill baby suggested the perp was an insider who wanted to frame Karl. But, the Easter eggs in the two files suggested the perp was someone in the Army. I hoped the entry records kept by the security guards would resolve the mystery.

We made it back to the trailhead by one o'clock so I offered to buy everyone lunch at Duffy's. As we neared Packwood and regained cell coverage, my phone beeped, telling me I had a message. When we pulled into Duffy's, I lagged behind and saw it was a text from Joan saying, "Call me ASAP." I joined Julie and the Andersons at an outside table under a shade umbrella. A few minutes later, buxom Rita came to our table, winked at me, and took our lunch orders. I told the others, "I just got an urgent message from my client. I hate to be rude, but I've got to make a quick call. Please excuse me."

Julie frowned. I imagined her thinking *David is never going to change.*

I went back out to the car and called Joan. "What's the emergency?"

She snapped, "What took you so long to call back?"

"I was out of range."

"Remember asking for the records of who was in the building early last Monday morning?"

It looked like I would finally get the last missing piece to the puzzle. "Did you get them?"

"I just got the logs from the head security guard this morning. Nobody from Braxter's Kilroy team was in the building during the time slot you gave me, but get this; Sam Tinker was. The night guard remembered it, too. It was just after one in the morning. He said Tinker told him he had forgotten his blood pressure medicine at his desk and needed to get it. The guard said Tinker didn't return for twenty minutes, which seemed a long time for Tinker just to go to his desk and back."

My mind raced ahead trying to process the implications. "That explains the Easter eggs. Tinker was probably leaking the Army's copies of the specs all along. When the Army's Defense Security Service intercepted the documents, Tinker tried to steer suspicion away from the Army by implicating Braxter."

"Makes sense."

Hoping I could be the one to tell Gross and rub his nose in it, I asked, "Have you told Gross?"

"When you didn't call back right away, I called him. He didn't believe it until he called the security guard who was on duty that morning. He still has some doubts because Tinker apparently does have high blood pressure, but Gerald wants to bring Tinker in for questioning. The problem is Tinker has gone off the grid."

"Maybe Tinker is out of cell range like I was."

"Maybe yes; maybe no. Gross said their policy is everyone is on call 24/7 unless time off is authorized. He's concerned that Tinker may be coming after you."

"After me?"

"Yeah, and according to Gross, Tinker has special ops training."

"I know I pissed him off, but why would he come after me?"

"You told them you had evidence that could prove the specs came from the Army. If Tinker can destroy your proof that the two files were added to Matson's drive while only Tinker could have done it, then there won't be any hard evidence against him. His story about the blood pressure medicine would stand up."

"I'll be careful."

"Gross told me to tell you he needs to see those events log files. He needs to see the discrepancy himself."

I knew that if Gross got the log files from Theron, then Tinker wouldn't have a reason to come after me. "He can get the originals from Theron."

"I told him that very thing at nine o'clock this morning. He called back at eleven and said the disk from the backup server has been removed. He called Theron, and Theron confirmed that he told Tinker about the backup server yesterday morning.

Looks like Tinker stole the disk. We'll probably never find it. David, you have the only hard evidence. You'd better be more than careful."

"Tell Gross I have the disks hidden in Packwood and ask him to get up here with a couple of his people as soon as possible. I'll turn them over to him, but remind him I expect him to sign the release my attorney is preparing."

"I'll call him right away."

"Text me with the time he expects to get here."

"Okay."

I hung up and took a couple of deep breaths as I tried to decide on my next step. The easiest thing would be to do nothing and to hope Tinker was on his way to Mexico, not to Packwood. Or maybe he was on his way to China or whatever country was paying him to commit treason. I hoped he liked Chinese food. Or maybe he was afraid if they learned he'd been discovered, they would try to silence him before he could finger them.

I walked back into Duffy's just as Rita served our burgers and drinks. I sat down and announced, "I have a big problem." Julie looked over at me as to say *"What's new? When did your work become a problem for you?"* I continued, "That was my client from Vancouver. Someone stole top-secret, military information from them and is apparently selling it; we think to China. I've been working with our government to identify the traitor, and I have the only evidence that can put him away. It's locked in Zeke's floor safe."

Julie said, "It sounds like you're the hero and can leverage this to grow your business. What's the big problem?"

Hoping the Anderson's didn't notice the sarcasm in her voice, I said, "The problem is they can't find the suspect. His name is Tinker, Samuel Tinker. Tinker knows about Zeke's place, and the feds think he may come up here to destroy the evidence; proof that would both convict him and save my client's Army contract. Of course, that's complete speculation, but just to be safe they're sending a team up here to intervene and secure the evidence. But, they won't arrive for several hours. The big problem is if I stay away from Zeke's, Tinker may find the floor safe and steal the evidence. If I go to Zeke's, and Tinker shows up, it could get ugly, very ugly."

They were each half way through their lunches by the time I filled them in on my problem. I took a bite of my lukewarm burger, and Carl said, "There's only one thing to do; we go up there and safeguard the evidence."

I replied, "Carl, I can't let you get involved. It's too risky."

Ignoring me completely he said, "Here's what we'll do. We drive in the back way to my house so no one will see or hear us going down the driveway. Angie and Julie will stay at our place, where they'll be safe. I'll camo up and sneak over to Zeke's through the woods and get into position to cover you with my Glock. David, you give me forty-five minutes to case the place and get into position and then you drive over to Zeke's like you don't have a care in the world. If Tinker's there, I'll have the drop on him. If he isn't there then I got some extra stalking practice for elk hunting."

"Carl, it's too dangerous."

"Trust me. He won't even know I'm there, unless I want him to."

I shook my head from side to side, but reluctantly agreed with Carl's plan. "Okay, but I'm taking my pistol, too."

I paid our bill, leaving Rita a generous tip, wishing she would use it to buy a blouse that fit properly, but knowing she wouldn't. Carl directed me along the route to get close to his place via the back way, and I wondered what awaited us.

TWENTY-SIX

I drove the car up a pot-hole ridden forest service road that wound through the woods behind Zeke and Carl's places. Carl pointed to a wide spot alongside the road and said, "Pull over there. We'll need to hoof it from here." Carl led us through the woods, and it's a good thing he knew the way, because we weren't following a path, not even a game trail. Carl pointed to a faded survey stake and said, "We just crossed the boundary onto our property. I know our property and Zeke's too, like the back of my hand. Zeke and I used to put on our camo and challenge the high school youth group from the church to an annual paintball contest. It was usually eight or ten boys against Zeke and me. Zeke, he and I never lost. Although one year, Zeke accidentally belly crawled over an underground wasp nest. A swarm stung him more times than he could count. He jumped up running and yelling like a banshee, and one of the boys nailed him. But I nailed that boy and all of his buddies."

When we got to the Anderson's, Carl disappeared upstairs. When he returned he looked like the poster child for camo gear; a camo balaclava covered his entire head, except for a small opening around his eyes, brown and green paint covered all the skin that was visible through the eye opening, a matched long sleeved tee shirt and pants covered the bulk of his body, and camo gloves, socks and boots covered the rest. I joked, "Don't get lost because if you do, nobody will be able to find you." He strapped on his camo holster and pistol and headed out the front door saying, "Don't leave for forty-five minutes."

I checked my watch and then said, "Angie, I shouldn't have gotten Carl involved in this. It's dangerous, and if anything happens to him it'll be my fault."

Angie replied, "You tried to stop him, but there isn't much Carl wouldn't do for you because Zeke was such a good friend to Carl and because Zeke and Carl prayed nearly every week for you since you were little. None of us could stop him, but we can pray for him."

Julie and I glanced at each other, and I think both of us wished we could camo up and disappear. Angie noticed our expressions and smiled. "Don't worry. I'll do the praying." She held our hands and started praying like she was talking with a good friend. "Heavenly Father, we don't know what could happen, maybe nothing, but You know all things. We ask you to watch over Carl and David. Protect them from harm. Help them to use good judgment. We ask these things in the wonderful name of your Son, Jesus. Amen."

Julie gave my hand a little squeeze, and I looked at my watch; thirty more minutes, an eternity. I felt like a bride groom waiting for the wedding ceremony to start. However, that would have been even scarier. I paced around the living room and rubbed my hands together. Julie said, "David, you're making me nervous. Either sit down or go outside and take a walk." I opted for the latter and headed out the front door to burn off my excess energy. I walked the opposite direction from Zeke's to make sure I didn't disturb Carl. I turned around after ten minutes and headed back to the house. I put Zeke's Springfield Armory pistol into the waistband of my pants, in the small of my back, covered it with my shirt tail, and looked at my watch. As I headed for the front door, I turned to Julie and Angie and said, "Call 911 if you hear any gun shots, and stay here."

Angie hollered after me, "Don't worry about us. I'm going to get my rifle, and don't think I don't know how to use it."

I backtracked to where we had left the car and drove down the forest service road to get back to the Highway and head up to the turnoff to Zeke's. I remember the two cameras I had set up to watch Zeke's place and regretted not telling Carl about them. He might have been able to sneak a look at them and see if anyone had been nosing around. I slowed the car to five miles per hour so I could search for anything out of the ordinary, but didn't see anything unusual until I arrived at Zeke's house. A dark SUV was parked by the car port and Tinker was sitting on the porch in one of Zeke's chairs like he owned the place. He was dressed in jeans and a plaid shirt, and was wearing a baseball cap. With his flat top hidden by the cap, Tinker almost looked like a normal guy.

I checked to make sure the pistol was in place and covered by my shirt and got out of the car. Tinker gave me a little wave, and I walked over to face him. "Samuel, what brings you all the way up to Packwood?"

"Gross sent me. He asked me to assure you that he's changed his opinion of you and is going to recommend you're on the short list to audit the security of companies contracting with the Army. He also wants you to give me the evidence you promised."

"There isn't any additional evidence. If you remember, I told Gross that after he signed a document clearing me of any wrongdoing, I would show him all the proof I have. I didn't say I had more proof. I said I would show him all I had.

There's a big difference, and I was very careful not to say I had additional proof. You can tell him to check the recording he made of the meeting."

"There is no recording."

"Yeah, there is. Neither you nor Gross were taking notes, and you both know neither of you are smart enough to remember everything said in the meeting. You recorded it." I hoped Tinker would believe me and leave without causing trouble. After all, if I didn't have more evidence, he didn't have anything to worry about. "It's too bad you drove all the way up here for nothing. Give my regards to Gross."

Tinker stood up as to leave and then quickly pulled a pistol from his back waistband. He aimed at my chest and said, "We both know you're too smart not to keep an ace in the hole until Gross signs the document from your lawyer. You have more evidence, and I'm not leaving without it. You can give it to me, and keep living, or you can keep your secret to the grave."

Just then Carl stepped out of the woods and stood within twenty feet of Tinker, his pistol aimed at Tinker's chest. Tinker's expression was one of disbelief, like he was seeing an apparition, a pistol toting phantom. Carl calmly said, "Drop your gun, or I drop you. Now!" I didn't doubt Carl was milliseconds away from pulling the trigger, and I don't think Tinker doubted it either. Tinker lowered his gun and bent over to place it on the porch floor.

Carl's pistol didn't waver as he said, "David, move his gun out of the way and then frisk him." I walked over to Tinker and keeping my eyes on him, I squatted to pick up his pistol. I backed up and put the pistol on the other chair. As I stepped towards Tinker to frisk him, I noticed a clear plastic tube coiled around his ear and realized he was wired for sound. I told Carl, "He's wired." Immediately Tinker said, "Shoot him." Without warning, Carl jumped behind me. I heard the unmistakable sound of a rifle shot, and Carl fell to his knees, dragging one hand down my back as he fell. Before I could react, Tinker made a quick move for his gun on the table. I heard another shot, this one deafening, and saw Tinker fall to the ground. Carl had shot him in the right shoulder before collapsing onto the porch.

I grabbed Tinker's pistol and ran for the edge of the deck, vaulted over the railing, and turned behind the corner of the house to put it between me and the unknown shooter. I heard another rifle shot, and felt wood chips from the house's siding brush past me. I was outgunned; two pistols that I had never even fired against a rifle. My best option was to circle around through the woods and try to sneak up behind the shooter. I ran deeper into the woods, making sure I kept the house between him and me. Once in the woods, I crawled out from behind the house to where I hoped to see the shooter. I kept moving until I saw the porch, carport, and the woods surrounding the carport. I found a good hiding place behind a clump of large ferns and waited, hoping Angie had heard the gunshots and called 911. I needed the police, and Carl needed medical attention.

I noticed movement on the porch and saw Tinker pull himself up to an upright position and lean against the side of the house. I felt like using him for target practice and would have, but I didn't want to reveal my position to the shooter. My position behind the ferns was well concealed from the carport and the woods, where I thought the shooter must have been; but it wasn't well concealed from Tinker. He pointed directly at me, and I saw his lips move as he said something into his hidden mic. I was afraid to move just in case the shooter hadn't seen me, but I knew I would be a sitting duck if he had.

I tried to hunker down a little lower and wait for the cops to arrive. However, I heard footsteps in the distance. The shooter was moving toward me, but I couldn't see him because of the trees between us. I needed him to get within thirty yards so I could have a reasonable chance to hit him with Zeke's pistol. I held my breath and saw him step behind a tree that was at least seventy-five yards away, too far for a pistol shot. I saw him look through his scope at the area around me. His scope quit moving. He was focused directly at me, but I didn't move a muscle hoping he hadn't zeroed in on me. I heard a rifle shot at the same time his rifle flew up into the air, and I saw him fall to his knees. Angie walked toward the downed shooter, never taking her rifle off him. He tried to stand, and Angie's rifle barked again. He fell to the ground. She walked over to him and poked him in the eye with her rifle's muzzle. His stillness seemed to convince her he was out of commission, if not dead.

I stood up and walked towards Tinker, keeping my pistol aimed in his direction. He put Carl's Glock on the floor and started yelling, "Don't shoot! Don't shoot! I'm not armed." I walked over to him and pistol whipped him into unconsciousness with one hit.

Angie looked towards the porch and saw Carl lying prone. She ran to him and hugged him and begged. "Carl, hang on. Help will be here soon."

In case Angie and Julie hadn't already done so, I called 911 and told them to send an Air Rescue helicopter because we had an injured federal officer; we didn't really have an injured officer, but I wanted them to rush. I gave them the address and told them to land the chopper at the graveled intersection where Zeke's and Carl's driveways diverged. Next, I called Julie and told her to find a first aid kit and bring it to Zeke's as fast as she could.

A cacophony of distant sirens announced help was on the way. Gross and two of his sidekicks, the Packwood Fire and Rescue unit, and the Lewis County Sheriff all arrived virtually at once. EMTs jumped out of the rescue unit, and I pointed them to Carl. They immediately checked his vital signs and worked to stop his bleeding and stabilize him.

The Lewis County Sheriff did his best to secure the area and preserve the crime scene, but his distraught expression told me he knew he was in over his head. I overheard him radio the State Patrol and tell them to send officers and their forensics team. Gross overheard him, too, and said, "Don't bother with extra manpower. This is a matter of national security, and the federal marshals will be here in a few minutes." It was going to look like a law enforcement convention; I hoped to see Tommy Lee Jones.

I heard the Air Rescue helicopter approaching low and fast, and ran down to the area to show them where I wanted them to land so they wouldn't waste valuable time. It landed, and the paramedics and I ran back to the house while carrying the stretcher. When we reached the porch, the head Air Rescue EMT asked, "Which one is the federal officer?" I nodded toward Carl, and Gross purposefully looked the other way and played dumb. The paramedics stabilized Carl the best they could, started an IV, and loaded him on the stretcher to carry him to the chopper. Angie trotted along beside them, and the paramedics helped her board the helicopter for the ride to the Seattle Trauma Center.

I wanted to ride in the chopper to the trauma center so I could comfort Angie while she was waiting to hear Carl's prognosis. However, Gross had other ideas. "David, you can't leave until the marshals arrive and get your complete statement. Judging from the carnage here, it's going to take hours, maybe until tomorrow morning."

"Gerry, can I call you Gerry?" Gross nodded and I continued. "Gerry, Carl Anderson saved my life. He didn't hesitate but immediately jumped between the shooter and me. His wife is scared to death that he won't make it. I need to be with them."

"Sorry, you are the only eye witness I can trust. You're staying put. You can't shoot people up and expect to go merrily on your way."

The chopper took off, making our argument moot, and Julie came over to stand beside me. As the chopper's sound faded in the distance, the Packwood Fire and Rescue loaded Tinker into their unit. Gross told one of his sidekicks to ride along to ensure Tinker didn't somehow escape custody.

"I didn't shoot anyone. Angie did, but not me, and she's going merrily on her way, if you want to call it merrily."

"She what?"

I pointed in the direction of the shooter and said, "She shot the guy over there who shot Carl. Twice."

282

"I shouldn't have let her leave. The marshals are going to read me the riot act."

"Yup," I said with no small measure of smug satisfaction. I added, "Gerry, can you have someone drive Julie to the trauma center to be with Angie? It's not right for Angie to be alone."

"Can Julie be trusted to keep an eye on Angie to make sure she doesn't run off?"

"Absolutely!"

"Good. She'll be a pseudo deputy. I'll ask one of the State Patrol officers to drive her. In the meantime, you wait here for the marshals."

TWENTY-SEVEN

The local police seemed to understand the importance of preserving the crime scene until the Marshals arrived; they wouldn't let me go on the porch or into the house. I sat on the hood of the Malibu, where I could watch and listen and maybe learn something new about Tinker or the shooter. While I waited, two federal marshals arrived in the requisite full-sized SUV with its dark, tinted windows, emergency lights, and multiple antennas. To my disappointment, neither of the marshals barked out orders like Tommy Lee Jones. The apparent person in charge was a middle-aged, petite blond woman dressed in blue jeans and a short sleeved golf shirt worn under a sleeveless vest striped with reflective material. The words *US Marshal* were emblazoned on the back. The other marshal, in his late thirties, also wore jeans, a golf shirt, and an official vest, but he also wore dark shades and a cool baseball cap with *Department of Justice – United States Marshal* printed on an official looking emblem. I coveted that cap.

Gross introduced himself to the Marshals, and the three of them talked in hushed voices for several minutes, before the two marshals left Gross and huddled with the local law enforcement. The local boys, seemingly dismissed by the marshals, shrugged their shoulders and drifted towards their vehicles and drove away. Gross walked over to me and said, "David, you need to cooperate fully here so we can get to the bottom of Braxter's leak and minimize the damage."

"It's the Army's leak; not Braxter's. I told you I would cooperate after you signed a document absolving me of any wrongdoing."

"Give me the document, and I'll sign it."

"Gerry, I don't have it yet. My attorney is busy."

"David, that's your problem. I need you to cooperate; starting right now."

Everything in me wanted to make Gross beg, but I decided it would be smarter to cultivate him as an ally. "I'll cooperate, but I need you to help me get more business with the Army's prime contractors. Maybe we can scratch each other's back."

The marshals joined us, and Gross introduced me to Marshal Elizabeth Annex and to Marshal Alex Bass. "Elizabeth and Alex, this is David Klein. He is one of the good guys so try to ignore his abrasive manner." We shook hands, and Elizabeth asked, "Is there a comfortable place we can talk and still keep an eye on things until the forensics team gets here? This could take a while."

I pointed toward the front door. "We can go into the house."

Alex shook his head. "Can't go through the front until forensics is finished. Is there a back door?"

"Follow me." We went around to the back door, and I led them to the living room where we could make sure nobody disturbed the yard. We each took a seat, and I waited for the questioning to begin. Elizabeth started with innocuous background questions; What's your full name, what number can we reach you at, who owns the property, and when did the altercation start? Gross looked relieved as I provided straightforward and detailed answers. This obviously wasn't the first time Elizabeth and Alex had worked together because they seamlessly shared the questioning and made it seem like a casual conversation, not an interrogation. I hoped that Gross was learning a few things to add to his repertoire.

Elizabeth and Alex both pulled out notebooks, and Alex asked, "David, give us a summary of what happened here today. We can drill into the details later."

I didn't know how much background Gross had already provided and didn't want to assume he told them very much. "I was hired by Braxter, one of the Army's key suppliers, to help them determine if someone was stealing top-secret documents, and if so, to identify the insider who was doing it. I collected evidence implicating Samuel Tinker, Gross' lieutenant, from the Army Defense Security Service. Tinker thought I had enough evidence to convict him, and I suspected he might come up here to get it.

"I told Carl Anderson from next door about the possibility that Tinker would come here to steal evidence, and Carl wasn't willing to let Tinker get away with treason. Carl snuck through the woods with his pistol to watch the house and back me up in case Tinker arrived. I gave Carl time to get into position and then drove over here. Tinker was waiting for me on the porch. He asked for the evidence, and I told him I didn't have it. He pulled a gun on me. That's when Carl appeared. He made Tinker put down his gun. But then somebody shot Carl. As Carl was collapsing, he shot Tinker. I ran into the woods to elude the unknown shooter, but Tinker and the shooter found me and pinned me down. Just as it looked like the shooter was going to take me out, Angie, Carl's wife, shot him. Tinker knew he was outnumbered and gave himself up."

Elizabeth and Alex glared at Gross because his phone's obnoxious ringtone interrupted us. Gross walked into the kitchen to take the call while we waited. He returned in a few minutes and said, "That was the trauma center. Anderson made it there alive. He's in critical condition; they rushed him into surgery. They'll know more in a few hours, after he comes out of surgery, assuming he does."

Words couldn't begin to express the relief I experienced. The dam holding back my feelings crumpled, and a wave of emotion washed over me. I lowered my head and covered my face with my hands and sobbed. Despite my embarrassment, I couldn't stop. One wave subsided and other, not quite as powerful, followed it. Through my bleary eyes I noticed Gross and Alex squirm uncomfortably in their chairs. Elizabeth quietly walked out of the living room and returned a minute later bringing a box of tissues to me.

I finally stopped crying and wiped my eyes. "I'm so sorry. I didn't expect that to hit me so hard."

Elizabeth said, "Don't think anything of it. You've had a traumatic afternoon." But I knew that it was more than a traumatic afternoon. Carl didn't have to take a bullet for me. I was overwhelmed.

I said, "One more thing. Earlier in the week I installed two motion-activated cameras to watch the house. Normally they just take a picture every second when they detect movement. But I set them to record thirty seconds of video if they detect motion in five consecutive seconds. Each frame is time stamped. "I'll show you where they are. After you review them, I'll try to fill in any missing details."

The marshals went outside to talk with the forensics team and to collect the two cameras while Gross and I remained inside. I enjoyed watching Gross cross and then uncross his arms and clench and unclench his jaw, apparently unsure of whether he wanted to pat me on the back or wring my neck. He finally spoke, "David, as much as you have vexed me I'm quite impressed with your creative approach to information security. Those Easter eggs were simply genius. And, making a backup copy of all the user activity to compare with the official copy so you could identify deletions; that was genius too. I encourage my people to be innovative, but they always go by the book. I could use someone like you, in a senior role of course. New blood would be good for my team, and I just happen to have an opening."

"I appreciate the thought, but my style would drive you nuts. Plus, I want to keep Klein InfoSec Associates independent. Of course that would be very difficult if you indict me. But if you indict me, it will get difficult for you, too. My attorney is a litigious buzzard who smells the carrion of a potentially big lawsuit from miles away. He would only need a few minutes to make a list of the wrongs done by the Army; improper employee vetting and oversight, not to mention recklessly endangering my life and mental anguish."

"You're right. Your style is already driving me nuts. I'm trying to hand you an olive branch here. I promise to refer Klein InfoSec to other Army contractors, and we may even use you ourselves if we get too busy."

"I appreciate your support. But, what about Carl? He took a bullet. Assuming he lives, he may suffer permanent disability. My lawyer would love to get his hands on Carl's case."

"I'll see what we can do. I want to do the right thing; out of court."

As long a Gross was in a conciliatory mood, I kept pushing. "And then there's Braxter. How are you going to make things right with them?"

"Braxter is up to General Matthews. I'm just following his orders."

"Joan told me he's out to get Braxter."

"Seems that way, but if the Army was the source of the leak, it would be difficult for him to terminate Braxter's contract. However, he could easily activate the 'Second Source' clause. It gives him the sole authority to designate another supplier as a Kilroy second source. Braxter would be required to share their specs, manufacturing processes, suppliers, and their profits with another supplier."

"That'd be very short sighted. Several Braxter employees have been harmed by the Army's actions, and my att –"

"Yes. I can imagine your attorney would love to get his buzzard talons on cases like that."

"Exactly. You probably know Harold Barry filed a harassment claim against Braxter before quitting. When he learns that the Army, not Braxter, was the leak, I'll bet his attorney amends the suit to include the Army. Then there's Karl Matson. I can only imagine what his attorney will demand."

Gross unbuttoned the top button of his shirt. "I can't control what their attorneys might or might not do."

"You may want to suggest to Matthews that he get Harold and Karl back on the payroll, with back pay, maybe even a little bonus. He owes Joan an official commendation for her foresight in retaining an outside information security consultant. He needs to relax the contract dates for the next Kilroy release; extend the milestones to something very reasonable. Finally, he needs to forget about the Second Source clause. Of course, these are just my recommendations."

Gross leaned forward and sighed. "I'm going outside to see what the marshals have found." I tagged along a few steps behind him to stay in the loop. Elizabeth and Alex were both looking at a clipboard when we walked up. Without being asked, Elizabeth pointed toward the paramedics loading the dead shooter onto their gurney, "His name is Lawrence Tinker; we're assuming he's Samuel's brother. He's been convicted twice for grand larceny and multiple traffic violations. Nothing with a weapon, until today. We're still gathering information on him."

I asked, "Anything on the cameras?"

Alex replied, "There are a few gaps, but they captured almost everything; just like you said. Samuel Tinker was shot in self-defense so Carl Anderson is in the clear. It looks like Angie Anderson shot Lawrence to protect you, so she's in the clear. Of course, the DA may see it differently, but we won't recommend charges."

Gross asked, "Anything else?"

"Tinker, Samuel, is in surgery and expected to make a full recovery. We should be able to start interrogating him tomorrow."

I touched Elizabeth on her shoulder and asked, "Can I go to Seattle, to the trauma center?"

"She nodded. "But keep your phone with you."

"Before I go, I have two disks containing important evidence implicating Tinker. Who gets them?" Gross and Elizabeth simultaneously said, "Me."

I turned to go into the house and said, "I'll get them while you two sort it out." When I returned with the disks, Elizabeth reached for them, and when Gross didn't object; I gave them to her.

I returned to the house to pack my suitcase and then took off for Seattle, anxious to learn how Carl was doing.

TWENTY-EIGHT

My phone's navigation app told me the fastest way to reach Seattle was to drive around the back side of Mt. Rainier using roads that were only open during the snow-free months. I sped through a number of small towns on country roads until I neared the Seattle metro area and its freeways. I arrived at the hospital in less than two hours, at nine fifteen. I parked the car in the hospital's parking structure and power walked to the information desk to get directions to the trauma center, which I was told was located on the second floor. I followed the signs to the family waiting room. Angie and Carolyn slouched next to each other on the long side of a small coffee table littered with old magazines, empty coffee cups, and wadded tissues. Julie sat with her back to the door at the end of the table. They all looked up at me as I quietly walked over to them. I swept the trash aside so I could sit on the table facing Angie.

I took Angie's hands in mine and said, "Angie, I am so very sorry. Any word?"

She sniffled and said, "He's still in the O.R. He's been in there for almost four hours, and they haven't told us a thing."

"Hopefully, that means they are busy saving his life."

Angie, Julie and I were still wearing the boots and clothes we had hiked in. Our morning hike to Shriner Peak seemed like it was days ago. Carolyn wore a tee shirt, jeans, and tennis shoes. No telling what she was doing when she got the call about her dad. Angie and Carolyn's red, puffy eyes renewed the guilt I felt about involving Carl with my problem. I didn't know what to say to either of them, and it didn't seem like the time to try and make small talk. I thumbed through a seven month old *People* magazine but didn't see a thing worth reading. A few minutes later, my growling stomach reminded me that I hadn't eaten anything since lunch. I said, "I need to get something to eat, can I bring back something for you?" Angie and Carolyn each shook their head, but Julie said, "I'll show you where the cafeteria is. It's at the other end of the hospital and hard to find."

I was surprised when Julie took my hand as we walked through the halls. She must have sensed how terrible I felt and how much my fragile emotions needed a comforting touch. I asked Julie, "How's Angie doing?"

"Seems to be holding herself together. I got here just before Carolyn arrived. When she saw Carolyn, they both lost it. They just held each other and bawled. Then I lost it, too. They pulled me into their hug, and we sobbed until we couldn't cry anymore. Two other people who were in the other side of the waiting room quietly slipped out to give us our space. While we were standing in each other's arms, Carolyn started praying God would spare her dad and give the doctors the wisdom and skill they needed to take care of him. Then Angie prayed for you; that you wouldn't feel responsible for Carl getting shot. They talked to God like He was right there in the room with us. Without even thinking about it, I prayed, too. I asked God to comfort them and to help Carl. I don't think I have prayed since high school, but right there with Angie and Carolyn it was so natural."

We were about to enter the cafeteria, but Julie stopped me and said, "Remember when you called me? You said Zeke's neighbors were born again Christians. I think you said you felt okay with them. Now I understand what you meant. I'm okay with them, too." We split up to get our own food. It was too late for anything but pre-packaged food so I opted for a tuna sandwich, an apple, and a cookie. Julie took a container of yogurt, and I added four bottles of water to our tray and paid the cashier. I carried the tray back to the waiting room and wished I had a third hand so I could carry the tray and walk hand in hand with Julie.

Julie and I sat down in the same chairs we had occupied earlier, and I nibbled on my sandwich until I had eaten most of it. I had just started on my chocolate chip cookie, when a very tired looking doctor wearing surgery scrubs walked into the room and said, "Mrs. Anderson…?" We all stood up. Angie's expression was a mix of hope and fear as she stepped toward him and silently nodded.

"I'm Dr. Jonathan Walters." He pulled an empty chair over to our table and we all sat down. "Your husband is a very lucky man. I've never seen anyone survive a gunshot wound as bad as that – of course he's still critical and anything could happen. But he made it through more than four hours of surgery, and I'm cautiously optimistic that he'll stabilize and start breathing completely on his own in a few days."

Angie leaned her head back as if to look toward heaven and tears silently streamed down both cheeks. Carolyn put her arm around her mother's shoulder and gently pulled her towards her. The doctor continued, "The bullet entered his upper back, just a few centimeters to the right of his spinal cord. He had a collapsed lung, three broken ribs, and significant soft tissue damage. We removed everything that wasn't supposed to be there and put everything else back together as best we could. For a man of his age, he's in excellent physical condition, so I'm hopeful he'll make a very near full recovery. Of course, the next three to five days are critical; anything could happen.

After that, he will get better week by week, but it will take months before he begins to feel like his old self."

I felt like a heavy load, twice as heavy as Zeke's backpack, had just been lifted from my shoulders. The doctor said, "Any questions before I go home and get some sleep?"

Angie said, "When can we see him?"

"He's going to be totally out for at least three more hours, and even when he starts to come around, he is heavily sedated and probably won't be coherent. He needs to rest, but family members can wait in his room as long as you're reasonably quiet."

Angie interjected, "We're all family."

"Okay. Follow me." We quickly cleaned up our mess from the waiting room, picked up our water bottles, and fell in line. As Dr. Walters led us through ICU to Carl's room he explained, "Normally only two people at a time are allowed in ICU, but since Carl's asleep I'll make an exception as long as you're quiet. Each of you needs to wear a sterile robe, gloves and mask. They're all hanging on the back of his door. One of our biggest concerns at this point is infection. Whenever you leave his room, take them off and discard them, and then put fresh ones on when you come back." We arrived at room 202 and gowned up as instructed. Before he departed for home, Dr. Walters assured us that he would check on Carl first thing the next morning.

The four of us quietly entered Carl's room and stood around his bed watching the nearly imperceptible rise and fall of his chest as the machine helped him breathe. Tubes and sensors sprouted out of his body like tendrils. I pulled a chair next to the bed for Angie so she could sit close beside him and hold his hand. Carolyn, Julie and I sat on a roomy couch at the end of the bed, where we could see Carl's slightly elevated head and torso.

I realized that Angie, Julie, nor Carolyn knew how Carl got shot. I whispered, "I need to tell you what Carl did for me." The all looked up at me, and I said, "When I got to Zeke's house, the guy who stole the top-secret documents was on the porch waiting for me. He demanded the evidence that would incriminate him, but I told him there actually wasn't any evidence, and I was bluffing when I said there was. He didn't believe my story and pulled a pistol on me. That's when Carl showed himself and told Tinker, the bad guy, to drop his gun. Tinker put his gun down. I hadn't noticed that Tinker was wired with a two-way radio. As I was about to frisk him, Tinker yelled into his mic, 'Shoot him!' Carl and I both instantly knew that Tinker had an accomplice who was going to shoot me. Carl jumped forward to stand behind me just as the shooter fired. He did it to save me. If he would have stayed put, the shooter would have had a clear shot at me.

"In the melee, Tinker reached to get his gun back, but before he got it, Carl shot him and then collapsed onto the porch. I ran around the corner of the house to get away from the shooter, but with Tinker's help, the shooter spotted me and was just about to take me out, when Angie shot him." I looked at Angie and said, "If it wasn't for Carl and for you, I'd be a dead man." A tidal wave of emotions hit me again. I started to cry like when I told the story to Gross, Annex, and Bass. However, this time was worse because I was looking right at both Carl and Angie. I asked, "Why did Carl do it? Why would he do that?"

Carolyn turned toward me but let me have a few minutes to compose myself before she responded in a whisper, "Because I know Daddy, I know why he did it, but it's difficult for me to explain, and may be even harder for you to understand." Carolyn took a couple of breaths before continuing, "EZ taught a six week Sunday school class. He repeated it every year in January, and when I was in high school, Daddy and I took it three years in a row. EZ called it *God's Invisible Kingdom.*

"You probably know that Daddy and EZ loved to hike and see the wildflowers, wild animals, and mountains. They loved to see the beauty of God's creation. Daddy even saved up for a nice camera so he could record what his eyes saw. EZ believed God's invisible kingdom was even more beautiful than the creation we can see with our natural eyes. In fact, EZ taught that we can't see God's kingdom with our natural eyes; God must first enlighten our eyes; give us eyes to see the unseen and ears to hear the kingdom's beautiful language. It's a kingdom of virtue where love overcomes hate, grace overcomes judgment, forgiveness overcomes retribution, and service overcomes selfishness."

I nodded, trying to comprehend the mystery of what Carolyn was telling me. She continued to whisper, "It's an inverted kingdom. Jesus, the king, became the servant of mankind by laying his life down for us. Jesus said, 'He who is the greatest among you shall be your servant.' Imagine a king being a lowly servant. He even washed his disciples' feet, a menial task normally relegated to humble servants. Jesus also said, 'Greater love has no one than this, than to lay down one's life for his friends.' That's why I think Daddy protected you. He loves you with a love that is so pure it can only come from

God's heart. Daddy was willing to lay down his life for you because you're his friend."

I hung my head in my hands with my elbows resting on my knees, completely overwhelmed by Carl's love. Julie gently put her hand on my back, and I leaned towards her. I knew I didn't have the kind of love Carl showed, nor could I imagine ever having it. We all sat quietly for several minutes, and then Carolyn said, "There's another thing EZ taught about the kingdom. He said that it's an enigma."

I muttered, "How do you mean?"

"It's a puzzle, a puzzle in several ways. Jesus said things like 'blessed are the meek for they shall inherit the earth,' which is at least counterintuitive. Most of us think the strong and the powerful and the assertive will inherit the earth, but Jesus said it is the meek and the gentle and the tame.

"I remember EZ teaching us about how Jesus paid the price for our salvation. Jesus said eternal life is the gift of God; it's free. But Jesus also said, 'He who loves his life will lose it, and he who hates his life in this world will keep it for eternal life.' EZ told us that Jesus was really saying that the kingdom will cost us our lives; the enigma is that salvation is free, but entering into the kingdom costs us our selfish lives. It's not very surprising that most people believe the talk about Jesus and his Kingdom is foolishness and that many professing Christians fail to enter it. The kingdom's entrance fee is very costly; it costs us our lives, the lives that most of us struggle mightily to hold on to. However, EZ said, 'Those who lose their lives find new, abundant life both in this world and in the next.' Daddy was willing to lose his life in this world because he was looking forward to his life in the next world."

Carolyn was right about the enigma part, because I was completely puzzled and clearly didn't have enlightened eyes required to see the kingdom. I reflected back on the last week and realized perhaps I had seen small glimpses of the invisible kingdom. I remembered the vacuum cleaner tracks Angie left in the hall carpets so Zeke's place would be spotless for my arrival. I remembered the gracious meals with the Andersons. I remembered Carl's invitations to join him on his hikes. And I remembered that Carl risked his life for mine. I thought back to the comments I made during my first conversation with Carl and Angie, the conversation where I said many Christians were asses. But Carl and Angie were the real thing, befriending and serving me in ways that I had never done for anyone, in ways that I couldn't imagine being able to do for anyone. If unselfish love was the kingdom's currency, I was a penniless pauper, totally bankrupt of love, grace, forgiveness, and service.

I looked at my phone and realized it was nearly eleven. I asked Angie and Carolyn if they were planning to spend the night in Carl's room and both were. Carolyn said, "If we change our minds, we can go to my place. It's only twenty minutes from here."

Julie and I wanted to give the Andersons their privacy so I called a Marriott which was near the downtown Nordstrom store and reserved two rooms. I didn't look forward to waking up and not having clean clothes, and I was sure Julie felt the same. Julie and I hugged Angie and Carolyn good night and asked them to call me if Carl's condition changed. Otherwise, we would see them the next day.

TWENTY-NINE

I awoke at eight, having slept much better than I expected given the prior day's chaos. I showered even though I knew I would be wearing the same smelly and dirty clothes I had worn the day before. Julie texted me while I was showering and asked me to come to her room so we could order breakfast from room service before our shopping excursion at Nordstrom. I dressed and walked down the hall to her room. She ordered granola with berries and coffee. My appetite had returned with a vengeance so I ordered an omelet with hash browns and toast, along with coffee and juice. If the menu had offered a logger's breakfast I would have gladly ordered it instead. Our breakfasts arrived twenty minutes later, and we had them polished off by nine fifteen and walked six blocks to the Nordstrom store, which opened at nine thirty.

I offered to pay for Julie's clothes and shoes, but she wouldn't hear of it. We split up and agreed to text each other when we had each purchased clothes for the next two days. Next, we found a Rite Aid and bought replacement toiletries, and Julie bought an inexpensive carry-on bag for her return trip to Boston. She also called the Butter Butte Lodge in Packwood and asked them to box the personal items she had left in her room and hold them for a couple of days until I could pick them up. We walked back to our rooms at the Marriott. I took another shower, put on my new clothes, stuffed yesterday's clothes in a laundry bag, and met Julie in the lobby. We checked out and drove up to the hospital to check on Carl.

Gerald Gross called me during our short drive to the hospital, but I let it go to voicemail. After parking the car in the hospital's garage, I asked Julie to go ahead into the hospital while I returned Gross' call from the car. He answered on the third ring, and I said, "This is David. What's up?"

"I am, but barely. I only got three hours sleep. I wanted to give you a heads up that I really need you here at Braxter no later than tomorrow morning. General Matthews will be here, and he wants to meet with you. If you can, please make yourself available."

"Wow. It sounds like the General is asking, not ordering. That's a big change."

"He's trying to get through this without having any of the proverbial excrement sticking to his uniform."

I couldn't help smiling to myself. "Sounds like this Tinker thing could be a career limiting fiasco for him."

"It depends on how he can spin it, and your cooperation will make a lot of difference."

"Let me guess. Worst case: the military gets blamed for a leak that was only stopped because one of their prime contractors, Braxter in this case, had the foresight to bring in an outside team that succeeded in stopping the leak in spite of the many obstacles the Army and the Defense Security Service raised. Best case: The military suspected a leak, and Matthews had the foresight to work with one of their prime contractors and bring in an outside team to lay a trap for the bad apple."

"That's about the size of it."

"This may shock you, but I'm willing to cut the General some slack, even help him spin the best case scenario."

I detected some skepticism in Gross' voice, but he said, "Smart move. Matthews is willing to issue Joan and Braxter letters of commendation. He also encouraged Braxter to do whatever it takes to get Harold back to work and to compensate Karl for his trouble."

"He's trying to avoid a couple of very public and very messy lawsuits."

"Could be."

"He's also willing to give Braxter three extra months to make the next Kilroy delivery, and if they meet the milestone, which they should easily do, he has authorized a million dollar bonus for them."

"And some of the bonus money will trickle down to Harold and Karl, if they play team ball."

"It's possible."

"Sounds like a win-win to me."

Relief had replaced the skepticism in Gross' voice. "I was hoping you'd see it that way... By the way, Tinker confessed; cut a deal to avoid the death penalty. He's been selling secrets to the Chinese for more than three years, and not just from Braxter; he stole from the other contractors he was assigned to inspect. Oh, and he turned over the eight disks he stole from your safe and gave us the number for a Swiss bank account. It has more than two million dollars in it."

"Sounds like everything can be quietly wrapped up for Matthews, but what about for Carl Anderson?"

"Matthews is checking with the Army's legal team, but expects to cover all of his medical bills, plus provide a generous amount for Anderson's pain and suffering."

"And Angie won't be charged for any wrong doing."

"Absolutely not."

"Please do whatever you can to take care of the Andersons."

"Will do... There are a couple more things. When you meet with Matthews tomorrow, he wants to personally thank you and express his desire that Klein InfoSec Associates will be available to work with the Army and their primes in the foreseeable future."

"Nice. What else?"

"Braxter is going to pay you for the full four months specified in your contract."

I was happy to hear that. "Sounds good. See you tomorrow."

"I'll be there by nine."

I was pleased to learn that both Braxter and my firm were going to come out okay, but Carl's condition remained my primary concern as I rode the elevator up to the second floor. I walked into Carl's room and immediately noticed relief on both Angie and Carolyn's faces. Carl's eyes were open, and he gave me a weak smile. I asked him how he felt, and he said, "Like I wrestled a momma bear, and lost."

Angie said, "You just missed Doctor Walters. He's amazed that Carl's color is so good and that he's already breathing so well."

Optimism and gratitude flooded me as I pulled a chair close to Carl's bed and said, "I can never repay you for saving my life, but if there's anything I can do let me know, and I'll do it."

"You don't owe me a thing."

"I just got off the phone with the Army. They're going to cover all your medical bills and will likely offer a generous compensation for all your pain and suffering. Of course, no amount of money can repay you."

Carl closed his eyes and appeared to drift off to sleep. Angie walked over and straightened his blankets. Then she squatted down beside my chair, and put her hand on my arm. "David, I was praying for you this morning and recalled Proverbs 16:9. It says, 'A man's heart plans his way, but the Lord directs his steps.' I think you have planned your life out, but it hasn't been going according to your plan. I think God has been directing, redirecting your steps towards Him."

I nodded and wondered if there wasn't some truth to what she had said.

Angie continued, "If you think there's a chance that I'm right, please don't ignore Him. There's a course I would encourage you to take. Carl helps out with it when our church runs it, so I know he would like you to take it, too. It's called the Alpha Course and it's for people who want to investigate the basics of Christianity. Churches all over the world offer it so I'm sure it's available in Boston. It usually meets once a week for about three months. There's no pressure, but I think you would enjoy it.

I replied, "Angie, I appreciate your concern. I really do, and I'll check into the course when I get back to Boston." We watched Carl for a while and then I said, "Julie's flight leaves in a few hours. We're going to get some lunch before I drop her at the airport. Then I'm going to head back to Zeke's for the night. I need to leave early tomorrow morning for a meeting in

Vancouver. I'll call you tomorrow to check in on Carl. Depending on how he's doing, I may head back to Boston."

Angie, Carolyn, Julie, and I all hugged each other and promised to stay in touch. Julie and I walked a half a block to a nice café near the hospital. We ordered our lunches, and I already started to miss her. "I am so glad that you came out, even though we didn't get to see most of what I wanted to show you."

"True, but think of the stories I'll be able to tell Laura about the Wild West. We went on a hike and were almost mauled by bears, had lunch in a saloon, and then there was a shootout at the OK corral." We both had a good laugh.

I said, "On a more serious note, I'm tired of being gone all the time, of making the business my only priority. I'm either going to hire some people and let them do most of the traveling, or I'll sell it and go to work for a corporation – maybe become a Chief Information Security Officer."

"Are you sure that's what you want?"

"Positive. I've given it a lot of thought, doing a lot of re-evaluating; trying to figure out what's important. Part of me wants to believe all the Jesus stuff that Carl and Angie believe, but it's too big of a jump for me. I have too many questions about myself, let alone about Jesus. I think I'm going to take Zeke's Bible back to Boston with me."

"Maybe we could take that Alpha Course together."

"I think I'd like that."

AUTHOR'S NOTE

I wrote *Uncle Zeke* out of frustration with my chronic inability to have meaningful conversations with my friends, conversation about the things that make me who I am, my aspirations, my problems, and my faith. I hope *Uncle Zeke* will be a conversation starter for me and for others as we look for opportunities to develop deep and fulfilling friendships and to discuss the seemingly taboo topic of the Christian faith.

If you are interested in learning more about the Christian faith I encourage you to start by reading the New Testament books *Matthew* and *John*. I also highly recommend the Alpha Course. Its low-pressure and fun approach has appealed to millions of people around the world. Additional information is available at: www.alpha.org and www.alphausa.org

A significant portion of *Uncle Zeke* takes place in the town of Packwood, WA. Anyone who knows the town of Packwood and the surrounding area will recognize the setting for this book, but will also note the many liberties I have taken with the geography. There is no road to Zeke's place, and Zeke's property is completely fictional as are the Packwood businesses mentioned in the book. I have visited the Packwood area many times and have hiked extensively in Mt. Rainier National Park, the Tatoosh Wilderness, and the Goat Rocks Wilderness. Additional information about the area is available at: www.destinationpackwood.com

www.ingramcontent.com/pod-product-compliance
Lightning Source LLC
Chambersburg PA
CBHW031122210626
46816CB00016B/1758